The CARMARTHEN
Underground

The CARMARTHEN Underground

Gaynor Madoc Leonard

y Lolfa

I thank, sincerely, those friends who were kind enough to read my first effort at novel-writing and who have given me so much support and constructive criticism. So, thank you Julie, Penny, Shelley, Peter, Adrienne and Daniel. Also, I am grateful to my editor, Eifion Jenkins, for taking on this task.

I would also like to acknowledge the website www.tylwythteg.com whose pages were invaluable for my research into pagan rituals.

First impression: 2009

© Gaynor Madoc Leonard & Y Lolfa Cyf., 2009

Cover image: Martha Burzynski
Cover design: Sion Ilar

ISBN: 9781847711625

Printed on acid-free and partly recycled paper
and published and bound in Wales by
Y Lolfa Cyf., Talybont, Ceredigion SY24 5AP
e-mail ylolfa@ylolfa.com
website www.ylolfa.com
tel 01970 832 304
fax 832 782

Oes trên tanddaearol yng Nghaerfyrddin?
Nac oes, y twpsyn!

Is there an underground train in Carmarthen?
No, stupid!

The Pan-Celtic Phrasebook
by William Knox

Chapter 1

'*DIAWL!*' ANEURIN COULD have kicked himself, if he hadn't already been so busy kicking the cat.

The surveillance operation was already going wrong and it was only half an hour after closing time. The streets, gleaming from the light rain falling on Aneurin's uncovered head, were empty, barring old Prothero sleeping it off in the Post Office porch, of course. Harmless enough, old Prothero had been sleeping there for years and the coppers didn't even bother to move him now – not that there were ever many coppers about these days. Prothero was supposedly from a well-off family and had been a wonderful pianist in his day. Although he had a home, it seemed that even he couldn't face the mess in it most of the time.

That bloody cat had to appear suddenly, didn't it? Aneurin knew he shouldn't have drunk that third pint of Twm Tomkins but the *Cwrw Nadolig* was his favourite and soon the springtime beer would replace it. Had to make the most of it, didn't he? The cat cared nothing for *cwrw*; he meowed maliciously and disappeared around the corner, seeking more congenial company at the back of Woolworths.

Aneurin tucked himself into the doorway opposite *Y Gegin Fach*, his eyes checking the length of Jackson's Lane for any suspicious movement. 'Shouldn't have had that beer… got to concentrate, Aneurin *bach*.' Time was that cat wouldn't have got near him but age and a weakness for the beer had dulled his senses; he knew he couldn't afford any more mistakes or he'd be sent to the old spies' home in Llanfihangel-ar-Arth, a fate worse than death. He shuddered at the thought.

'*Calon lân… yn llawn daioni…* ' A drunken voice sang the old hymn. The sound was coming from King Street.

Aneurin tensed, wondering whether to risk a look, but the voice, repeating and not getting further than the first line of that glorious refrain, faded into the distance, probably heading towards Nott Square and one of the late-night drinking dens in Little Bridge Street. Besides, the target was likely to come from Red Street, in the other direction.

'Relax, Aneurin *bach* – you're getting jittery in your old age.'

That was his last thought before a blow from behind knocked him flat. He felt neither the hard cobbles of Jackson's Lane, nor the ropes that bound him. Nor did he know anything about being carried gently to the waiting van and taking the long drive to the seaside.

His attacker had some sympathy as he watched his accomplice drive the small blue van away. '*Duw, duw,* Aneurin, you've really lost your grip, boy *bach*.'

He shrugged, sighed and headed toward Red Street and Guildhall Square, humming under his breath, '*Calon lân…* '

Chapter 2

G UILDHALL SQUARE WAS deserted; the good people of Caerfyrddin were either tucked up in bed, like good chapel people should be, or pissed in front of a late-night, post-watershed *Pobl y Pentref* (the unexpurgated, raunchy version). As for the bad people, they would also be indoors, but at the unauthorised bars and seedy strip-joints lining the back streets leading down to the river.

Wyndham (not his birth name of course, but the one by which he'd become generally known) headed across the square toward St Mary Street, that by-way which looked so innocent but concealed a great secret. He slipped into the narrow doorway next to the Wimpy bar and, after quickly entering his code on the electronic pad, with the odour of fried onions assailing his nostrils from the now closed café, went through the door to a hallway. Passing the stairs leading upwards, he went to the back of the hall and pressed a panel on the wall. Another door slid to one side and he went through, the door closing behind him with a swishing sound.

'*Shw mae'n mynd*, Wyndham, *cariad*?' The voice belonged to one of the leading lights of the old St Peter's Operatic Society, Meinir Arian. Now stout and in the late autumn of her life, she still had a voice to shatter the glass in St Peter's Parish Church. A bit of a glamour-puss in her day, she showed a fine leg and enjoyed her job as part-time doorwoman at CIHQ. Many of the incumbents there remembered her rousing version of 'You'll Never Walk Alone' in the historic production of *Carousel* which had launched the stellar career of Caitlin Gamma Evans, Carmarthen's only Oscar winner.

Meinir put down her copy of *À La Recherche du Temps Perdu* (the Welsh translation), which she'd been reading ever since Wyndham could remember, and pressed the button for the lift. She winked at Wyndham as he pressed the button for the fourth floor down and he blew her a kiss in return. Friendliness costs nothing, after all, and Meinir had done him a few favours over the years – not that she was one to remind him of that.

Before Meinir had picked up her book again, the lift had arrived. The doors slid open to an empty, seemingly blank corridor. Opposite the lift there was an almost invisible keypad on the wall. As Wyndham entered the code, the keypad automatically checked his fingerprints and a tiny camera checked his eyes. A door opened and allowed him through to the hub of operations.

This was the central nervous system of Carmarthen Intelligence.

Chapter 3

WYNDHAM HEADED STRAIGHT to his desk at the rear of the room; no 'hot-desking' for CI, each operative had his or her own space.

He always wondered how they managed to make a room so deep underground seem so light and airy; it never felt claustrophobic. He sat at his ergonomically-designed desk and speed-dialled The Boss. As usual, she picked up her phone immediately and he said, without preamble, 'It's done; he'll be in the safe house in Porthgain before dawn.' She replaced her phone without speaking so Wyndham knew she was satisfied. Now for the damned paperwork.

First he checked his e-mails. Geraint in IT was organising another coracle party, despite the fact that the last one had ended up with everyone floating downstream as far as Llansteffan and the beer had run out halfway. Wyndham knew he shouldn't do it but he signed up for the party, throwing caution to the wind. 'We only live once, after all,' he muttered, 'but I'll take an extra flask of Penderyn whisky this time and wear a thicker vest.'

The second e-mail really got his blood pressure up; it was from Emia, The Boss's PA. Emia, the vamp of the first floor down, all silk stockings and slim skirts made from Welsh plaid. He'd once seen her in Welsh costume at an office *Noson Lawen*, complete with the black stovepipe hat and white lacy bonnet, and his heart had flipped over. All his years as one of CI's up-and-coming operatives had not prepared him for his first sight of Emia. In the field, he was tough; in front of Emia's desk on the first floor down, he was a bumbling schoolboy.

Her e-mail was formal, congratulating him on his recent promotion, but he knew that there was an underlying message. If he started thinking about it too much, he'd never get his work done.

The report on Aneurin's kidnap was short and to the point, thank heavens. He clicked to send it to The Boss's e-mail and reverted to thinking about Emia.

His phone buzzed, startling him out of his reverie. It was The Boss and she wanted to see him, pronto. If he was seeing his boss, then he would be seeing Emia beforehand. A quick glance in the mirror he kept in a small drawer confirmed that he looked more than acceptable.

This time, he used the inner lift to go to the first floor down; cameras outside the lift and within it watched his every move. Within seconds, the lift door opened again at his destination and he was faced with The Boss's receptionist, Iori. Not Wyndham's favourite person; indeed, probably not even Iori's mother's favourite person.

An upbringing on a remote farm near Star and a third-class degree in *Welsh Love Spoons in History* from the University of Wales (Treorchy campus) had left Iori bitter and regretful. A closet Bonnie Tyler fan, he expressed a public preference for the music of Dafydd-y-Pwll, an obscure 14th century bard; in fact, he was so obscure that no one else had ever heard of him. Iori lived in a small studio flat above one of the charity shops on Nott Square and the only joy in his life came from playing 'The Man That Got Away' on his Irish harp.

Wyndham decided to make an effort. '*Shw mae'n mynd,* Iori?' Iori merely sneered and buzzed through to Emia to tell her that 003½ had arrived. 'There's gratitude for you,' thought Wyndham, 'I won't bother another time.'

He walked through the doorway to Emia's office and caught his breath. She was a vision standing before him; silky red hair brushing her alabaster face and neck. She must have been to TP Hughes in Haverfordwest again, as she had the chic-est of Welsh plaid suits on, her long, slender legs clad in her favourite seamed stockings and her delicate little feet in the latest *Swanci* Heels shoes. He'd been past *Swanci* Heels the other day and stood looking at the shoes in the window, until he'd noticed the shop assistant smiling at him and had retreated, embarrassed.

Emia, in turn, looked at him with a raised eyebrow and a smile playing on her glossy lips. What she saw was pleasing to her. Wyndham had once played at number 12 for the local rugby team and his training had resulted in a compact and muscular body. Not too tall – she knew from his records he was 5ft 10in. And she didn't object to strawberry blond hair on a man, after all she was a redhead herself. Not much cop in the clothes department, of course, but that could be dealt with and there would be the interesting part where he might be without any clothes at all. Her eyebrow lifted even higher.

She spoke softly. '*Shw mae'n mynd*, Wyndham?' Her voice was like velvet and her mundane enquiry sounded like seduction; certainly a voice like that would be illegal in several American states. He blushed and croaked, 'Grand, *diolch*, Emia.' He felt the sweat break out on his brow and the blood rush to his groin as her eyes swept over his body.

She chuckled throatily and indicated that he should go through to the inner sanctum. Clearing his throat, he walked past Emia, feeling her eyes on his tightly-muscled rear, and reached the sanctuary of The Boss's office, closing the door behind him with a mixture of reluctance and relief, hoping that any evidence of his confusion had subsided.

Chapter 4

THE BOSS WAS nobody's fool. The only daughter of an old farming family in Trelech, she'd abandoned the cowshed to her brothers and headed to the University of Wales at Lampeter where, in the great Llanbedr tradition, she'd been recruited as a spy by Welsh Intelligence. With a first class degree in Celtic linguistics and a *gwregys ddu* in the ancient Welsh art of *llaw gwag* for which she had won several medals at the Inter-Celtic Games, she was a natural for the spying game and she'd proved a dab hand at it. She had a lighter side and was known to enjoy the fruits of the Welsh vineyards, as well as doing some stand-up comedy at the *Chwerthin* club in Brechfa during her student days. But, at her desk, she was the true professional and stood no nonsense. She rose from her chair to greet Wyndham.

'Well, Wyndham, you did your job well tonight. You didn't allow sentiment to get the better of your professionalism – I knew I could count on you.'

'All in a night's work, ma'am – it helped that Aneurin had had too many pints of course.'

'The very reason we had to do it, although I am of course sad it had come to that. In his day, Aneurin was a good man for this game. Dewi rang to say they'd got as far as Camrose and Aneurin was still well out of it. I never like sending anyone to that safe house, but Aneurin was getting to be a danger to himself and the rest of us.'

'Will he end up in Llanfihangel, ma'am?' Wyndham shivered at the thought.

'We must hope not, Wyndham, but this is his last chance now.' She sighed and moved back to her chair.

Wyndham couldn't help but admire this good-looking woman; she stood about 5ft 5in, slim but strong without losing any femininity. Like Emia, she dressed in an understated but chic way. Word was that she was conducting an affair with RSJ Williams, the suave Deputy Speaker of the Welsh *Cymanfa* or Senate, known for his bespoke wardrobe purchased from the finest cutters on Tailors' Row in Loughor. If so, RSJ was a lucky man.

'Wyndham,' The Boss's voice jerked him back to reality, 'you've earned your promotion but you know that it puts you into more dangerous situations. I have a new task for you.'

Wyndham immediately gave his whole mind to The Boss's instructions; he hadn't reached this level in CI without proving himself a tough and bright operative who could leave all personal issues aside and attend wholeheartedly to the job in hand, Emia notwithstanding.

One hour later, he was leaving the first floor down with a false ID and instructions for his toughest job yet. Only Emia's soft words of '*pob lwc*, Wyndham' and the electric touch of her skin as she handed him his papers disturbed his concentration. Disturbingly, Iori gave him a toothy grin.

Half an hour after that, he had cleared his desk and left CIHQ via the St Mary Street door, pausing only to kiss Meinir Arian swiftly on the cheek as he made his way out again past the hated onion smell.

He walked steadily but quickly up St Mary Street and turned right into Quay Street. Moving silently to the end of the street, constantly aware of any shadows, he could see the river beyond Coracle Way, shining in the moonlight; that

.

ancient movement of water had carried his Celtic ancestors, the Romans and other invaders over several millennia and would shortly carry him to his next operation. He turned to the door at his right, entered a code on the keypad behind the house sign and went in.

Wyndham had only moved into his new flat a few weeks before and he had still had no time to sort out his personal belongings. The flat had come with a new kitchen and bathroom so all he'd really done was ensure that his bed and bed linen were installed, along with a chair and table in the living room. For the first time, he really felt a need to settle down and have a proper home. Perhaps he'd ask Emia to help him choose the decoration... no, that way lay madness!

He stripped off, revealing a superb physique. Tightly muscled with a firm, flat stomach, he set to shaving his legs and armpits; fortunately, his body wasn't very hirsute although his head boasted a thick mane of hair. Next he found a bottle of blond hair dye in the bathroom cupboard and dyed first his heavy mane, then his eyebrows and lastly his pubic hair – matching the collar and cuffs was essential. While waiting for the dye to take, he wandered naked into the kitchen and made a large mug of tea. Booze would have to wait until the operation was over, unless it was essential for cover purposes. He turned on the gas under a small pan to heat up the remainder of the *cawl* he'd bought from the elegant *siop fwyta* by the market. They did a good selection of *cawl*, both meat and vegetarian; he'd chosen the lamb version this time. By the time the dye had taken, he'd eaten his *cawl* with some thick slices of bread, washed the dishes and put everything away.

He showered and dried his hair, finding that the blond colour had taken just as he'd wanted it and would probably last very well for the length of the operation. Time for a couple of hours' sleep.

At 5am, his alarm buzzed and he dressed in the anonymous uniform of jeans and hooded sweatshirt and packed a couple more versions of the same thing into a light bag, along with his toiletries and some disposable, but washable, underwear. The passport went into a hidden pocket inside his sweatshirt. Warm socks, desert boots and a padded jacket finished the outfit, along with a sharp knife in a sheath strapped to his left ankle; the gun was in his bag, in a special pocket made just for the purpose.

There was no question of taking any risks by going back into the street so, having closed the door of his ground floor flat, he turned to his left in the hallway, away from the street door, and opened the entrance to the cellar, using a special code on the near-invisible keypad and giving the password, '*Barry John*,' in a whisper.

There was a slight swooshing sound as the door opened and he moved quickly down the steps, the door closing behind him. At the bottom of the short flight, a lift door opened and Wyndham entered, pressing the number -5 on the wall of the lift. A few seconds later, the doors opened again and Wyndham found himself in the most secret part of Carmarthen: the Quay Street Underground station.

Wyndham had worked for CIHQ for two years before he even knew about the Underground, let alone seen it. Even among the Intelligence workers, the Underground was 'need-to-know' and only those on special operations, the management and certain of the town *crachach* used it. And only people in the very highest echelons knew how far it extended, though rumour had it that it spread its tentacles as far as Llansteffan in one direction, Llandeilo in another,

Newcastle Emlyn in yet another, and all stations in between. Perhaps it even made it as far as Swansea. Impressive indeed. Designed by the late, great Sir Clough Williams Ellis, the underground passages that Wyndham had seen had the elegance of an Italianate villa and were lit by antique-style lamps.

The train was waiting for him. Constructed in the 1920s, it was light and comfortable inside; although Wyndham didn't have to go far, he appreciated the warmth and soft upholstery.

There was one other person in the carriage, the man whom Wyndham knew as Will 'Front Row'. Built like a brick outhouse, Will had been part of the great 1970s Scarlets front row. No hair graced his head and he had no discernible neck. He was not known for his repartee or sense of humour but he was the man to have beside you in a crisis and Wyndham felt very grateful to be on the same side as Will; certainly the alternative was not to be contemplated. Will nodded to Wyndham and the train moved off with a slight jerk.

Chapter 5

Four minutes after leaving Quay Street Underground station, the train arrived at its slow pace on the far side of the river, beneath the *Pont* King Morgan. Will Front Row showed Wyndham out of the carriage and took him to the lift door at the end of the platform, merely grunting as Wyndham thanked him, '*Diolch*, Will; *pob hwyl*.' The lift took him up to directly beneath the bridge, the lift entrance disguised as part of the bridge itself. There he found a female operative waiting for him, code-name Myfanwy Fach (there was also a Myfanwy Fawr, but her name was only whispered in corners by the very brave). She cautioned him to be silent although it was still only 5.40am and he could see no one around. Quickly, she showed him some steps cut into the riverbank and motioned him to get into the coracle below. He couldn't see the coracle-man's face but he had a feeling it was Dai Sewin, a legendary fisherman on the Towy.

Within moments of sitting down, Wyndham found himself being rowed upstream in the coracle, with the monolithic hulk of County Hall far above and the windows of Towy Works glinting in the street lights of Coracle Way. Around them was gloom, cloud had obscured the moon and a light rain had begun to fall again. Wyndham made sure both the hood of his sweatshirt and the hood of his jacket were pulled up over his head and he felt almost invisible to the rest of the world.

Dai Sewin was no young man but he was certainly powerful and the coracle moved easily up the river. At last they reached White Mill, Wyndham very impressed that Dai

Sewin had managed to row so strongly and so far. The sky was getting lighter and Wyndham was anxious to leave the coracle. They drew up at the bank where Wyndham could see a small motorboat with a cabin. He climbed onto the bank and signalled his thanks to Dai Sewin, who touched his cap in response.

Moving over to the motorboat, Wyndham climbed in and was surprised to see his old pal from the rugby team, Aled 'Hook' Thomas. They shook hands and Wyndham went inside the small cabin where there was a flask of tea for them both. In the meantime, Aled pushed off from the bank and set off further up the Towy.

Wyndham poured tea for both of them and sat in the cramped cabin next to Aled, as he piloted the little boat so expertly and gently upriver. In quick succession, they passed by the tiny village of Llanegwad, then Felindre and the beautiful ruin of Dryslwyn Castle in its exquisite setting. Despite his work, Wyndham had the Welshman's natural appreciation of beauty and he loved the Towy Valley. Aled, never a great one for small talk, said little but grinned occasionally at Wyndham, who knew better than to discuss Aled's involvement with CIHQ; that could wait for another, more appropriate, time.

At last, just south west of Llangadog, they drew in to the riverbank. Aled caught Wyndham in a big bear hug and helped him off the boat, telling him to climb up to the road where a blue van would be waiting. '*Hwyl*, Aled.'

The bank was wet from the rain and Wyndham had to struggle up it. As he'd been told, the van was waiting at the side of the road. He ran and got into the passenger seat. He didn't recognise the small, thickset young man in the driving seat but the man introduced himself as Walter and gave the password: '*Alf*.'

Walter drove confidently but carefully through Llangadog, not wanting to draw attention. He headed left on a B-road, taking them past Cilgwyn, then turned right at the next junction. Within minutes, they had arrived at Wyndham's destination. Just outside the village of Myddfai, Walter dropped him off and sped away eastward.

Chapter 6

A NEURIN'S HEAD WAS aching. An attempt to raise himself from the narrow bed ended in groans and he slumped back onto the pillow.

'*Bore da*, Aneurin, *shw mae'r pen y bore 'ma?*' a not unfriendly voice enquired. Nobody I know though, thought Aneurin. He was sure that if he closed his eyes tight, he would wake again in his own bed in the small flat in Little Water Street. Slowly, he opened his eyes again, one at a time, and had to concede that he was not in his own bed, not in his own flat and not even in Carmarthen by the look of it. He thought he could smell the salt air of the seaside.

His interlocutor was a thin man. Indeed, everything about him seemed to be thin: his hair, his lips and his laugh. Aneurin noticed the man was wearing a white coat. Had there been an accident? He tested his legs and arms and decided everything was working, despite the pounding in his brain.

'Water… ' Aneurin croaked. The man held a glass to Aneurin's mouth and he took grateful sips.

'Aneurin, I'm Doctor J Thomas Thomas, and I'll be looking after you for a while… you're going to have a nice seaside holiday.'

'Don't remember booking anything!'

'Don't worry, it was all done for you and it won't cost you a penny. It's like a prize. Now, I've put a couple of aspirin into that water so your head should clear up nicely. Once you've had a good rest, we'll talk about the rest of your stay.'

'Anything you say, Doc,' murmured Aneurin, as he drifted off to sleep once more.

Two hours later, he woke up and managed to finish off the rest of the water and aspirin before dragging his legs off the bed and sitting up. A cursory look at the room convinced him that he was not in luxury accommodation, although he could see a small shower room in the corner and an easy chair opposite the bed. He stood up unsteadily and shuffled to the window. Opening the curtains, he could see wrought-iron bars on the other side of the glass and, beyond, a view of Porthgain's small harbour, the waves crashing against the rocks and the harbour walls.

He shuffled back to the bed, sat down and put his head in his hands. He now realised that the attack had been from his own side and that he had been set up for a spell of rehabilitation in the Porthgain safe house. There would be no Twm Tomkins to tempt his palate here. A few tears wet his cheeks. What had he come to? What had happened to Aneurin Ebenezer Hopkins?

'*Duw, duw*, Aneurin, what's this?' a kindly voice asked. 'See, I've brought you a nice pot of tea and lovely ham sandwiches… made them myself for you.' He looked up to see a motherly woman in a nurse's uniform; her badge identified her as Mair Beynon.

'*Diolch*… I'm quite hungry now. What day is it?'

'You've only been here since the middle of the night, *bach*. Plenty of time to get acclimatised and rest, get some good sea air. You won't know yourself after a while.'

She put the tray down on a small table by the window and poured him a cup of tea. He sipped it quietly, feeling the comforting warmth.

'I'll leave the tray for you and come to fetch it later. You rest now, get as much sleep as you can today.'

She left the room, the door clicking behind her. Aneurin knew it was no use trying the door as it would be locked. He'd never been to the Porthgain safe house before but he'd heard things about it. At least it wasn't Llanfihangel... He sighed with relief and poured himself some more tea.

He didn't remember falling asleep after eating the sandwiches and drinking all the tea. Nurse Beynon came to take away the tray but he didn't know it. He dreamed, he dreamed.

In his dream, he sat in a comfortable leather chair, his feet up on a large stool. He was in such a nice room – must have been a study. A fire burned in a large grate, the wood giving off comforting scents.

'Relax, Aneurin, you don't have to lift a finger.' The voice, definitely North Wales now that Aneurin thought about it, was deep and friendly. A face came into view; a man in his sixties perhaps, thick grey hair and moustache – not unlike David Lloyd George.

'I wanted to welcome you here, Aneurin, to our lovely house by the sea. You'll be staying with us for a while; lots of healthy walks on the cliffs and good food and you'll be back on top before you know it. You won't know yourself.'

'I won't know myself... ' murmured Aneurin.

'That's the spirit; just do what the doctor tells you and all will be well.'

The kindly Lloyd George face, like a doting grandfather, swam before his eyes and when he awoke, he was still in the narrow bed in his room. He felt better, if still a little removed from reality.

Some clothes had been left for him, hanging behind the door. Just some underwear, a pair of jeans, a T-shirt and a warm fleece. There were no shoes, only some slippers. He drew back the curtain and looked out.

'Must have slept the rest of the day; too dark to see the sea out there.'

At that moment, the door clicked open and Nurse Mair Beynon popped her head in. 'Oh good, Aneurin, I was just coming to fetch you for your supper – you'll enjoy meeting some of the other people who are taking a little holiday with us.'

He stepped outside into the corridor and followed the nurse along a passageway lined with doors, presumably to rooms just like his own, then through a fire door and down a flight of stairs to a large hallway. To the left was the busy dining room and Mair took his hand, leading him in. There must have been about twenty other people there, although they did not raise their heads to see the newcomer.

'Now then, Aneurin, come and sit with Mr Goronwy Evan Evans. *Noswaith dda*, Mr Evans, here's Mr Aneurin Ebenezer Hopkins to meet you… I'm sure you'll have a lot in common.'

Aneurin looked at the man sitting opposite him while Nurse Beynon bustled away to find him some food. She came back with a tray bearing a laver bread omelette, a baked potato and peas, and a small pot of Beddgelert green tea.

'You get that down you now, *cariad*; you need building up,' she said.

Mr Evans looked down at his plate while sipping his green tea. He was probably in his late sixties, with thinning hair and a jowly face which had probably been quite jolly in its time.

As yet, he had not so much as looked up at Aneurin, but after Mair had left them alone, he spoke quietly; Aneurin had to lean forward to hear him.

'Do you know yourself, boy?' Evans asked.

'Sorry, what do you mean?'

'I asked if you know yourself. All the time they tell me that I won't know myself.'

'It's only a figure of speech, isn't it, Mr Evans?' said Aneurin, looking a little blank.

'Ah, is it now? And am I really Mr Evans?'

Aneurin felt uncomfortable. 'If you are not Mr Goronwy Evan Evans, sir, then who are you?'

'Ah, there you have me, boy. Every so often I feel a name on the tip of my tongue and I spend my nights dreaming of mathematics, although I'm told that I'm a shepherd so you would think I'd dream of sheep.'

'Well, I know who I am and I'm still the same person I was yesterday before I came here,' said Aneurin, although a smidgen of doubt was beginning to filter into his brain.

'But who will you be tomorrow, boy? That's the riddle, you see.'

Aneurin decided to concentrate on eating; at least the food was real, or so it seemed. Mr Evans lapsed into silence again and finished his tea.

At last, Mair returned. 'Had a lovely chinwag, have we? Time for you to go back to your room now, Aneurin; there's a good film on your personal screen tonight.'

As he was leaving, Aneurin turned to Mr Evans and said, '*Nos da*, Mr Evans, see you tomorrow.'

Mr Goronwy Evan Evans looked at him doubtfully and

blinked back tears as Aneurin walked away.

Back in his room, Aneurin changed for bed again and was surprised to see a screen, like a plasma TV, drop down slowly from the ceiling. Mair tucked him in and said, 'Now, there's some water on the bedside table for you; make sure you drink plenty while you're enjoying the film. Then you must rest.' She left him and the door locked automatically behind her.

Aneurin drank some water and relaxed. Perhaps this wouldn't be so bad after all, being looked after day and night, with plenty of food and a comfortable bed. The film started.

The music seemed to cradle him, rocking him from side to side like a lullaby. The images on the screen were soothing: a long, empty beach with waves gently lapping the shore and trees waving in the breeze. Then a voice began narrating a story. The voice was familiar, with a slight North Wales accent; a comforting voice, a voice you could trust implicitly.

'Aneurin, Aneurin! Wake up, lazybones, it's time for breakfast.'

He opened his eyes to see Nurse Nest Jones smiling at him. 'Must have fallen asleep during the film; don't remember anything after that,' he muttered.

'Come on and have your shower now and get dressed; I'll see you down in the dining room,' ordered Nurse Jones with a grin. She looked like a nice, jolly, down-to-earth girl.

After washing – surely his face was rather red today – and dressing, Aneurin noticed a notebook on the bedside table. It appeared to be a diary and in his own writing. He put it in his pocket and tried the door, expecting it still to be locked. It opened easily and he followed the signs to the dining room.

There seemed to be some new faces in the dining room

and some of those he remembered from the previous evening had gone. He looked around for Mr Goronwy Evan Evans but there was no sign of him.

There was a window seat available so he sat down and a waitress brought him a plate of poached eggs on toast with mushrooms and tomato and a pot of green tea. 'I'll bring extra toast in a few minutes,' she said.

Aneurin thanked her and looked out of the window at the view. The waves still crashed against the rocks and small boats bobbed in the harbour; one or two people seemed to be out and about, braving the wind. He tucked into his breakfast and the waitress brought him the extra toast, as promised, with jam and butter and more tea.

He remembered the notebook and took it out of his pocket. It was a diary of his time at Porthgain. According to this, he had been at the clinic for a week. He read of his walks on the cliffs and down at the harbour, the meals he had eaten and the people to whom he had spoken in the dining room and sitting room.

The notebook fell from his hand onto the table, knocking over his cup. The waitress came and wiped the table, replacing the cup and smiling. Aneurin asked her, 'Where is Mr Goronwy Evan Evans?' She frowned and said, 'Oh, I think Mr Evans left us three days ago. A quiet man, wasn't he?'

Aneurin thought back to Mr Evans's comments at supper and his hands shook. He had no memory of the past few days or of any of the events in the diary that he appeared to have written about. He knew better than to dispute the waitress's version of events; that way lay trouble and he couldn't let them know he suspected anything. He had to think. He ate some more toast and drank down his tea and then made his way to the residents' sitting room, following the signs. He thought to himself, 'If I'd been here a week, I'd know the way without using the signs, surely.'

He sat gazing out of the window and thought about all he could remember since waking up at the clinic the first time. He'd eaten supper with Mr Evans, then gone back to his room and drunk water and watched a film. No, he'd taken a few sips of the water and only remembered a couple of minutes of the film. He couldn't have been asleep for six days. He realised that he was wearing shoes today, rather than slippers; it hadn't occurred to him that new shoes had been provided. He looked at the soles; they were a little bit worn and there appeared to be earth and sand stuck in the treads. Had he really been out walking or had someone else worn them first, to make him think that?

'Hallo there! Good to see you again today. That was quite a walk yesterday and you caught the sun a bit.'

The voice was warm and friendly, and Aneurin turned to see a short middle-aged man with receding, nondescript hair and a smile revealing several missing teeth.

Aneurin returned the smile warily. 'I thought my face was a bit red when I looked in the mirror this morning,' he said.

'Get Nurse Jones to give you a bit of cream for it or you might peel,' the man advised. 'Ah, they do a good breakfast here, nothing to complain of on the food front.' He sat back, comfortably.

Aneurin decided to go along with his companion and replied, 'Yes, it's been good so far and I'm getting used to the Beddgelert green tea.'

'Amazing how they grow it in North Wales, isn't it? Something to do with the microclimate. I'm no scientist though, I don't really understand these things,' said his new friend.

Nurse Jones appeared. 'Aneurin, I'm glad to see that you and Mr Brynaman are getting along so well but it's time for your visit to the doctor now. And I'll give you something for the windburn on your face.'

Aneurin made sure that the notebook was safely in his pocket before getting up and following the nurse. Mr Brynaman waved to him with a grin, showing his vacant gums.

Fear gripped Aneurin. What was happening to him and all the other patients here at the clinic? Where had Mr Evans gone? And, more importantly, where had those six days gone? He braced himself and reminded himself that he was a spy and, if he kept his nerve, he would solve the mystery and get back to Carmarthen and safety.

A few moments later they reached a set of double doors. Nurse Jones knocked and the voice with the North Wales accent said, 'Please come in.'

Nurse Jones opened the door and ushered Aneurin in. 'I'll be giving Aneurin some cream for his face afterwards, Dr Owain ap Owain.'

'Very good, Nurse Jones, you can leave us now. Aneurin and I will have a nice little chat.'

The door closed and Aneurin was alone with Dr Owain ap Owain. The fire burned in the remembered grate, the wood giving off that comforting scent.

'Sit down now, Aneurin, we don't stand on ceremony here. Well, I have to say that you've improved by leaps and bounds in the week you've been here; you are a big success for us.'

Somehow, those last words made Aneurin feel afraid, but he held his nerve and smiled at the good doctor. 'Does that mean that I can go home soon, Doctor?'

'We mustn't rush things now, must we? Give yourself another couple of weeks and then we'll think about home. I hope you are comfortable here, Aneurin; we do our best you know, to make you feel comfortable.'

'Yes, I'm sure, Doctor. The food is good and I seem to have slept very well. I was sorry not to see Mr Goronwy Evan Evans again before he left though.'

Was that a glint of steel Aneurin saw in the good doctor's eyes, just for a second? But Dr Owain ap Owain smiled and said, 'Such a pity not to see your new friend again before he left but his niece came to fetch him and take him home with her for the final part of his recovery. Another success story for us, I'm happy to say... oh yes.'

The crackling of the fire and the scent of the wood were soporific; the grandmother clock ticked. The doctor's voice seemed distant as Aneurin's eyes closed. He thought his sleeve was being rolled up, and was that a small jab in his arm? Nothing seemed to matter anyway, he was so comfortable and he wanted to sleep. He tried opening his eyes and he thought he saw Mr Brynaman's gums grinning at him but then the face floated away and became Dr Owain ap Owain with his friendly moustache, a moustache you could trust. Aneurin's eyes closed again and he slept.

Chapter 7

I T WAS STILL very early in Myddfai and the only inhabitants Wyndham could see were some lethargic cows desultorily munching grass, as though they wished they could have something different for a change but would make do for now.

He could see down Myrtle Hill, toward the village. The ancient and great estate of Llwynywormwood lay to his left; home of myth and legend and the birthplace of the Physicians of Myddfai. This was to be his bolthole for the next few days. Above the ruins lay a place of safety, should he need one, and he now went to prepare it for any emergency.

He moved quickly through the grounds, keeping as far as possible from open areas, until he reached the ruined keep. He slipped inside and found the entrance to the great hall. A doorway on his left, blocked off to general visitors by a metal gate, showed some steep steps leading into a tower. He used the key he'd been given by Emia to open the gate and climbed carefully to a room high above the grounds, having locked the gate behind him. This was a place used by CI when they were on operations so there were already some supplies there: a brazier with some fuel, a chest containing a sleeping bag, water and packs of dried food for emergencies, along with some equipment which would be useful for Wyndham. There was also a small tent to shelter from the worst of the wind, although the roof had been partially restored to keep off the rain.

Wyndham took out one set of clothing from his bag and

placed it in the chest. He could not enter Myddfai with a gun so he hid it behind a stone in the wall. Then he sat down to wait.

He thought about the Physicians of Myddfai and their father, whose beautiful wife had returned to her lake, taking her livestock with her, thereby ruining her husband and leaving him broken-hearted. The sons went on to become famed healers. Wyndham had read about some of their medicines and was very relieved that he would not have to consult them.

He dozed for a while, then thinking that 9.30am would be a suitable time to enter the village, he went back down the stairs and let himself out of the tower, locking the gate carefully behind him. Again, he kept to the shelter of the ruins and trees before finding himself on the road leading to the village. It was still quiet and he walked casually down toward the main street.

Myddfai had a private volunteer police force made up of local inhabitants. Strolling up the main street was the man known as the Sheriff of Myddfai, with his deputy.

Sheriff Iwan ap Rhys was a former entrepreneur and amateur rugby player who had won two caps at international level. The details of his business practices were hazy but he'd apparently made enough money to retire to Monaco, or so the local bush telegraph had it. However, he had chosen to stay in his birthplace and the villagers had been happy, at least initially, for him to take over the security of their picturesque home.

His deputy, David Davies, or 'Dai Sluice', the local plumber, enjoyed the importance his position gave him and he swaggered along beside the sheriff. He called out to

Wyndham, '*Bore da*. Good morning, sir. On a walking tour, are we?'

Wyndham approached him and replied, '*Bore da*, I'm looking for somewhere to stay for a few days. Someone told me the pub in Myddfai was a good place. I hadn't expected to arrive so early but I managed to get a lift from Llangadog.'

The sheriff looked at Wyndham quizzically, but clearly chose to believe the story for the moment. '*Y Ceffyl Du* is a very good pub, just over there.' He pointed. 'They'll put you up and give you a good breakfast. Just knock on the back door.'

'Thank you,' said Wyndham, 'I'm looking forward to exploring the countryside around here.'

The sheriff looked flint-eyed. 'Are you now? Well, be careful, we've had people suffer unexpected accidents around here in the past.'

Wyndham waved as he walked to the pub and said, 'Thanks for the warning; I'll be careful.'

The sheriff narrowed his eyes as he stared after Wyndham. 'Keep an eye on him, Mr David Davies; we don't want anything happening to him, do we? And see what you can find out about him on the database; if he's not on it, put him on.' Dai Sluice grinned and nodded. 'Righto, Sheriff.'

High up in the church tower, Merle Jenkins looked thoughtfully at Wyndham, via the camera obscura. A fine figure of a man, she thought. 'I'll go to the pub later and check his credentials,' she chuckled to herself. Then she watched the sheriff and his deputy saunter along the main street and she knew in her bones that Wyndham was going to find himself up against them.

Wyndham found the back door to the pub and knocked.

The door opened almost immediately and a pleasant middle-aged woman, teacloth in hand, appeared. '*Bore da*, what can I do for you?'

'My name's Haydn Jones,' Wyndham said. 'Someone recommended this pub to me. Have you got any spare rooms going, please?'

The woman smiled and said, 'You're in luck, Mr Jones, we have a choice of rooms at the moment. How long were you thinking of staying?'

'Oh, probably four days or so, if that's all right.'

'That's fine; I'll show you a nice room now. I'm Betti Williams, by the way. My husband and I have only been here two years and we're doing up the pub as we go along.'

She indicated that he should follow her up the steps outside the back door. A door at the top of the steps opened into a charming room with a large bed, easy chair and table. Wyndham could also see a small shower room leading off the bedroom. There was a large window on one side of the room and a smaller one near the table.

Wyndham said, 'This is perfect, thank you, very nice indeed. Shall I pay you something now?'

Mrs Williams answered, 'We have to charge £25 a night, including breakfast. I hope that will be all right for you.'

'I'll pay you for two nights in advance and we'll go from there, shall we? If possible, I'd love some breakfast now too.'

Mrs Williams took the proffered £50. 'No problem at all, Mr Jones, make yourself comfortable and come down to the back door again; I'll have a good breakfast ready for you in ten minutes or so.'

She left him alone and he went to the large window, from where he could see part of the main street and Dai Sluice looking up at him. A warning bell rang in Wyndham's mind; that man would be dangerous.

Ten minutes later, Wyndham was back downstairs and sitting at a worn, scrubbed kitchen table with a pot of tea. Mrs Williams was at the stove, cooking a fried breakfast for him while bread toasted deliciously under the grill.

'There now, you won't find a better breakfast than that this side of Llangollen,' she said, putting a large plate of eggs and bacon in front of Wyndham. She was right, it was delicious, and Wyndham tucked in, dunking toast into the runny egg yolk.

'Mrs Williams, I met two men in the street; one was wearing a ten-gallon hat and cowboy boots. Who are they?'

Mrs Williams gave a wry laugh. 'That's the sheriff and his deputy! Mr Iwan ap Rhys is our sheriff and Mr David Davies, the local plumber, is the deputy. They are the leading lights of the local volunteer police force. Don't say anything, but they think themselves very important. They started up the force about a year before my husband and I came here and there've been rumours because three people have gone missing mysteriously since then.'

Wyndham said, 'Oh, really? Surely it's just coincidence. Were they local people then?'

She answered very quietly and Wyndham had to strain to hear her.

'No, they were visitors, rather like yourself. Walkers, hikers. People won't talk about it publicly but there's a lot of suspicion and the villagers don't know who to trust. Trouble is, we can't see any motive for the sheriff and his deputy to do anything with the hikers... ' She stopped talking and put her finger to her lips, moving to the back door and opening it quickly. 'Oh, Merle, I thought I heard something moving outside and it was only you!'

Merle Jenkins entered the kitchen. 'Sorry, Betti, didn't mean to startle you. Were you up to something you shouldn't have been, then?' she laughed. 'Oh, I can see you have a gentleman caller… Hallo, I'm Merle Jenkins, the vicar's daughter.'

Wyndham stood up and wiped his buttery hands on a napkin. He extended his right hand and said, 'I'm Haydn Jones; doing a bit of walking in the area so I'm staying here for a few days.'

Her hand was warm and dry as she clasped his. She was about twenty-four years old, of medium height, with a round, buxom figure, clear pale skin and lustrous dark hair. She was what used to be called 'pert' and Wyndham could see that she was interested in him. He returned the compliment and thought that his stay in Myddfai might become a great deal more pleasant than he had expected. Better watch out for the vicar, though!

Merle sat at the kitchen table without invitation and Betti gave her a cup of tea.

'So, Mr Jones, if you're interested in the history of Myddfai, I could show you around the church… and other places.' She grinned invitingly.

'Very kind of you, Miss Jenkins, I'd be pleased to see the church and anywhere else you think appropriate.'

Betti Williams cleared her throat and rolled her eyes upwards at this flagrant flirtation. She knew Merle's reputation, even if the vicar didn't, but she had to admit there was real chemistry between these two.

'No time like the present, then, Mr Jones. Finish your breakfast and we'll go.'

Wyndham obeyed with a grin at Betti Williams, who couldn't help being amused.

A few minutes later, Wyndham and Merle were walking to the church. Wyndham could feel someone staring at him but didn't turn to look back until they had reached the gate to the churchyard. It was Mr David Davies, plumber and deputy sheriff.

Merle said, as they walked up to the church door, 'Have you met Dai Sluice, then? I mean Mr David Davies, deputy sheriff!'

Wyndham replied, 'I've had that dubious honour, briefly on my arrival. I also met Mr Iwan ap Rhys, the Sheriff of Myddfai.'

'Oh, you are honoured, Mr Jones. They'll be checking you on their database before the morning is out.'

'Database? Are they a branch of the FBI, then?' Wyndham spoke light-heartedly but warning signals flashed in his mind.

'I wouldn't be surprised… but don't tell them I told you, Mr Jones.'

'I wouldn't dream of it, Miss Jenkins. Now, what are you going to show me?'

She giggled.

Chapter 8

G ULLS SCREECHED SOMEWHERE close by and the smell of the sea reached into the room, along with some feeble rays of sunshine.

The man in the bed groaned as he awoke. His left arm was stiff – he must have slept on it awkwardly. He looked at the arm and noticed a large bruise inside his elbow.

Slowly, he dragged himself into a sitting position and tentatively put his feet on the floor; good, well-kept feet. He raised himself up from the bed and shuffled toward the shower room in the corner. Switching on the light, he looked in the mirror. The face that looked back at him was red with sun and windburn, his greying hair was cut short and there was small scar on his temple. Otherwise he looked fairly fit.

He switched on the shower and washed quickly. After brushing his teeth, he looked for his clothes in the bedroom. There were jeans and a sweatshirt hanging on the back of the door, and a pair of desert boots with some clean socks inside them on the floor.

He dressed and looked out of the window. The scene was familiar: the waves breaking onto the stones of the harbour and a few people braving the wind.

A quick knock on his door before it opened and there was Nurse Mair Beynon. '*Bore da*, Rhodri, time for breakfast now. You don't want to miss that lovely fry-up, do you?'

He hesitated. Who was Rhodri? Was that his name? Something was missing but he couldn't put his finger on it. 'I'm coming, Nurse,' he replied, but without conviction.

He followed Nurse Beynon down to the dining room and went straight to the window seat; he remembered liking that seat until his cup had fallen over. Why had the cup fallen over?

'*Bore da*, Rhodri. How are you today? Still a bit sunburnt, aren't you? Nurse Jones will have to give you some more of her special cream!' The man speaking to him was short, middle-aged and had several teeth missing.

'Hallo. I think I shall need some more cream.' He felt muddled; perhaps a good breakfast would sort it out for him. Yes, he'd feel better after some solid food. Mr Brynaman grinned his toothless grin and waved goodbye.

'Oh, Rhodri, I'm sorry I forgot to give you back your notebook. I found it in the sitting room yesterday and you'll want to carry on writing your diary.' Nurse Beynon handed him the notebook.

He looked at the diary; it was vaguely familiar. According to his notes, he had been at the clinic for three weeks and had enjoyed a number of bracing walks, good meals, some films on his personal screen and chats with his fellow patients. He didn't seem to remember any of those things, though.

A waitress brought his fried breakfast and a pot of Beddgelert green tea, and he ate. The food was good and he didn't mind the taste of the tea. He gazed out of the window. Had he really been here three weeks? What had he been doing before that? What would do when he was allowed to leave?

He finished breakfast and took his notebook to the residents' sitting room. At first he just sat staring out of the full-length windows toward the sea. He rolled up his sleeve and looked at the bruise on his arm; there was a mark, as though he'd been injected with something. He rolled up his right sleeve and saw a faded bruise in the same position within his right elbow. He didn't remember any injections. What was happening to him?

'Good morning, Rhodri.' A thin man, with thin hair and thin lips was speaking to him. He wore a white coat and his badge displayed the name Dr J Thomas Thomas. 'Something wrong with your arms, Rhodri? Let me have a look.'

He felt he had no choice but to hold out his arms for inspection. He seemed to remember this doctor from a long time ago but the memory kept slipping from his grasp.

'Only some light bruising, Rhodri. Nothing to worry about. But I'll get Nurse Jones to give you more of the face cream to put on before you go out for your walks.'

'How many walks have I been on, Doctor?'

'Well, I'm told you keep a diary, so you should know better than I do! But you've been very keen on the outdoor activities over the past three weeks. Don't overdo it now. If you keep up this level of recovery, you'll be going home before long.'

'Really? I'd like to go home.'

'Yes, I'm sure you'll be pleased to see old Aberteifi again.'

'Aberteifi? Oh yes, of course… ' Further doubt seeped into his mind; he didn't remember Aberteifi at all.

'Well then, you make the most of this period of rest and you'll be off home.' With that, the doctor left him alone.

It was only then that he noticed the shrunken figure of a man in the far corner of the sitting room; a familiar figure, somehow. He was in his sixties, with thinning hair and a jowly face, and a scar on his temple.

'Hallo,' he said to the man, 'don't I know you from somewhere?'

The old man gazed back at him and said very quietly: 'You are Mr Aneurin Ebenezer Hopkins and I'm told that I am Mr Goronwy Evan Evans, a shepherd.' Tears fell down the old man's face and he muttered, 'But who will we be tomorrow? Who will we be?'

Aneurin's blood ran cold. Was he Rhodri or Aneurin? He felt pity for the older man and patted his shoulder, but Mr Goronwy Evan Evans said, 'Go now, they mustn't see you speaking to me – get out of here any way you can, if you can escape Llanfihangel.'

'We're not in Llanfihangel, we're in Porthgain,' said Aneurin. But the older man had slumped in his chair.

What did he mean about Llanfihangel? Aneurin could see the sea outside the windows, see the plants and trees being buffeted by the wind. He could smell the salt air and hear the gulls crying. It was time to pull himself together and find out what was happening to him. But he mustn't let the staff see that he had any suspicions. He had to clear his head; he wasn't even sure who he was. The staff were calling him Rhodri but the old man had stated with certainty that he was Aneurin Ebenezer Hopkins and that name certainly had a familiar ring to it.

He left the sitting room and walked back to his bedroom. An orderly was cleaning it and changing the sheets. 'Only be a couple of minutes now and you can have your room back,' he grinned.

At last the room was finished and Aneurin was alone. He opened the window and put his head outside, breathing in the ozone. It was refreshing but there was something odd; the waves continued to crash against the harbour walls and it seemed as though the same few people were out in the village as had been out earlier that morning and they were in the same positions. The scene never changed.

He closed the window and sat in his chair staring out, trying to make sense of it all. He became filled with horror. If this wasn't Porthgain and he was really in Llanfihangel, then what were the odds of him ever getting out? Why had they changed his name and why could he not remember the past three weeks?

Chapter 9

WYNDHAM, NOW UNDERCOVER as Haydn Jones, felt a kind of liberation in being another character. As he climbed the steps up into the church tower behind Merle Jenkins, he wondered why he felt so at ease with her when he felt anything but with the glorious Emia. Perhaps it was just because he wasn't being Wyndham at the moment; or, perhaps, it was this girl's lack of sophistication and her earthiness that made him feel relaxed in her company.

At last they arrived at the top of the church tower and Merle revealed her secret to him. 'This is the camera obscura,' she said.

He was astonished; he knew of such devices but had never seen one. He could see the entire village and a good part of the surrounding area. In fact, he could see Dai Sluice on his beat in the main street.

'Merle, does everyone in the village know about this?'

'No, only my father and me... and a couple of good friends. Dad was going to open it as a tourist attraction, but after Mr Iwan ap Rhys became sheriff, he thought it was best to keep it to ourselves for the time being. He's never really trusted the sheriff and he thought that the camera obscura would be handy to keep an eye on things.'

'Very wise, I should think. I can't say that I took to the sheriff or his deputy on my first meeting with them. The sheriff even gave me a warning.'

'Did he, now?' Merle frowned. 'Then I would heed him,

Haydn Jones, and keep an eye in the back of your head, if you can.'

'Do you come up here very often, Merle?' asked Wyndham.

'Oh yes, quite a lot; but not always to look at the camera obscura, you know!' she giggled.

Wyndham laughed along with her. He really liked this girl.

'So, Mr Haydn Jones, what are your plans for the next few days?' Merle asked, coming to stand close to him. He could smell the faint scent of roses in her hair.

'I'm going to explore the countryside around Myddfai, Miss Merle Jenkins.'

'Well, don't forget to let me know if I can help you,' she said with a soft smile. 'Perhaps you'd better get going then, or people will talk.'

He followed her down the steps again and they walked out into the churchyard, among the falling, fading gravestones. Her hand brushed lightly against his as they walked and he liked the sensation. At the gate, she said, 'Goodbye for now, Mr Haydn Jones – you'll be seeing me again.'

'I hope I will, Miss Merle Jenkins, I hope I will.'

He headed back to the pub and let himself into the kitchen. Betti Williams was making sandwiches ready for the lunchtime drinkers.

'Mrs Williams, is there any chance I could have one or two of those as a packed lunch, please?' Wyndham asked.

'There's every chance, Mr Jones! I'll have some ready for you in a few minutes now and you can get going on your walking. Er, just for one person is it?'

'Just for one, Mrs Williams,' he laughed.

Chapter 10

A NEURIN THOUGHT HARD. It was still difficult to grasp some things, but by now he was certain that the bruises on his arms were from hypodermic needles. He'd been drugged. But what if other things were drugged too? Perhaps the food or the drink. The Beddgelert green tea, of course, must be very suspect. Whoever had heard of tea growing in North Wales? Well, he would make sure not to drink the tea from now on, and eat as little as possible. What if the tap water was drugged? He'd have to risk some of that, or find some water used by the staff. And he wouldn't watch the films on his personal screen any more because they must be used for hypnosis.

He sat for some time, slowly putting things together in his mind, like a jigsaw. He felt as though he were climbing a very long and difficult ladder from a dark place into the sunlight. Bit by bit, things were becoming clearer.

Then there was Mr Goronwy Evan Evans (or whatever his name really was); he felt sure he'd been told that Mr Evans had left but there he had been this morning, in the sitting room, looking wasted and frightened. If Aneurin could only come up with a plan, then he'd do his best to get Mr Evans out too.

The first part of his plan was to find out where he actually was. Was the clinic in Porthgain or was it really in Llanfihangel-ar-Arth? The thought was terrifying. Was it possible that they had deluded everyone into thinking they were by the seaside when, in fact, they were in a country village?

He went to the window and opened it wide. The bars outside meant that he couldn't get out and could only reach out so far. The sun was higher in the sky now but, when he put out his arm, he could feel no warmth from it. There was a breeze, but that could come from a giant fan for all he knew. The plants outside looked real enough but he was struck, again, by the harbour scene looking the same as it always did with the same people outside. Granted, the boats bobbed up and down on the water and the waves smashed into the rocks and harbour walls, but that didn't mean it was real. No doubt the smell of salt water could be manufactured too.

'All right, Aneurin, much as you want to get out and get out fast, you'll have to take your time about this,' he said to himself. 'Can't arouse any suspicion or you'll be going out in a pine box.'

A sound outside his door had him turning quickly and moving back to his chair.

'Hallo, Rhodri,' said Nurse Jones. 'I've brought that cream for your face. I've been looking for you; Dr J Thomas Thomas said you were in the sitting room.'

'Oh, Nurse Jones, thank you. Yes, I was in the sitting room but I fancied being on my own for a bit, just enjoying the harbour view.'

'Yes, I don't blame you. It's lovely, isn't it? Now then, put your head back and I'll put on the cream for you.' She spread the cream gently on his face. 'I'd advise you not to go on one of your walks today because of the windburn. Leave it for a couple of days.'

She sounded so kind and gentle that he found it difficult to believe she could be involved in such deceit. But he hardened his heart and decided that he could trust nobody at the clinic, not even Mr Goronwy Evan Evans for the moment.

'I'll do as you say, Nurse. Thank you for looking after me so well.'

'It's my job, Rhodri, but it's always nice to be appreciated. I'm sure you feel that in your line of work, too.'

'I don't know if I'll have a line of work when I leave here,' Aneurin answered sadly.

'Come on. There's no shape on you today and I thought you were coming along nicely. Don't let us all down now.'

'It's important that I don't let myself down, Nurse Jones,' Aneurin said, 'and all those that have relied on me.'

'That's the way – good fighting talk,' she said firmly. 'Keep that up and you'll be out of here before the week is out.'

'Do you mean that I'll be able to go home and live normally?'

'Well, don't say that I said anything but they seem very pleased with your progress.'

With that, she left the room quickly and Aneurin was left wondering if she was trying to tell him something. For all he knew, her comments could all be part of the deceit. It was still difficult to think straight after what must have been three weeks of drugs and hypnosis – that is if it really had been three weeks. He really had to concentrate hard to make decisions but he was determined to succeed.

He closed the window and locked it, then moved his easy chair and placed it firmly against the door. He moved slowly around the small room and the shower room, ensuring that there was no other entrance, including through the floor or ceiling. He was tired so he lay down for a while and slept.

Whispering disturbed him. What was it? Where was it coming from? He opened his eyes and could see that the screen had been lowered from the ceiling. Immediately he jumped up from the bed, slid across the floor and dashed to the shower room to fetch some tissues. He tore up a couple and stuffed as much as he could into his ears so that he couldn't hear the voices. Tentatively he looked up at the screen again. This time it was showing a swirling kaleidoscope of colour so he turned away. He'd sit in the chair, up against the door, that's what he'd do! That way, he wouldn't see the screen and he'd know if anyone was trying to come into the room.

After a time, perhaps fifteen minutes, the screen withdrew into the ceiling again and he removed the tissue from one ear. The voices had gone. He threw away the tissues and put the chair back in its normal place. Then he lay on the bed.

A few minutes later, he heard voices outside his room so he closed his eyes almost completely. The door opened and two hefty orderlies entered on tiptoe. He'd never seen these two before. By this time, there was one on either side of the bed and he could just see that they'd brought in a wheelchair. The lifted him easily into the chair and Aneurin was careful to appear to be a dead weight.

'He's out, all right, Gav,' said one of the orderlies.

Gently, they wheeled Aneurin out of his room and down the corridor to a lift. They must have gone down two floors but Aneurin couldn't be sure. Next they wheeled him along another corridor to those familiar wooden doors and knocked.

'Come in, come in,' the North Wales voice called out.

Gav opened the door, took Aneurin into the room and lifted him into a leather chair. Then both orderlies left with the wheelchair.

'You can come back in twenty minutes, lads,' said the voice.

Silence. Aneurin kept his eyes closed and feigned sleep.

'Rhodri, I am your friend, Dr Owain ap Owain. Do you remember me?'

'I remember you,' said Aneurin sleepily. 'You are the doctor, you are my friend.'

'Excellent, Rhodri, excellent. Now I'm going to remind you about our little plan.'

Aneurin was hard put to keep his eyes closed and his body relaxed but he forced himself to sit still.

'Rhodri, you'll be going home this week but there's just one little thing you need to do when you leave. Do you understand me?'

'One little thing to do... ' Aneurin murmured.

'That's right. When you leave, a friend will take you to Carmarthen to see a lady. This lady is not kind, Rhodri, and she wants to harm you and to harm me. That's not nice, is it?'

'Not nice... '

'Very good. So when you see this lady, Rhodri, you must shoot her. That will stop her doing these bad things to you and me.'

'I must shoot her... ' said Aneurin.

'That's right, Rhodri, you must shoot her dead. You will be given a gun. And when you hear the words "Macsen's sword" you'll know it's the time. Do you understand?'

'Macsen's sword. I must shoot her dead with the gun,' muttered Aneurin.

'Excellent. Well, it's been nice talking to you again, Rhodri. I won't be seeing you again before you leave but it's been a pleasure to have you here at our little clinic. You've been a very good patient.'

The door opened and the two orderlies came back in with the wheelchair. They lifted Aneurin and wheeled him back to the lift. Dr Owain ap Owain had told the orderlies he wouldn't need them again that day.

'Well, Gav, we'll be able to leave a bit early tonight and get to the disco at Llandysul.'

The two orderlies discussed their plans for that night as they took Aneurin back to his room. Having laid him on the bed again, Gav and his companion left and the door clicked softly behind them. To be on the safe side, Aneurin lay still for some minutes, in case someone else came in.

He had a lot to think about. It appeared that he need not make an attempt to escape as he would be released very soon. That was a relief and made everything that much easier. But what struck him most forcibly was the fact that the orderlies were going to the disco at Llandysul that night. Llandysul was very close to Llanfihangel-ar-Arth and nowhere near Porthgain, so his suspicions were correct. Even if he had been at Porthgain to start with, he was now in the dreaded rest home at Llanfihangel.

He had a strong feeling that the woman he was to kill was someone in Carmarthen Intelligence. If that was the case, who was Dr Owain ap Owain working for?

The door opened; it was Nurse Jones. 'Hallo, Rhodri. Have you had a nice sleep again? It's time for lunch now.'

Aneurin yawned and slowly sat up. 'Would you please walk with me, Nurse Jones? I just feel a little bit light-headed at the moment. Perhaps I've been sleeping too much.'

'Well, I'm sure you needed it, Rhodri. But I'll come with you. I've been told you're leaving in two days so that's good news for you. We'll miss you though.'

She held his arm companionably as they walked to the staircase and down to the hall where Mr Brynaman nodded to them and watched them go by, grinning gummily.

Chapter 11

GUILDHALL SQUARE WAS still busy when Iori left CIHQ for home the evening after Aneurin's kidnap. He'd put in a double shift and he was tired. The Boss and Emia had been in conference all morning and they had both gone home after lunch, weary after the previous night's work.

'Lucky they can rely on me. If everyone there had my attitude, the place would be much more efficient,' he thought to himself as he walked in front of the Guildhall and up Hall Street to Woolworths. If he hurried, he'd be in time to get some pic'n'mix to enjoy that evening. The Bonnie Tyler Show was on at 8pm so that was something to look forward to.

A few minutes later he was letting himself into his flat, complete with a large bag of sweets. He flicked the light switch by the door and nothing happened; the flat remained in darkness.

'Damn, the bulb must have gone. Where's my torch?'

At that moment, the table lamp by the window came on and Iori gasped with fright. Someone was sitting in the easy chair. He turned to run back down the stairs, still gripping his bag of sweets, but a large figure put a hand on Iori's shoulder and steered him back into the room.

'*Noswaith dda*, Iori. Nice little place you've got here. Bit small for my taste but you've done it up nice, and this is a comfortable chair,' said a voice.

'Who are you?' Iori managed to croak.

'I'm your friend, Iori, and the gentleman behind you wants to be your friend... don't you Harri?'

Harri grunted but Iori's attempt to look behind him to see Harri's face was discouraged by two strong hands on his neck.

'Now then, Iori, let's make ourselves comfortable and have a chat. What's that you've got, pic'n'mix is it? I'm partial to a few sweeties myself and Harri is fond of those triangles from Quality Street, aren't you, Harri?'

Harri grunted again and removed the bag from Iori's hand, pouring the sweets onto the table by the man whose face was still in darkness, despite the lamp. Iori wondered if fainting might be a good idea at this point but Harri returned and pushed him over to the bed, the only other place to sit. So Iori decided against fainting and sat on the edge of the bed, nervously. Harri went back to the table and took all the green-wrapped triangles from the sweet selection in his great paw and then stood guard at the door, munching contentedly.

The man in the chair chose a tiny Bounty bar. 'Oh, you don't mind do you, Iori? Plenty for us all, I think.'

Iori opened his mouth but couldn't make up his mind what would be the right thing to say at this stage, so he closed it again.

'Had a little look round at your cosy home, Iori. Like the harp very much – very cultural. Not a fan of Bonnie Tyler myself, though you seem to have all her records and that's a good picture of her on the wall. But you must be wondering why we are here so let's get down to business. One of your colleagues has gone on a little trip, we think. You know the one we mean: the tall, red-headed one. All we want to know is where he's gone and why.'

Iori's heart sank; he was only a receptionist, not an intelligence officer, and he'd never expected to get into a situation like this. 'I don't know what you mean,' he said.

'Oh, come on now, Iori, you might not be an intelligence officer but you've got a bit of brain about you. You see who comes and goes.'

'I'm not told about all the details of operations. I'm not meant to know, it's safer that way.'

'Yes, Iori, but you are in a position to find out, aren't you? And that is what you are going to do for me. Tomorrow you will find out where your man has gone and why, and you'll tell me everything you know. I know that you get a lunch break, so Harri will meet you in the café in Welsh Home Stores tomorrow at 12.30pm and you will have the information for him.'

'But... if they find out, it'll be the end of my career – in fact, the end of everything. I could end up dead or even in Llanfihangel.'

'I don't think I explained myself properly, Iori. If you don't do this little thing for me, CI is going to find out about that night in Blackpill, on the beach, and your career will definitely be over then.'

Iori went pale and shook with fear. How could they have found out about Blackpill? It was all so long ago. He tried to brazen it out. 'I don't know what you're talking about. You must be confusing me with someone else.'

The man was disapproving, 'Now, now, Iori, don't be silly. We had a little word with a young gentleman from Betws who remembers the incident very well and even mentioned a small birthmark in an interesting place.'

Iori slumped and a tear came to his eye.

'I think we understand each other now, Iori, so we'll leave you to enjoy your evening. Still plenty of sweets for you.'

The table lamp went off and a small torch lit the man's steps to the door while Harri held Iori firmly down on the bed.

'Come along, Harri. We'll leave Iori to think about our conversation. I'm sure he'll be sensible.'

Harri followed the man out of the room and closed the door firmly behind him. A few moments later, Iori heard the outer door close and knew he was alone, but he couldn't find the strength to run to the window and look out. Perhaps it wouldn't have been wise anyway.

How could they know about Blackpill? The question kept going round and round in his head. The man had been right; if CI knew about that, his career and reputation would be gone in a second. He'd spent the past few years building a reputation for strict morals, so if the Blackpill incident got out he would be destroyed and all the people he'd rubbed up the wrong way at CI would have a good laugh. He lay down on the bed and wept as he had not done since childhood. The pic'n'mix lay spread out on the small table, forgotten, and Bonnie Tyler was of no comfort, staring out from her picture as she always did, with big hair.

Outside, the two men crossed Nott Square and went through the old keep gate to the ruined castle, a short cut to the council car park. There a dark, unmarked car awaited them with the engine running and a driver in place. Harri and the man got in the car and they left the car park, turning right and joining the evening traffic going down Jail Hill and heading for Coracle Way.

The driver looked in the rear-view mirror and said, 'How

did he take it, boss? Going to co-operate is he?'

Mr Brynaman smiled, revealing his chocolate-covered gums. 'Oh, I think he will see sense. Yes, I think Iori will be a nice little asset to us,' he said, and unwrapped another tiny Bounty bar with obvious pleasure.

Chapter 12

WYNDHAM WENT BACK up the outside steps to his room and unlocked the door. Before he went in, he checked the floor and saw that he'd had a visitor in the time he'd been in the kitchen and with Merle. He'd sprinkled some talcum powder on the floor just inside the door and it was this that revealed a large footprint. The print had come from a heavy walking boot, definitely not from Betti Williams's little shoe. So, Dai Sluice had looked in, had he?

Stepping over the print, Wyndham went over to the wardrobe and looked inside. The blond hair he'd left on his bag had gone but the bag had not been opened. As a matter of course he always used special numbered plastic tabs on the lock as they had to be cut off in order to open the bag. The tab was still there. He took his smaller day bag out of the wardrobe and a few items he'd hidden under a loose floorboard beneath the bed, and went back downstairs to the kitchen, having spread a little more talc on the floor.

Betti had left his sandwiches on the table in a sealed bag, along with a small bottle of water. He could hear voices from the bar and realised the pub was now open and busy so he packed his lunch into his bag and went out the back door. He headed out on the road to Llangadog to find the site of the first murder.

Watching him, along the street, was Dai Sluice, wearing a distinct frown. He was annoyed that he hadn't been able to find anything in the new visitor's room, but had decided that the tab on the bag meant that Wyndham was up to something and Dai would find out what in due course. First he had to unblock Mrs Beer's toilet and he was cross about it. He was a deputy sheriff, so he would have to get in another assistant as unblocking drains was beneath him now. He fancied getting some of those cowboy boots and a stetson too, like Mr Iwan ap Rhys, but perhaps he ought to tread carefully with the sheriff to start with; he didn't want to rub him up the wrong way.

He looked at Wyndham with longing, like a dog confronted with a nice, tasty, smelly bone. If he'd been a real deputy sheriff he could have shot him, or at the very least stopped him and put him in jail. He growled with frustration and went to put on his overalls and unblock Mrs Beer.

Wyndham could feel eyes on him as he walked away from the village, and as he looked behind him he could see Dai Sluice walking away reluctantly. A flash, like a mirror in sunlight, made him look up at the church tower and he thought he could see Merle looking down at him. He couldn't give any thought to Merle right now; he was working and he had to find the site of the first death to have taken place during the new sheriff's reign. Plenty of time for fun later on, he hoped.

He walked swiftly up the hill for a mile and then climbed a gate into a field and walked close to the hedge. He hadn't been followed and the traffic had been very light, but he wanted to keep out of sight just in case the sheriff was about. He came to another gate and climbed over. This was the field where the first hiker had been found by a farmer fourteen months ago. The body had been in a deep ditch at the side of the field beneath a high hedge. It had been there for about three weeks, steeped in water. Not a pleasant sight. Carmarthen Crime Scene Unit (CCSU) had been over the area but Wyndham needed to see exactly how and where the murder had been committed.

After wrapping his boots and the lower part of his jeans in the kitchen film he'd brought in his day bag, and removing his jacket, Wyndham looked down into the ditch. It was surprisingly dry for the time of year and it would be easier to search than when the body was found. He put on some latex gloves and dropped down into the ditch, pleased that the ground was fairly firm beneath him. He hadn't really expected to find anything so he was taken aback to see something metallic sticking out of the drying mud in the bottom of the ditch. He pulled at the metal and almost fell backwards when the mud released its treasure suddenly. It was a knife, a large hunting knife. Placing it carefully on a piece of cloth, Wyndham took out his Blackcurrant and photographed it, then e-mailed the photo to The Boss, Emia and the CI weapons department with the message: 'Found at first site, deep in mud.' Then he placed the knife in an evidence bag and put it in his day bag.

He lifted himself out of the ditch and sat on the grass for a moment to collect his thoughts and look again at the murder site. His Blackcurrant vibrated and he saw the message: 'Evidence collection Llangadog Church 45 minutes, password Bedwyr.'

He got up immediately, made sure he had all his equipment and, still keeping close to the hedge, headed for the far gate which would put him on the right road. Before he climbed the gate, he removed the kitchen film from his shoes and jeans and put it in his pocket. Then he set off westward to walk the three miles to Llangadog.

He made good time and arrived at the church with several minutes to spare.

Wyndham spent a little time looking at the graves in the churchyard before trying the big west door of the church. The handle turned easily and he went in. At the far end of the church, in front of the altar, a black-robed figure knelt. Wyndham walked quietly, almost on tiptoe, toward the front pews and sat. He removed the evidence bag holding the knife from his day bag and placed it by him, on the side nearest the aisle, then he bent forward with his head resting on one hand, as though praying. The other hand lay lightly on the evidence bag at his side.

The black-robed figure stood up, walked backward a couple of paces and bowed to the altar, then he turned and walked toward the pew where Wyndham sat. He stood in the aisle and whispered, 'Bedwyr.'

Wyndham removed his hand from the evidence bag and the priest said, 'Bless you, my son, go in peace.'

Wyndham nodded, got up and walked out of the church slowly and without looking back. The priest, in the meantime, bent down as though to tidy the hassock where Wyndham had been sitting, and slipped the evidence bag into his wide sleeve. Then he turned back to the altar, bowed again and made for the vestry.

Outside the vestry window was a man waiting by a small blue van. The priest handed him the evidence bag and closed the window. He heard the van leave and breathed a sigh of relief.

Wyndham had waited in the church porch and saw the van leave, driven by Walter, and also felt some relief. Time to eat his lunch now. He found a bench and sat to eat the excellent cheese sandwiches Betti had made him and drink some water. The way the investigation was going was almost too easy; he was certain that the rest of it would not be so straightforward but he felt satisfied with his first morning's work.

He thought he could have a few minutes to himself so he walked along the road and then the public footpath that passed by the old castle. In fact it wasn't so much a castle now as a barrow which was covered in trees, but there was an atmosphere there that held some fascination for him. For a few minutes, he stood looking at the hill where the castle had stood so many centuries before. Then a voice said, 'Something haunting about it, isn't there?'

Wyndham, who had sensed someone coming up the path toward him and had seen, out of the corner of his eye, a middle-aged woman in walking clothes with a dog, said, 'Yes, you can almost feel the history emanating from it, somehow.'

'Funny you should say that,' she replied, 'that's almost exactly what that young man who went missing said to me.'

Wyndham turned to her. 'What young man was that, then?'

She looked serious. 'Young North Wales lad down here last year, in April it was, and he was a walker. Seemed very harmless and pleasant but the next thing I knew, he was on the news as being missing, and as far as I know he was never found.'

'I'm a walker,' said Wyndham, 'I hope that doesn't happen here all the time!'

'No, of course not,' she said, 'but it would be wise to keep your eyes open all the same. We get plenty of hikers down here but there are some strange people about.'

'I'll keep my eyes peeled, then,' said Wyndham. 'Er, did they find out where he was last seen, or anything?'

The woman thought and frowned. 'In fact, strangely enough, I think he was seen trying to get up to the mound there, to see if there was anything left of the castle. The owner of the Lion was out walking his dog and thought he saw someone who looked like him going through those trees one evening.' She turned and called to the dog, which had run ahead excitedly. 'Good luck and enjoy your walking,' she said.

'Thank you. I think I'll keep away from the mound though!' said Wyndham, good-humouredly.

She smiled and the dog ran up to her, then they both turned back toward the village.

So, thought Wyndham, there was something about the mound and the old castle that needed investigating. The hikers had clearly just been visitors to the area but both of them must have stumbled across something and paid for it. It was wiser to continue this investigation at night, he thought. Time to get back to Myddfai, catch up on a little sleep and make friends with the locals.

He went back to the road and set off eastward again. He walked further east so that he entered the village from the opposite direction from the one he'd used when leaving earlier. As he walked along the main street, he noticed some curtains moving in a house on his right and wondered if Dai Sluice was watching him again.

A few people were coming out of the pub and another few were going in. He headed for the back steps and went straight to his room, where he could see that the talc had been disturbed again. The deputy sheriff certainly wasn't very bright. He wiped up the talc and checked the shower room where he could see that some of his toiletries had been moved. Then he looked under the bed and very gently moved it slightly to get at the loose floorboard, where he replaced his kitchen film and one or two other items he'd taken out with him. He moved the bed back quietly.

Before lying down for some sleep he undressed partially, leaving his jeans and T-shirt on, then placed a chair under the door handle as well as locking the door. He emptied the carafe of water that sat on the bedside table, rinsed it thoroughly and refilled it from the bathroom tap. He checked his Blackcurrant which showed one message: 'Evidence safe.' He deleted the message and the previous instruction, sent a message confirming his arrival back in Myddfai, then plugged in the Blackcurrant to recharge and lay down. He was asleep within minutes.

Chapter 13

IN THE SMALL studio flat in Carmarthen, sleep did not come as easily to Iori. He may have worked at CI for several years but his life experience hadn't prepared him for blackmail and treason.

For a long time he lay weeping. He was very tired but sleep eluded him and the TV show he'd so looked forward to and the sweets he'd planned to eat no longer appealed. He had no one to turn to and who could he have trusted anyway? He had no friends, despite belonging to the Irish Harp Society; none of the other members socialised with him. All he had was his work and this little flat. Not a lot to have accumulated in his twenty-eight years. He could go to The Boss, perhaps, but then he'd have to tell her about Blackpill. What a mess.

The only other thing he could do was to kill himself. They couldn't do anything to him if he were dead. He got up slowly and went into his tiny bathroom. He opened the cupboard but there were only two soluble aspirin in there – hardly enough to send him to oblivion. He had no alcohol in the flat; he rarely had more than a half of shandy at most, even at the office parties.

He went to the kitchen and looked at his chopping knife. It would be so messy and painful and drawn out. Besides, he didn't have a bath he could sit in like the Romans used to do when they killed themselves, only a shower. And there was nowhere strong enough to hang himself from in the flat; in any case, that didn't appeal very much. He'd seen films where people had hung themselves and the result was always horrible.

He could go to the supermarket and get some pills and vodka but what if they were watching him? If they saw him buying those things, they'd know what he was going to do.

He went back to the bed, reluctant to sit in the chair where his nemesis had sat. For the next ten minutes he sat staring out of the window, unable to stir himself to any action. There was nothing else for it; he would have to betray Wyndham. Not that he liked Wyndham – he was too good-looking, fit, popular and a favourite with the girls. He was everything that Iori was not. But betrayal was a big thing.

He spent the next hour justifying his decision to himself, then he went and washed his face and changed for bed. Eating was out of the question; he felt nauseous and his sweets had been contaminated by that Harri and the strange man.

He lay under the duvet in his fake silk pyjamas and stared at the ceiling, willing time to reverse so that Blackpill had never happened. Eventually he fell into a disturbed sleep.

It seemed as though only five minutes had passed before the alarm went off. Iori sat up sharply, then remembered the previous night and buried his head in his hands.

He took a shower and dressed. He was still nauseous but there were also pangs of hunger in his belly. However, he couldn't stand the thought of eating. Again he sat on his bed staring out of the window, waiting for the time when he could reasonably go to work.

It was a fine day but as far as Iori was concerned, it might as well have been bucketing with rain. He walked slowly down Hall Street. There was a man standing in the doorway of Woolworths who might have been watching him. Iori tried not to look at him as he walked past and the man continued reading his copy of the *Carmarthen Journal*, seemingly unaware of anyone else. Iori walked faster and headed straight for CI's door in Guildhall Square. At last he felt safe, but then he realised he was anything but safe. Indeed, there was nowhere safe for him.

The doorkeeper this morning was Bert, a former policeman who took a dim view of Iori and seldom bothered even to be polite to him. Iori said, 'Hello, Bert,' much to the doorkeeper's surprise, as Iori rarely took the time to acknowledge his existence. He stared as Iori entered the lift and pressed the button for the first floor down. 'Must have found a girlfriend,' thought Bert, 'that'll be the day!'

Iori was early enough to be alone in the office that morning. Taking a deep breath to calm his nerves, he unlocked his desk drawer, picked up some files and took them into Emia's office, accidentally knocking some to the floor as he reached her desk. As he knelt to pick them up, he realised this was his chance to see if Emia's computer held the information he needed. Quickly, he clicked the mouse to open Emia's e-mails and saw a message from Wyndham, the one where he'd attached a picture of the knife. Iori pressed 'print' and the picture came out of the printer. The subsequent message to Walter regarding the evidence pick-up followed and he printed that too. Making sure that both pages fell on the floor, he picked them up with some files and took them back to his desk. He sat heavily in his chair and took deep breaths, afraid that he was going to vomit. He was sweating so he took out some moist wipes from his top drawer and wiped his face and, opening his shirt, under his arms. It was done. All he had to do now was go out to lunch as arranged and hand the pieces of paper over to Harri; then it was up to them to find out more. After a few minutes he felt calmer, although the feeling of nausea hadn't really subsided.

He had to look busy for when Emia and The Boss arrived so he went through his work and his e-mails. He never received social e-mails from the other employees at CI; he had never been invited to the coracle parties. At that moment he had never felt so lonely.

Eventually Emia arrived, immaculately turned out as always. '*Bore da*, Iori,' she said. 'How was Bonnie last night?'

Iori cleared his throat and looked at her blankly.

She said, 'Ground Control to Iori, how was Bonnie last night?'

'Oh, she was very good, of course,' said Iori hastily, 'she always is.' He turned back to his work.

Emia blinked at him. He never usually admitted watching Bonnie Tyler so that was a first. 'What next?' she thought. 'Perhaps he'll give us a performance of "Total Eclipse of the Heart"!' She decided not to pursue the subject and went to her desk. 'Thanks for these files, Iori,' she said as she sat down. Her beautifully shod foot slid on something beneath her desk – a piece of paper. She bent down and picked it up; it was a blank sheet from the printer. 'That's funny,' she thought, 'the cleaners should have seen this but I'm certain it wasn't there when I left yesterday.' She looked at Iori but he was engrossed by his work. She made a mental note to speak to The Boss about it.

The Boss was at an important meeting all morning so both Emia and Iori got on with their separate tasks. The two pieces of paper Iori had printed were folded up in the inside pocket of his jacket. At 12.25 he said to Emia, 'I'm just popping out for a lunch break, if you don't mind; I didn't have any breakfast this morning and I'm getting hungry.'

She replied, 'That's all right, Iori, I'll go when you come back. I've got plenty to keep me occupied.' She watched him leave and thought, 'Another funny thing; he's always going on about how important breakfast is and he didn't have any today.'

Moments later, Iori was crossing Guildhall Square to Welsh Home Stores on the opposite side. He went straight upstairs to the café but Harri wasn't there. Perhaps he wasn't coming, perhaps it was all a horrible dream. He bought a cup of coffee and a cheese sandwich, then sat down with his back to the wall and waited.

Just before 12.35 the large presence that was Harri made himself known to the café staff. He got himself a cup of coffee and sat at the adjoining table to Iori. The pieces of paper were on the banquette between them, under Iori's hand. Harri said, 'Sugar,' and nodded to the bowl on Iori's table. Iori passed it to him and said quietly, 'This was all I could get.' Harri grasped the papers and stuffed them into his jacket pocket. Then he slurped down his sweet coffee and left the café.

Iori had a horrible feeling that he was going to wet himself. He breathed deeply and noisily to the astonishment of the cashier, then got up, his legs feeling weak, and walked slowly out of the café, leaving his sandwich and coffee behind. He walked out through the store and into Guildhall Square. It wasn't yet 12.45 so he had time to go home and freshen up a bit.

At 1.25 Iori returned to his office. Emia looked up from her work and said, 'Feeling all right, Iori? Had something to eat? I'll go out for a quick break now as The Boss is due back at 3pm.'

Iori nodded, still feeling exhausted and weakened by his adventure.

On her way out, Emia stopped to talk to Bert, who was just finishing up his shift.

'Bert, *cariad*, I'm a bit worried about Iori; he's not himself today. Did you see where he went for his lunch break?'

Bert was always ready to talk to Emia, whom he admired from afar in a fatherly way.

'He went across to Welsh Home Stores, Emia, but the funny thing was that he came out a few minutes later without any bags or anything and then went up Hall Street, as if he was going home. He was a bit strange this morning, he said hello to me!'

Emia frowned; this was peculiar. 'Thanks, Bert, you're a star, as ever! Let me know if he does anything else that's odd, will you?'

'No problem, Emia. Perhaps he's in love,' he laughed.

Emia didn't think so; she was sure something else was going on. She left the offices and went across to Welsh Home Stores. If Iori was getting something to eat, he'd have gone up to the café, perhaps. She went up the stairs and got herself a cup of tea. As she was paying the cashier, she said, 'Oh, I was hoping I wasn't too late for my friend; I was supposed to meet him earlier here and I couldn't get him on the mobile phone to say I'd be late.'

The cashier said, 'What does he look like then?'

Emia went on to describe Iori and what he was wearing and the cashier said, 'I know who you mean; he came in about half-past twelve, got himself a coffee and a cheese sandwich and left them on the table!'

'Do you mean he just put them down and walked out?' Emia asked.

'No, *bach*, he sat down and waited and a really big man,

70

like a nightclub bouncer or something, came in, bought a coffee and sat at the table next to him. Then this man asked your friend for the sugar, even though there was a bowl on his table. And your friend gave it to him. The man drank his coffee straight down and left and your friend went really pale and he was breathing as though he'd run a race. Then he got up and walked out, looking a bit wobbly.'

'Well,' said Emia, 'I'll have to ring my friend when I get back now.'

She was thoroughly bewildered by this behaviour but she was very suspicious of the big man the cashier had described. She sat and drank her tea, left a good tip for the cashier and left. As soon as she got back to the office, where Meinir Arian was now installed as doorkeeper, she went straight to the security room. Alun, the head of security, looked at Emia in astonishment and appreciation; she didn't often go down to his office.

'Alun, it may be my imagination but I think something strange is going on,' she said. 'Can I see the tape for Guildhall Square from 12.25 to 12.50, please?'

Alun knew that she wouldn't ask for such a thing unless it was important, so he said, 'No problem, Emia, nothing easier.'

He typed something on his keyboard and the screen showed Guildhall Square at 12.25. He ran the film forward a little and they could see Iori walking across to Welsh Home Stores. Emia asked him to fast forward a little and then said, 'Stop there!' A very large man was walking into Welsh Home Stores a few minutes after Iori. Shortly afterwards he came out again with his right hand in his pocket, as though he was making sure that something was there. Very soon after that,

Iori emerged from the store and walked up Hall Street.

Emia asked Alun if he could find out where the large man had gone. He typed again and his screen showed several pictures from various cameras in town. Eventually they found the pictures showing the entrance to the castle from Nott Square. The large man went through the keep gate. Then Alun found the pictures for the council car park and they saw the large man walk toward a dark-coloured car and get in; the car then drove away. Yet again, Alun was able to follow the car as it went down Jail Hill and on to Coracle Way and headed westward. Alun tried to find a picture of the car's registration but didn't seem to be having any luck.

'Alun, I'm not joking when I say that we need to find out more about that car. Can you put someone on it for me, please?'

'You're serious, aren't you?' Alun replied. 'Don't worry, I'll put my best man onto it now and get back to you. How do you want me to contact you, if you're worried about Iori?'

'Just ring me direct and say that you've found the old file I was looking for – thanks, Alun.'

Emia went back to her office and gave Iori no more attention than usual. Her mind seethed with theories as to what was happening and she could scarcely wait for The Boss's return.

Eventually, at 3pm, The Boss arrived and went straight into her office. Emia followed her in with some memos for signature and closed the door. Iori was at his desk, his heart thumping. If he could just get through today, he was sure to be all right.

Emia signalled to The Boss that she was going to write something down for her to read. The Boss took the hint and just chattered about how dreary meetings were for a few moments. When she read the note, she looked steely. 'Is Alun on to this?' she asked.

Emia nodded and said she'd instructed Alun to find out about the car but it was a matter of waiting. For the next half an hour, they got on with work and Emia returned to her desk. Shortly afterwards, her phone rang and Alun told her that he'd found the file. Emia went into The Boss's office and told her and The Boss instructed her to have all the pictures e-mailed directly to The Boss's office, and only her office. A few minutes later, all the pictures had downloaded and The Boss's face was pale. Emia had never seen her like that.

The Boss turned to Emia, saying, 'This is very, very serious and I'll have to speak to Swansea about it as we'll be swimming in deep waters with this.' Then she suddenly said, 'Warn Wyndham that someone may be on to him and it's dangerous, do it now!'

Emia hurried back to her desk, trying not to arouse Iori's interest, but he seemed to be completely enthralled by his work. Within moments, she'd sent off a coded message to Wyndham's Blackcurrant and she prayed he'd be in a position to see it straight away.

The Boss called her in again and told her that they would both have to take the Underground later that afternoon, after Iori had gone home; she didn't like spoiling Emia's evening but there was no choice – this was an emergency.

Iori left the office at 5pm and then Emia and her boss got themselves ready for their trip. Emia was still no wiser as to what had happened but she knew The Boss wouldn't be reacting like this if it hadn't been very important.

At 5.15pm, they both descended to the Quay Street

Underground station and boarded the express train to Swansea. This was the first time that Emia had been to Swansea on the train and she felt a frisson of excitement that she would be travelling underground in a secret train. The Boss said little on the journey but they both drank tea, brought to them by a young woman dressed in a Welsh plaid skirt, white frilly blouse and buckled shoes. In twenty minutes they were in Swansea and they disembarked to be met by a stern-faced young man in a tailored suit and wearing a personal communicator behind his ear. He was obviously an agent from the WBI – the Welsh Bureau of Investigation. He indicated that they should follow him and he took them to a lift.

The lift rose swiftly and they found themselves on the top floor of Swansea's only skyscraper, with a view of Swansea Harbour and the sea. Emia was thrilled. They were in a vast room, dotted with Modernist furniture. The agent invited them to sit on a long sofa near the window and offered them some Ty Nant water. A moment later, a man entered, followed by two female agents who went to stand on either side of the doorway. Emia and The Boss made to stand but he said, 'No, don't get up, ladies. We're meeting up here so we can feel a bit more relaxed than in my office.' He turned to the agent who had brought them up in the lift. 'Special Agent Lewis, I think we can do better than water, don't you?'

The agent turned and went to a large cabinet. He poured a large Brecon gin and tonic for Emia, with ice and a slice of fresh lime, and a large Penderyn whisky for The Boss, with a slice of orange and ice. A third drink, a dry Martini with a couple of olives, was poured for the man in charge. He brought over the tray and put down the drinks on the table.

'That's better,' said the man, 'now we can talk turkey, as they say in America!'

Emia was impressed, if a little taken aback, that her favourite drink, and that of her boss, was known to the WBI. Still, it was delicious and very welcome after the day's events. She sat back and relaxed a little. The Boss was giving the details of what they had discovered that day to the man in charge.

Emia looked at him and wondered what she was supposed to call him. He was about 6ft tall, perhaps a little less. He was slim, lightly tanned and he had grey hair very expensively cut. He was rather attractive and exuded power. She realised that she should be listening to what her boss was saying.

'Director, I'm very concerned about what has happened today. Iori, while never very popular at the office, has always been reliable and trustworthy, so I can only assume that something very dramatic has happened to him. We're certain that he printed something from Emia's computer this morning; he went to have lunch at the Welsh Home Stores opposite CI's offices and was followed in there by a very large man who I believe is Harri Harris.'

At this, the Director really sat up and paid attention. The Boss continued, 'Harri came out just a few minutes later and Iori shortly afterwards. Enquiries made by Emia revealed that Iori had bought himself a sandwich and coffee but left them untouched on the table, and he behaved very strangely according to the cashier at Welsh Home Stores. When he left the store, he went home and returned to the office at 1.25pm. Cameras in Nott Square and at the council building show that Harri went straight to the car park and got into a dark car which then drove off westward, out of Carmarthen.'

She waited for the Director to say something but he indicated that she should continue, while sipping his Martini. The Boss took a sip of her drink and went on.

'Alun, in Security, set someone to looking at the video tapes for yesterday evening in Nott Square. Iori had stopped at Woolworths on his way home to buy sweets and went home. About twenty minutes later, two men came out of Iori's street door and walked straight to the council car park where they got into the same car. Security then looked back at slightly earlier tapes for yesterday evening and saw the two men going into the building where Iori lives. One of those men was Harri Harris and the other I believe to be the person known to CI as "Mr B", although the photographs we have on file for him are old so I'm guessing.'

The Director looked serious and waved to Special Agent Lewis to show the pictures The Boss had given them on the large LCD display on the wall. Harri Harris and Mr B loomed large above them. The Director frowned and turned to Emia. 'I understand that it was you who initiated enquiries, Miss Glas. Can you tell me what made you suspicious in the first place?'

Emia put down her drink and sat up straight. 'Director, when I went into my office and sat down this morning, there was a plain sheet of paper on the floor under my desk. I knew for a fact that it hadn't been there the previous afternoon when I left and the cleaners had been in since then anyway; so my immediate thought was that someone had been using my printer. Before that, when I arrived, I'd asked Iori about the Bonnie Tyler show on the TV the previous night and he said that he'd enjoyed it. He's never admitted watching Bonnie Tyler before so that immediately told me that something wasn't right. And, what is more, I discovered later that the show had been cancelled because of an emergency political debate being shown. When I went out to have my lunch, I spoke to Bert, the doorkeeper, and he said that Iori had said hello to him that morning. Iori never normally acknowledges him. Bert told me that he'd seen Iori go across to Welsh Home Stores on the reception cameras so I decided to go and do some investigating myself.'

The Director gave her a long look and Emia felt herself colouring.

'I'm impressed, Miss Glas; that was very good work. It's always wise to listen to one's instincts and, by doing so, you could have stumbled onto something very important.' He carried on, 'Do we know what Iori printed from your computer?'

Emia looked at her boss, who nodded. 'I believe that two items were printed. One was a picture taken by our operative Wyndham of a hunting knife found at the site of a murder near Myddfai. The other was a message instructing him to take the knife to Llangadog Church for collection. The knife was collected successfully and we know that Wyndham returned to Myddfai because he checked in as soon as he arrived back at the village.'

'So,' said the Director, 'we can safely surmise that Iori took those print-outs to Harri at the café and both Harri and Mr B can now work out where Wyndham is.'

Emia picked up her gin and tonic and drank deeply. The Boss said, 'Wyndham was warned immediately, of course, but he's an experienced operative and he'll know best what to do next. Can I take it, Director, that you agree that the second man is Mr B, then?'

The Director nodded. 'I'm 98% certain from the pictures you've shown me.' He turned to the agent. 'Special Agent Lewis, would you have the pictures of that man compared to the old pictures we have of Mr B, please; perhaps our technology can see how well they match. It's as well to be 100% certain.'

The agent nodded and went to a keyboard and mailed the pictures to the laboratory for matching. He also sent pictures of the car so that the lab could try to make out the registration number. Lewis then returned to the drinks cabinet, poured out another round of drinks and brought them to the table with some bowls of Teifi Valley olives, crisps and nuts, as well as some small sandwiches made with Towy Valley smoked salmon.

The Director said, 'We may have to wait a while for the results so we might as well have a little something to eat and drink.'

Lewis stood imperturbably by the window, neither eating nor drinking. They made conversation for about fifteen minutes and then there was a sharp buzzing sound and the big screen flashed.

Onto the screen came an old picture of Mr B and, alongside, there was a picture showing how he would look twenty years later; alongside that was a picture taken by the Nott Square camera the previous evening. There was no doubting that it was Mr B.

Next there was a fuzzy picture of the car used by Harri and Mr B; the picture slowly cleared and the registration number could be seen. Further pictures of the same car were shown going through Haverfordwest and taking the B4330 toward the Pembrokeshire coast. Lastly there was a picture of the car arriving in Porthgain, at the safe house.

The Boss gasped. 'Oh no, that's where Aneurin was taken!'

The Director cautioned her to wait a moment as further pictures were shown of Dr Owain ap Owain greeting Mr B.

He signalled to Lewis to pause the film.

'So, your agent, Aneurin, was taken to the safe house and the senior doctor at the clinic there is clearly friendly with Mr B,' said the Director very seriously. 'This means a conspiracy within the agency and I fear that your agent, Aneurin, may become mixed up in it.'

The Boss protested: 'Aneurin may be many things but he's loyal. I only sent him to Porthgain as a last resort because his drinking was making him a bit sloppy. He's always been a trouper apart from that.'

The Director waved his hand. 'Forgive me; I didn't mean to question Aneurin's loyalty but he may find himself unable to do anything but comply. Dr Owain ap Owain is well known for using hypnotherapy in his treatments and, if he's conspiring with Mr B, anything is possible.'

The Boss calmed down. 'I'm sorry, Director, I realise that you weren't questioning my judgment, but I'm now very concerned indeed about Aneurin as well as Wyndham. It seems that we don't know who we can trust any more.'

'I'm going to send in one of my best agents to see what is going on at Porthgain. He'll report directly to me and I'll pass on all the information directly to you and Miss Glas,' said the Director. 'That way, you'll be kept in the loop but your office won't be directly involved; I think that's safer.'

The Boss nodded her agreement, although Emia could see her suppressed anger and concern.

The Director stood and Emia realised that they were now being dismissed. By now it was dark outside and she could see the glittering lights of Swansea spread out beneath them and the moonlight on the sea. She was sorry to leave but, equally, she was anxious to reach the safety of her own home and block out the events of the day, if only for a few hours. She doubted that The Boss would have that luxury; she would probably be up all night looking at ways to help Wyndham and Aneurin and worrying about them both.

Special Agent Lewis escorted them back to the express train underground and about twenty minutes later they were back in the Quay Street Underground station in Carmarthen. The Boss, who had not spoken on the way back and had refused the tea offered by the train's kitchen staff, turned to Emia and said, 'Go home and get a good night's sleep; tomorrow is going to be a very busy day.'

Emia knew the tone of voice and obeyed. A few minutes later she was leaving the office via the Guildhall Square door and walking home to her flat in Picton Terrace and a restless night.

Chapter 14

WYNDHAM WOKE AT 5.30pm and stretched. He glanced over at the door and could see that nothing had been disturbed. He checked his Blackcurrant but there had been no updates since the message at about 4pm regarding Iori, so he would carry out his plan to visit the mound in Llangadog again that night. Time for a shower and a look at the little TV set in the corner, over which he'd put a T-shirt in case the sheriff's surveillance was more sophisticated than it looked.

After showering and brushing his teeth, he changed into clean clothes, removed the T-shirt from the TV and switched it on. The local news was on, although there had been nothing exciting happening. He sat in the chair with his feet on the bed and, with one eye on the TV, he collected his thoughts. The woman to whom he'd spoken in Llangadog said that the man who had gone missing had never been found; there might be something to see at the mound though and it was a good lead, one worth following. First he had to appear in the pub that evening and he needed a proper meal again.

He finished dressing and ensured that all his belongings were either locked up or hidden away under the floorboard before going downstairs. This time, he went round to the front of the pub and walked in. There were already a few people enjoying an evening drink. There was a man behind the bar; Wyndham guessed it must be Mr Williams, Betti's husband. He went up to the bar and introduced himself.

'You must be Mr Williams, sir. I'm Haydn Jones and I'm staying in one of your rooms.'

Mr Williams turned back from the till and put out his hand to shake Wyndham's. 'Glad to have you here. What are you drinking tonight, then?'

Wyndham decided that it was important to appear relaxed so he ordered a half of Twm Tomkins *Cwrw Nadolig*, remembering that it was Aneurin's favourite and feeling a pang of regret at having to treat Aneurin so badly the previous night.

'Mr Williams, is there a chance of getting something to eat tonight, please?'

'My wife said you had a hearty appetite,' he laughed. 'I know that she's done a nice stew – local lamb with carrots and potatoes and such – so I'm sure she'll do you a big plate of that if you like. I'll let her know now.'

'Sounds wonderful,' said Wyndham, 'thank you very much, Mr Williams.'

He nodded to a couple of men standing at the bar and found a seat in a corner, with his back to the wall. He sipped the beer; it was delicious with a slightly spicy flavour that went down well on a cold evening. In a few moments, Mrs Williams emerged from behind the bar, with some cutlery and a napkin for him.

'I hope you can wait another 15 minutes, Mr Jones, then I'll be able to bring you a nice plate of stew,' she said.

'Please call me Haydn, Mrs Williams. And I'm happy to wait for your wonderful stew. Thanks for the lovely sandwiches you left me for my lunch, they went down a treat.'

She smiled happily at him, glad to be appreciated. In the meantime, he sat and studied the patrons of the pub; all of whom looked perfectly innocent and ordinary. Then Dai Sluice arrived, in his uniform as deputy sheriff. The other people didn't seem bothered by his arrival and didn't even make room for him at the bar; Mr Williams seemed to busy himself deliberately with doing something at the till for a few moments, ignoring the new arrival. Wyndham couldn't help smiling as he lifted his glass to his lips. He decided to stay tucked in his corner and just observe.

Eventually, just as it seemed Dai Sluice would explode with frustration, Mr Williams turned and said, 'Oh, Dai, didn't see you there. What are you having?'

Dai said, 'Well, I'm on duty so I'll stick with a spritzer please, Siôn,' managing to control his temper.

Wyndham almost choked on his beer. A spritzer? Mr Williams poured some wine into a glass full of ice and some lemonade on top; then he added a slice of lemon and a small, colourful cocktail umbrella and handed it over to Dai. At that moment, Dai was busy looking around the pub to see who was there, and his eyes alighted on Wyndham. He stared at Wyndham for a long moment then turned back to the bar to see his drink in front of him. Everyone else in the pub was either looking away from Dai or studying the ceiling with quizzical looks and pursed lips.

Dai removed the umbrella from his drink with a hiss and slammed it down on the bar. Then he walked over to Wyndham and sat opposite him, having first turned the chair around so that he was sitting astride it and leaning on the back of the chair. From somewhere in the pub there was a burst of laughter which the person attempted to cover with a cough, and then everyone else started talking nineteen to the dozen about nothing in particular.

'So, Mr Haydn Jones, how is the walking going?' asked the deputy sheriff. 'I hope you are staying on the straight and narrow, no trespassing.'

'I'm an experienced walker, Deputy Sheriff Davies,' said Wyndham, 'I don't go where I'm not allowed.'

That was the truth, but as an agent of Carmarthen Intelligence there weren't many places he was not allowed to go. Not that Dai Sluice knew that; at least Wyndham hoped not.

'I understand you are a plumber, Deputy Sheriff; that must be a busy life, in addition to your deputy sheriff duties.'

'Don't you worry about my life and my duties, young man, they are all under control, just like this village is.'

'That's very interesting, Mr Davies; am I to understand that you and the sheriff have absolute power in Myddfai?'

'You'll know how much when the time comes, young man, so just watch your Ps and Qs. I know your sort, of old.'

Wyndham replied, 'I don't know what "sort" I am in your eyes, Mr Davies. What I do know is that I'm just an ordinary person exploring the lovely Welsh countryside. And now here is Mrs Williams with some of her delicious stew for me, so if you'll excuse me, I'd like to eat it on my own and without supervision. Thank you for your company and your conversation, it's been very enlightening.'

Dai Sluice got up and picked up his drink. He seemed put out by Wyndham's cool demeanour. He was hoping that his position and attitude would scare Wyndham or at least make him reveal what he was really doing in Myddfai, but it seemed that Wyndham might be exactly what he purported to be. The deputy sheriff swallowed his drink and banged the glass on the bar, then he walked out with an attempt at a John Wayne lope. Needless to say it was a hopeless attempt.

As soon as he'd gone, the pub erupted with laughter

and one drinker called for another half pint for the brave newcomer in the corner.

Wyndham settled to eat his stew, as good as promised and with a basket of fresh bread, made that day by the same Mrs Williams. He ate slowly and supped at his beer. A second glass appeared at his table and he thanked the person who had bought it for him. He finished his stew and pushed the plate away with satisfaction.

'Don't think that you've finished yet, Haydn.'

Mrs Williams had appeared at his side. She came bearing another plate with a slice of Myddfai Tarte Tatin, made with local apples and served with cream. She placed the tart in front of him and removed the bread basket and the stew plate.

'Now, get that down you and you'll be set up for the rest of the night, whatever you get up to!' She laughed and nodded toward a new arrival in the pub, Merle Jenkins. Wyndham blushed and tucked into the tart; Mrs Williams was a superb cook.

Merle looked at him and grinned, the dimples showing in her cheeks. Wyndham got up and asked her what she would like to drink and she chose a half of *Cwrw Nadolig*.

'I'll bring it over now, Haydn,' said Mrs Williams, 'you sit and enjoy your food.'

He sat down and Merle sat opposite him, returning the chair to its correct position. He felt shy and could only think to offer her some of his pudding, but she shook her head.

'I'll be making something for Dad when he gets home so I'll wait for my supper until then,' she said. 'Betti is a wonderful cook, though.'

A half pint arrived at Merle's elbow and she thanked Mrs Williams prettily, then raised her glass to Wyndham.

'*Iechyd da*, Mr Haydn Jones, and may you get whatever you want in life.'

He blushed again, returned her smile and said, '*Iechyd da*, Miss Merle Jenkins. I think I'm doing very well to be going on with!'

She giggled and Wyndham finished his tart with her watching him.

Chapter 15

WHILE THE BOSS and Emia were with the Director in Swansea, Iori had gone to do some food shopping. He hadn't eaten breakfast and had left his cheese sandwich on the table in Welsh Home Stores. In fact he hadn't eaten since lunchtime on the previous day, but despite the lingering nausea he knew he would have to have something. While he longed for his cosy home, he also dreaded going back in case he found Harri and that frightening man there again.

Having picked up some ready meals, he went slowly back into Guildhall Square and up Hall Street, towards Nott Square. Everyone who passed him seemed to look at him with curiosity and suspicion, as though they knew about the previous evening and the incident in Blackpill. Two young women went past him, laughing, and he felt as though they were laughing at him. He glanced at the doorway of Woolworths and he thought he saw the same man who had been reading the newspaper outside that morning.

He almost ran up Hall Street and to his own front door. Just as he had put in the key to open the door, someone tapped his shoulder and he leapt a few inches in the air.

'Sorry,' said a voice, 'but you dropped this in Hall Street.'

A middle-aged man handed him a glove and smiled at him, revealing several missing teeth.

Iori reddened. 'You just took me by surprise,' he said, 'but thank you.'

'Not at all. We're here to help each other, after all.

Otherwise, what is the point of life?' said the man.

He turned and left Iori at the door and Iori hurried inside, closing and bolting it after him. He rushed upstairs, let himself in through the inner door and found his little home just as it should have been; no visitors.

He changed and put one of his meals in the microwave before laying the table. Then he put on a Bonnie Tyler CD, heard the 'ping' from the kitchen and put out his meal on a plate. Despite his nervousness, he ate hungrily and soon the meal was gone. As soon as he'd washed up the plate and cutlery, he sat with a small glass of shandy and some of the sweets he'd bought the previous evening and listened to Bonnie with his eyes closed.

Suddenly he sat up, spilling his shandy on the carpet. The man who had given him his glove! The man's voice had been the same as the voice of the man who had sat in that very chair last night. He was sure of it. But why had he come back? They must be keeping an eye on him.

He went to the window and looked out but he couldn't see the man with the missing teeth or big Harri. That didn't mean that no one was watching him, of course. He could see part of the way down Hall Street, but not as far as the doorway of Woolworths; he could also see almost all of Nott Square. Everyone down there seemed ordinary. There were a few people standing outside the Angel Vaults, smoking. One of them looked up and stared at him, but that was surely just coincidence.

Iori stood back from the window and then drew the curtains, shutting out the night. He moved his easy chair over to the door to the stairway and pushed it hard against the frame; no one would come in that way now and they could hardly climb up to the windows without someone seeing them. His heart was pounding but he made himself get changed into his pyjamas. He was so tired that he thought he would lie on the bed and watch TV. He switched on and was surprised to see the Bonnie Tyler show starting. An announcer said, 'And now, the show that was postponed from last night due to the political debate… '

Iori sat up again in astonishment; he'd told Emia that he'd enjoyed the show last night and it hadn't even been on. His head fell to his knees and he rocked back and forth, realising what a terrible mistake he'd made in admitting he'd watched Bonnie Tyler in the first place. Surely Emia would find out that the show had been postponed and she would wonder why he had admitted to liking Bonnie, never mind watching a show that hadn't been broadcast.

He got up and went to the window again, pulling the curtain away from the window frame a little. He looked out and could see that all the smokers outside the Angel had gone, but now there was someone standing smoking outside the photo shop further along the square, although whoever it was didn't look up toward Iori.

There was nowhere Iori could go and nothing he could do; his mother had gone to live in Ibiza with some New Age people and he'd never kept in touch with any other relatives. His only hiding place was under his duvet, so he left the TV on and snuggled down under the quilt, shivering with fear. As Bonnie crooned on the TV, his exhaustion overcame him. Some time later, Iori could be seen curled up in the foetal position with his thumb in his mouth.

In the early hours of the following morning, Iori's TV set showed a screen full of snow and static; it was that short break between the late-night fare and the kids' television. But Iori's screen changed from static to a rainbow of colours, swirling around in circles. Then whispering started and it continued for about fifteen minutes. Iori slept on, his thumb firmly in his mouth, but his eyelids flickered restlessly while the whispering voice spoke to him.

At 7am, Iori awoke and stretched. He was surprised to see he'd left the TV on and immediately switched it off at the plug. 'That wasn't very green of me,' he said to himself, 'I must have been very tired last night.'

He got up, showered and dressed and ate a good breakfast. He did wonder why his easy chair was up against the door but forgot about it as soon as he got outside to Nott Square and walked down to CI. He didn't notice the man standing in Woolworth's doorway reading the paper, or the tramp sitting on the Guildhall steps. He walked into the reception area at CI where Bert greeted him, and only gave the vaguest attention to the doorkeeper before taking the lift to the first floor down. Bert thought, 'Back to normal today, then. At least I know where I stand with him!'

When he reached his office, Iori was surprised to see Emia and The Boss there already. They both wished him a good morning but returned to their work immediately, so Iori sat down and looked at some new files on his desk. There was a note on top saying, 'Iori, would you please look through these expenses files as the accounts department is short-handed and they know that you understand them.' It was signed by The Boss. He looked through to Emia's office but it seemed that The Boss had already disappeared into her own room so he made a start on the files; it had happened before so he wasn't put out.

A little later, Emia went out of the room and came back with a cup of tea for herself and a cup of coffee for Iori.

'What did you think of the Bonnie Tyler show last night, Iori?' she asked.

'You know I don't watch that kind of thing, Emia, I'm more into classical stuff.'

'Of course, Iori. Forgive me for forgetting that. I only saw a bit of it myself; I was expecting another programme but Bonnie Tyler had been postponed from the previous evening because of a political debate. You probably watched the debate, didn't you?'

'Oh yes, I think I saw a bit of it but I had other things to do.'

Emia gazed at him and Iori felt uncomfortable. He didn't know what all this was about. 'Well, excuse me, Emia, but I have to get on with these expenses. Thank you for the coffee,' he said.

Emia just looked at him and then walked away. Before she reached her desk, she turned and said, 'Sorry to interrupt you again, Iori, but would you recommend Welsh Home Stores for a nice lunch?'

He looked surprised. 'I don't believe I've ever been to the café in Welsh Home Stores, Emia, and I wouldn't have thought it was your sort of place either.'

Emia turned back again and went to her desk, picking up a note pad, and then she walked through to The Boss's room. Having closed the door behind her, she told The Boss about her conversation with Iori.

'There's something odd about it all; he really believes what he's saying, I'm sure of it.'

The Boss picked up the phone and dialled Alun in Security. 'Alun, it's time for someone to go into Iori's flat and have a good look around. Test everything for surveillance and any devices you can think of, and even those you can't think of.'

Emia could hear Alun's voice murmuring at the other end of the line. Within seven minutes, a team of specialists was walking up Hall Street to Iori's flat.

In the meantime, Iori sat at his desk, immersed in CI's expenses files and thoroughly pleased with himself, as usual.

At the skyscraper in Swansea, Special Agent Lewis stared at his computer bank and watched as the specialist team entered Iori's home on one screen and Mr Brynaman entered the Llanfihangel clinic on another.

Chapter 16

WYNDHAM HAD ENJOYED his first evening at the pub, although he was careful not to drink more than the two half-pints of beer. Merle had left to prepare her father's supper at about 8pm and Wyndham stayed a little longer with the other villagers before pleading tiredness after a long day and going up to his room.

He checked his Blackcurrant again and sent a coded message saying that he would go to the mound in Llangadog and return to Myddfai before dawn. In the meantime he lay down and slept for two hours, having placed the chair against the door again for extra security.

At about 11pm his alarm woke him and he got up. Very quietly, he moved the bed and got out the equipment he needed for that night from under the loose floorboard and dressed in dark clothing with a woollen balaclava pulled down on his head. Having looked out of the windows to check for anyone walking about, he tip-toed in his rubber-soled shoes to the door and moved the chair. He heard a sound outside and stopped, holding his breath. It was a scratching noise. Wyndham opened the door a little and peeked outside, only to see a large ginger cat sitting at the top of the steps. He sighed with relief and stroked the cat; it purred with pleasure at this unexpected attention and tried to get into the room.

'No, Puss, not now; come back later and you can have a nice snug bed. Just not now.'

The cat settled itself at the top of the steps as Wyndham locked the door behind him, having sprinkled talc again on the floor. Then he crept slowly and carefully down the steps and checked the street before looking back up to see the cat still sitting at the top of the steps, its eyes glinting. Keeping to the shadows as much as possible, he moved quickly out of the village and took the road back to Llangadog. The village was silent and, apart from the cat, the only eyes that glimpsed a dark shadow passing along the road belonged to someone sitting up in the church tower.

This time, Wyndham took another road to Llangadog, initially following the way to Llanddeusant and then turning right about two miles beforehand. The road was steep from this direction but he was less likely to meet any traffic this way. Wyndham thought the gradient must be at least one in five and he thanked his rugby training for being fit enough to deal with the hill at a trot. About half an hour later, he found himself just south of the old castle. There was only a half moon and the night was a bit cloudy so he felt reasonably safe from enquiring eyes.

The mound itself was covered in trees and undergrowth but all around it was open ground. He spent a few moments composing himself and checking to see if anyone was about, then he ran very quickly over the open ground to the mound. Again, he stopped to compose himself and check that no one was following him. Everything appeared to be clear around him.

Taking his day bag off his back, he found his infra-red goggles and, starting at the base of the mound, moved in an ever-decreasing circle while checking the ground. The work was slow and painstaking and he didn't want to use an ordinary torch unless he really had to, certainly not at the base of the mound where it would be more visible. It took two hours for him to reach a place where he felt reasonably confident of the torch not being seen; he had checked the ground thoroughly, as well as the tree bark, and found no clues to the walker's disappearance.

He sat for a few minutes, resting and listening out for any unusual sounds, having taken off his goggles and turned off the torch. Then there was a slight creak and a sound like the air being let out of several cans of soda water simultaneously. The sound was near him and he lay close to the ground, thankful that he was surrounded by shrubs. There was a sudden sneeze and a voice said, 'Shut up, you idiot!' Wyndham held his breath and he could just see a shape moving away from him, through the trees. The same voice said, 'Leave the door open just a little bit, to save us trouble when we get back.'

Wyndham saw a second shape moving toward the first and another voice said, 'Okay, but I hope no animals get in there; we won't be back until mid-morning at this rate.'

The first voice said, 'Never mind about animals; it's such a job getting the damn thing open from the outside and it'll make it quicker for us to get in when we get back.'

The second man muttered something that Wyndham couldn't catch and the two shapes moved off as though going away from the mound. Wyndham sat up slowly and he could just see the two shapes as they moved very quickly across the open ground surrounding the old castle and disappeared toward the town.

Wyndham waited for five minutes and replaced his infra-red goggles. Moving slowly and carefully, and making no sound, he crept toward the place where the two shapes had appeared. Then he could see what appeared to be a trap door in the ground which, had it not been open, would have been entirely invisible under the plants and grasses growing there.

The door had been propped open with a small branch. Quietly he bent down and opened the door, keeping the branch in his hand. With his goggles, he could see metal steps leading downward so he stepped down and, having got far enough inside, he pulled down the door again and put the branch back in place. There were about a dozen steps down to the inside of the mound and there was some electric light down there, but he was grateful for the goggles and his torch. At the bottom of the steps, he found himself in a corridor about five feet wide and only about six feet high as he almost reached to the roof of the underground passage.

He walked forward slowly, keeping one hand on the passage wall. About fifteen feet from the steps he found a metal door with a bolt on the outside. There was no way of seeing through the door, there being no keyhole or window, so he had to risk there being someone on the other side. He took his hunting knife from the sheath around his calf and pulled back the bolt slowly; fortunately, it had been oiled and made no noise. Then he pushed down the lever to open the door and slid through. He almost gasped at what he saw.

In front of him there was a large workstation with a bank of computers on the wall, all state-of-the-art equipment. The room was not very large, perhaps twelve feet by fourteen feet, but there were other doors leading off it. Swiftly, he opened a door to his left and saw a kitchen, complete with fridge-freezer, microwave, kettle and sink; there was also a small washing machine with a tumble dryer. A quick look in the fridge told him that these people were prepared for a minor siege. Another door on the same side of the room revealed a shower room and loo.

He crossed the room and opened yet another door. From this, a short passageway led downward, with half a dozen steps at the end. He went down, listening carefully in case someone was behind the door at the end. There was no sound. This door, like the one to the inner computer room, was bolted from the outside and he slid the bolt back, holding his knife ready in his right hand. There was still silence and he moved quickly through the doorway, alert to an attack, but on the other side was another room, one with two single beds and a space for clothes, in which he could see several pairs of jeans, some camouflage outfits, T-shirts, sweaters and underwear.

Opposite the beds, on the right-hand side of the room, was another door; again, it was bolted from the outside but in this case there was a small barred window toward the top of the door, rather like in a prison, and another opening in the middle of the door, presumably for passing things through. Wyndham looked through the barred window and caught his breath. A young man, as far as Wyndham could make out in the poor light, was lying on a narrow bed and he looked unconscious. He was also cuffed to a chain on the wall. Wyndham remembered the story of the missing hiker and concluded that this must be him.

He ran back to the main computer room to check that no one had returned and, relieved that there was no sign of anyone, he started to check the computers. All the screens were blank and he didn't dare try to turn them on as that was bound to alert someone to an intruder. There was no paperwork anywhere either. So he had to content himself with taking photos of the room. Then he ran back down to the cell and opened it. The young man on the bed didn't stir but Wyndham approached him cautiously; the prisoner may have been cuffed to the wall but that didn't mean that he couldn't react violently. Reaching forward, he grasped the prisoner's free arm firmly but the young man didn't react at all.

Moving back, Wyndham took out from his bag some heavy-duty tape and taped the young man's arm to his side and his leg, then he photographed him for identification purposes. He went back out to the sleeping area and looked for a set of keys. There was one hanging from the wall between the beds so he grabbed it and went back into the cell where the young man didn't appear to have stirred. He tried the keys and the second one opened the cuff. The young man's arm fell down, a dead weight, and Wyndham taped that arm also. He then tied the man's legs with some rope and placed some more tape on his mouth.

Having replaced the keys in the sleeping area and put his day bag back on, Wyndham picked up the prisoner and put him over his shoulder. He was obliged to walk with his knees bent as the ceilings were quite low, but he took the prisoner back to the computer room and put him in a chair, then ran back, bolted the cell door and the door to the sleeping area and went back to the computer room. He took a small device from his knapsack and, looking around the room again, he placed it on top of a cupboard to the left of the door, facing the computer banks. He couldn't be sure that any signal from the viewing device would be received at HQ but it was worth a try.

The prisoner still seemed to be unconscious but Wyndham pulled back the young man's eyelids to check; he didn't seem to be faking.

Next Wyndham picked up the young man again and, knees bent, took him back through the door to the main passageway. Having stopped to lean the prisoner against the wall in order to bolt the door again, he set off, carrying the lad on his back and leaning forward with his knees bent. It was gruelling but there was really no other way. At the steps, he stopped and listened for any unusual sound but there was nothing. With difficulty, he climbed up with the lad on his back and pushed open the trapdoor with his shoulder. Then he pushed out the prisoner onto the ground and climbed out himself, returning the door to its original position with the branch holding it open slightly.

He took a few seconds to recover but knew that he couldn't afford to wait too long. The men had said that they wouldn't be back until mid-morning but Wyndham couldn't count on that and someone else might come in the meantime. He put his infra-red goggles back on and lifted the prisoner up again. Fortunately, the young man had a small build and was underweight, but it was still a struggle to get through the undergrowth and trees. At the bottom of the mound, Wyndham set his burden down in the shadow of a tree and took out his Blackcurrant.

Quickly he sent an emergency message to the Welsh Assault and Rescue Force (WARF) in code, giving them his position and stating that he had an injured man with him. Within seconds, an acknowledgement appeared on his Blackcurrant with the password 'Grand' and his response 'Slam'. He sat back to wait, knowing that he could do nothing until WARF appeared. Fifteen minutes later, he saw a light flashing from the direction of the town; it was flashing Morse code and spelling out the letters of the password. He flashed his response with his torch and saw several dark shapes running across the open area toward the mound, two of them carrying a stretcher. He flashed his torch again twice and in a couple of seconds they stood in front of him in combat gear. A voice whispered, 'Wyndham, it's me, Ryan!' Wyndham felt a great sense of relief; it was his pal from the rugby team. 'Where's your injured party, Wyndham?' said Ryan.

Wyndham showed the men where the lad lay under the tree and they lifted him onto the stretcher and set off at full pelt across the field toward the town. Ryan indicated that Wyndham should move further into the shelter of the trees while two other uniformed men patrolled the base of the mound. Then Wyndham explained about the rooms under the mound and the young man being kept prisoner and that he had probably found the walker who had gone missing the previous year.

Ryan asked if they should go back into the mound to have another look but Wyndham said that he couldn't be sure when the men would be back. So Ryan contacted his superior by radio and told him about the room, asking for instructions. His superior officer recommended leaving the room for the moment and getting Wyndham safely back to Myddfai.

Ryan, Wyndham and the two soldiers ran back toward the town and leapt into the Jeep waiting for them. They were to take Wyndham closer to Myddfai so that he could sneak back to his room quietly. As they drove, Wyndham told Ryan to keep The Boss at CI informed of the young man's destination and progress. Ryan nodded seriously. Then Wyndham told him about the sheriff and deputy in Myddfai and Ryan laughed but also said, 'Be very careful, Wyndham, that sort of idiot is always the most dangerous – get in touch if you need any help.'

At that point the Jeep stopped and Wyndham slapped his pal on the back and jumped out. He only had about a mile to walk to the village now but he took just as much care as he had when leaving earlier that night; he kept to the shadows and at last reached the steps at the pub's back door, leading up to his room. The cat still sat at the top of the steps, inscrutable.

Wyndham stopped to stroke the animal, which responded as before and led the way into the room after Wyndham had unlocked the door, making straight for the bed. Wyndham switched on the bedside lamp and checked the talc by the door; there were only markings from the cat's paws. Either Dai Sluice had not paid a visit that night or he was getting more clever.

He was tired but Wyndham had to make sure that everything was put away properly before he went to bed. He moved the chair to the door again and lifted the bed gently to replace the equipment he needed to keep hidden under the floorboard. The cat looked surprised at this but settled down once Wyndham had put the bed back and spoken soft words of reassurance. Then Wyndham undressed, washed at the basin, not wanting to disturb anyone by running a shower at that time of night, and got into bed, ensuring that he didn't disturb the cat too much. The animal clearly approved of this courteous behaviour and snuggled up to Wyndham, purring. Before setting his alarm for 9am, Wyndham sent a message to CI confirming his safe return to Myddfai and attaching the photos he'd taken in the underground room and turned out the light. He was asleep in moments and so was the cat.

Chapter 17

'EMIA, WITH ALL the other problems we've had, I haven't had a chance to bring you up-to-date with Wyndham's mission.'

The Boss was talking to Emia in her office at CIHQ while the specialist team was searching Iori's studio flat.

Emia looked alarmed but The Boss said, 'No need to worry so far; Wyndham is doing a good job. As you know, he found that hunting knife and forensics are still looking at it as there are some strange traces on it. However, Wyndham has found a young hiker who went missing almost a year ago in Llangadog. We are now certain that it is the same young man but he's very ill at the moment and we can't question him. Apparently the site of the old castle in Llangadog, which, as you know, is just a mound covered in trees now, conceals a secret room.' At this, she turned her computer screen around to show Emia the photographs that Wyndham had taken, including the one of the young man. 'Wyndham managed to leave a camera device in the room so we also have some film of the men who work there,' she added.

She showed Emia some rather grainy film of the men returning, making tea and sitting down at their computers. Then the film showed one of the men leaving the room toward the right-hand side and coming back at a run just a few moments later, yelling something at his colleague. They both dashed out of the room and came back again, yelling at each other. There was no sound but Emia could tell that one was saying, 'They'll kill us for this.' They both ran out of the room again and returned shortly with bags out of which were spilling clothes and personal possessions. And then they disappeared out of view.

Emia realised that she was sitting on the edge of her chair and settled back. 'Did they escape, then?' she asked.

The Boss said, 'Fortunately, Wyndham's camera surveillance meant that the men were picked up in Llangadog this morning; I've just had confirmation from WARF. It's only a matter of time before their superiors discover their underlings are missing and that their prisoner is also gone. So close surveillance is taking place now and WARF have swept the underground rooms and removed the hard drives from the computers. Wyndham may have stumbled upon something even more important than a missing hiker, although whether it has any connection with our other problem is another matter.'

'How long before we know what's on the hard drives?' asked Emia.

The Boss pursed her lips. 'The experts are on it but we can only wait and try to be patient. In the meantime, I am concerned about Aneurin. He isn't at Porthgain any more so we must conclude that he has been transferred to Llanfihangel.'

Emia gasped with horror. Like all the employees of CI, she had heard stories of the dreadful things that happened at Llanfihangel, although no one knew how true they were. She liked Aneurin and had felt really sorry when he'd been taken away.

At that moment The Boss's phone rang. She pressed the speaker phone button and a voice said, 'Ma'am, we've ascertained that Aneurin was definitely moved to Llanfihangel but the good news is that he's leaving in two days. We managed to find out that Aneurin has been subjected to hypnotherapy so we can't be certain that he'll know who he is when he gets out. According to our contact, he'll be driven back to Carmarthen so we'll keep him under surveillance from the moment he leaves.'

The Boss said, 'Well done – you've done a great job finding all that out, keep us informed. I'm very relieved that Aneurin is being released, whatever shape he's in, Special Agent Lewis.'

Lewis continued, 'There is something else you should know. There's a man being held there, and he too was previously at Porthgain. He's known at the clinic as Mr Goronwy Evan Evans, a shepherd.'

'Should that mean anything to me, Special Agent Lewis?' asked The Boss, frowning.

'I'm sending you a picture of the man now, Ma'am, although it's not a very good one as it had to be taken from a distance. It seems that he's been either at the safe house or at the clinic for some time,' said Lewis. 'Let me know if you need anything else, otherwise I'll be in contact as soon as I have more information about Llanfihangel and Llangadog. We are also looking closely at the so-called "Sheriff of Myddfai".'

'Thank you, Special Agent Lewis.' The Boss turned to her computer and waited for the message to come through. At last, a picture came up on the screen and she went pale.

Emia said, 'What is it? Are you all right?'

'I can't believe it. I thought he was dead! Look at the picture, Emia. That is a prize-winning mathematician, Sir Geraint Williams-Jones; he was also head of CI and my mentor when I joined the service. I went to his funeral, Emia; it was four years ago and he was supposed to have died of some terrible cancer. All this time, he's been held at that house of horrors.'

Emia was shocked at her boss's demeanour; she had never seen her like this. She went to the drinks cabinet and poured her a stiff brandy. 'I know it's a bit early, but you've had such a shock, it'll do you good.'

The Boss took the glass gratefully and sipped a little of the brandy. The colour started to come back to her face. 'Just give me a minute to collect myself, Emia. I know my behaviour isn't very professional but this is a dreadful shock to me, a very personal shock.'

Emia said, 'Don't worry, Boss, I think your reaction does you credit.'

'We'll both sit here for a few minutes,' said The Boss. 'We still can't be sure of our friend out in reception so we must look as normal as possible.'

Emia nodded, silently agreeing.

'At the moment,' The Boss continued, 'I feel as though we have a huge jigsaw without a picture to go by and without any edges to guide us. Whether all these different elements we've encountered in the past couple of days will come together, I don't know, but my gut feeling tells me that there is a link between the underground rooms in Llangadog, Mr B and his cronies at Porthgain and Llanfihangel, Iori's strange behaviour and Wyndham's mission in Myddfai, including the sheriff and his pal.'

Emia said, 'I'm going to draw a diagram, like you taught me, to see if I can spot any connections. If you do the same, Boss, we might come up with something.'

The Boss nodded. 'I agree; let's get on to it straight away.'

Emia left The Boss's office and went back to her desk. She looked over at Iori but he was still immersed in expenses and humming softly to himself.

Up at Iori's tiny flat, the specialist team had taken everything apart and were slowly putting it all back together again; they were very experienced and would leave his home looking as though no one had visited it during his absence. As it was, the one thing they had found was a connection in the TV set leading to a transceiver and a small computer hard drive. They connected the hard drive up to a laptop and found on it a hypnotic voice, whispering, and a kaleidoscope of colours whirling around the screen. The medical specialist called The Boss and explained what they'd found. They'd managed to decipher the whispering voice and found that it was telling Iori to forget the visit to his flat and the meeting at Welsh Home Stores. The medic explained that he could put in his own instructions, if she wanted. She told him not to do anything immediately but to ensure that there was a camera recording anyone who entered the flat; the camera could be installed at the top of the stairs from the outer door.

After speaking to the specialist, The Boss, now somewhat recovered, rang Special Agent Lewis in Swansea and explained what had been found at Iori's flat and what she had told the medic. Lewis asked her to hold while he spoke to the Director and was back on the line within a minute. He put her through to the Director straight away.

'Special Agent Lewis has told me what's been found at the flat. As soon as that transceiver and the computer hard drive are returned to your offices, I'd like them sent to us on the Swansea express. As this is obviously linked to Mr B, we'd like to examine all the evidence. I'd be grateful for your cooperation on this.'

The Boss nodded and said, 'Anything we can do to help each other is useful, Director. In the meantime, Emia and I are working on what the connections could be between Mr B, Porthgain and Llanfihangel, Iori and Wyndham's mission. There's also the small matter of the underground rooms in Llangadog and the missing hiker. We hope that WARF will come up with something soon as I'm concerned about Wyndham now.'

The Director responded, 'We are all working hard on this. I think you can rely on Wyndham not to do anything silly; he's clearly a very good operative. And you and Miss Glas are a formidable team. I'll be in touch.'

The line went dead and The Boss sat back and sipped some more brandy, thinking about Sir Geraint and what he must have been through in the past four years. Putting her glass down, she sat up and took out a large sheet of plain paper. Then she started to draw a diagram, linking all the elements of this strange case.

One hour later, the evidence from Iori's flat was on its way to Swansea, carried by Alun from Security. On his return, he rang Emia to confirm that he'd handed the package over to Special Agent Lewis at the Swansea Underground station. Emia got up from her desk and went to look at Iori again. He seemed to be enjoying his task and continued to hum. So, he had been hypnotised but that must have happened last night; Iori's behaviour the previous day had had nothing to do with hypnotism but everything to do with fear. That Mr B and Harri had something they could use against Iori but what on earth was it?

Emia went back to her desk and brought up the special files on employees. Only a few people could access these at CI and she was one of them, although she'd rarely felt it necessary in the past. Checking that Iori was still busy with his work, she entered the password and typed in Iori's name. His photograph and employee details came up on the screen but she wanted to see his history and she clicked on the 'Education' window. He'd been at Treorchy and lived in digs there; nothing special about that. She tried clicking on 'Other details' and noted that he'd spent a lot of summers in the Gower, particularly at Blackpill. Probably nothing special about that either, she thought. There were a few photographs in this section so she pulled them up; there was Iori grinning next to a nice-looking young man and two girls – so far, so ordinary. Another picture of the young man, drinking beer at the seaside; yet another of the same person, possibly in a caravan.

Emia sneaked a look at Iori; these pictures looked ordinary but Iori was not known for being ordinary in that way. He didn't seem to have friends and he socialised very little. She enlarged the picture of the male friend in the photos and printed it out. Then she ensured that her screen was clear of the personnel files and locked and she went to knock on The Boss's door.

'What is it, Emia?'

'Boss, I think I've got something that might take us further regarding Iori, but I need your permission to contact someone who could help us.'

She showed the photo to The Boss and explained that there had been several pictures of this young man taken in Iori's student days. She also explained what had prompted her to look and The Boss gave her permission to look into it further.

Chapter 18

A BOUT THIRTY-ONE HOURS after he had sent Aneurin off on his trip to the seaside, Wyndham felt something tickling his face. He opened his eyes, only to find himself staring into two saucer-like green ones. It was the cat who had been nuzzling his face to wake him gently.

'Hello, nuisance,' he said, 'I suppose you want to go out now, just when I was deeply asleep too.'

He got out of bed and moved the chair a little to open the door. The cat jumped down from the bed, rubbed up against his naked legs and with a soft meow, it went down the steps. Wyndham closed the door against the chilly air and replaced the chair against it. It was still quite dark so he went back to bed. Before going back to sleep, he checked his Blackcurrant but there were no more messages. Two minutes later, he was fast asleep again.

The cat trotted confidently through the village to the vicarage; this was his domain, his manor, and all other cats stood aside for him. He'd enjoyed his snooze with Wyndham but now it was time to go home. He climbed the wall into the garden; a small rodent dashed past him but the cat wasn't in the mood for hunting anyway, he was on his way to Merle's bed where he knew he would be welcomed. He ran across the garden and climbed up to the shed roof, scrambling up the trellis to Merle's bedroom window where he meowed to be let in. Merle came sleepily to the window and opened it.

'So, you've decided to come home, have you, wicked one,' she said as she held him and buried her face in his fur, much to the cat's pleasure.

At 9am, Wyndham's alarm sounded and he groaned. He was aching a little from the previous night's exertions; carrying the hiker had been awkward in the underground passages. He checked for messages but there were none. Fifteen minutes later, he was showered and dressed and he went down to the kitchen for breakfast.

Betti Williams was already busy kneading dough for the day's bread but she had the ingredients for his breakfast ready and she smiled at him when entered. 'Hope you had a good night's sleep, Haydn, that mattress is a new one.'

'I slept like a log, Mrs Williams, except for when the cat wanted to go out at about 6am! Do you know who the ginger cat belongs to?'

Mrs Williams grinned. 'It's Merle's cat and his name is Hannibal – don't ask me why! He normally sleeps with her but sometimes he comes to the pub to see who's staying and how soft they are! Looks like he found a real softie in you.'

Wyndham reddened at the thought of the cat going home to sleep with Merle after being with him; somehow it seemed so intimate, as though he had slept with Merle not the cat. Betti Williams got on with preparing his breakfast while he wondered about Merle, then he told himself to stop thinking of girls and start thinking of what he would do that day.

The other death had taken place close to Llandovery so he intended to walk that way today. Luckily the weather was still dry. He ate his breakfast with relish and left some more money with Betti Williams for all the food he'd eaten the previous day, telling her to expect him for supper that night.

Back in his room, nothing had been disturbed. He made the bed and left everything quite neat, having taken some equipment from under the floorboard beneath the bed.

At 10.30am he set off with his knapsack to walk to Llandovery, via Bron Farm. It was about five miles and he planned on having a snack lunch in Llandovery. Only a handful of people were about in the village, including Sheriff Iwan ap Rhys who stood leaning back on his gate, watching Wyndham go by.

'Mr Jones!' the sheriff hailed him, 'I hope you are enjoying your stay in Myddfai.'

Wyndham eyed him warily. 'Yes, thank you. I had a good walk yesterday and the food at the pub has been wonderful. Had a good night's sleep too.'

The sheriff gave him a smile which revealed Hollywood-white teeth in an alligator-skin face, a smile that was menacing rather than friendly. 'And where are you off to today, Mr Jones?'

'I thought I'd go up to Llandovery today but I'll see how it goes.'

Wyndham wondered if the sheriff was planning to pay a visit to his room in the pub.

'Well, I hope you have a good, safe day, Mr Jones. And I hope you find what you're looking for.'

'I don't know that I'm looking for anything in particular, just a good day's walk and good food and pleasant company when I return,' said Wyndham.

'Well, I'm sure you know best,' said the sheriff and he turned and walked away from Wyndham.

As Wyndham left the village, he could feel the sheriff's eyes on his back and knew that he had met a serious enemy, although he didn't know why.

The road was fairly quiet, only a few farm vehicles passed

him as he took the road toward Halfway. He would be turning north about two miles before Halfway, to pass by Bron Farm and onto the campsite where the other murder had taken place.

A short distance before the turning he heard a motorcycle revving. There was a farm gate to his left so he jumped over this and hid behind the hedge. The motorbike came along the road in the same direction that Wyndham had used and it was slowing down but it passed the gate and went to the turning leading to Bron Farm and stopped. Then the bike revved up again and came back along the road and disappeared. Wyndham had managed to see the registration number and got out his Blackcurrant. He sent a message to CI asking them to look up the registration and, less than minute later, he got his answer. The motorbike belonged to Mr David Davies of Myddfai, otherwise known as Dai Sluice, the deputy sheriff. Wyndham acknowledged the message and decided that he would stay in the field for a few minutes. He looked around and he could see another gate leading out onto the road to the campsite so, keeping by the hedge, he walked around to the other gate and waited for another couple of minutes but there was silence. He hopped over the gate and set off again at a brisk pace, keeping to the side of the road.

Wyndham made good time. As he passed Bron Farm, a farm worker raised his arm to wave and Wyndham waved back. The campsite was a little further on the right and was for both caravans and tents. At this time of year, he didn't expect to see many people but he was surprised that there were some hardy souls camping and staying in the caravans. He slowed down as he walked toward the entrance and then stopped and sat on a milestone as if having a rest. He took out a bottle of water from his knapsack and drank.

'Hallo there.' It was an Englishwoman's voice. 'Been walking a long way, have you?'

Wyndham looked up to see a middle-aged woman in combat trousers and a fleece; she looked quite pleasant.

'Hallo, I haven't walked that far yet today but I was thirsty and thought I might as well sit,' said Wyndham. 'I'm Haydn Jones, by the way.'

The woman put out her hand and introduced herself. 'Cheryl Kent; I'm camping down here with my husband – we like the outdoor life, get fed up of houses after a while!'

Wyndham shook her hand; she had quite a fierce grip.

'I'm not a great camper myself,' he said, 'I like to walk and then have a good hot meal served to me and a warm bed at night!' Then he said, 'Didn't I read something about this campsite a while ago?'

Cheryl said, 'Yes, some poor lad got himself killed here last year, just up by the trees. Turns out another walker got killed somewhere else in the area and a third young lad went missing. We don't let it worry us, otherwise we'd never go anywhere.'

Wyndham replied, 'Oh, I think I remember that now. I thought the young chap who got killed here was a walker not a camper, though.'

'That's right. He wasn't camping, just hiking and staying in pubs and B and Bs. It's very strange but if you start thinking about these things too much, it'll get you down.' Cheryl seemed to be very matter-of-fact. 'What about joining us for a cup of tea then?'

Wyndham thought it would be a good idea to get into the campsite in such an innocent way so he followed Cheryl to her tent. Her husband came up and introduced himself.

'Hallo, I'm Richard Kent. Come and have a cup of tea with us, we like to have visitors.'

Another couple also came to join them and Wyndham sat and listened to their chatter while he sipped his tea; they didn't seem very curious about him and he was glad of that. As he sat there, he thought he heard the revving of a motorcycle; he told himself it could be anyone as they were near Llandovery, but he looked over to the entrance to the campsite and the bike and rider looked remarkably similar to his earlier pursuer. Then the bike revved again and disappeared toward Llandovery.

Wyndham stood and thanked the Kents for the tea and said goodbye to the others who had joined them. 'I think I'll cut across the field if there's an exit towards Llandovery,' he said.

The others assured him that he would be able to get out of the campsite easily that way and he set off. He took his time crossing the field and responded to greetings from other campers cheerfully. He managed to get close to the area where the body had been found but decided that he would leave a search until his return later that day.

Llandovery, a delightful market town with its own ruined castle, had a welcoming air. He walked down to Market Square and found a very attractive pub; it was lunchtime and he thought it would be as good a place as any to have lunch. He hadn't seen the motorbike or its rider in the town, so far, but he would keep his eyes peeled.

He went up to the bar and ordered a large St Clement's and a ham and cheese sandwich and went to find somewhere to sit outside. It was unseasonably mild after the chilly night and it was pleasant to sit watching the people of that small town go by. A girl brought him his sandwich and he settled to eat and drink. He had only been sitting for about ten minutes when he sensed someone coming up close to him.

'Good morning, Mr Haydn Jones. Had a nice walk then?'

It was Dai Sluice; his helmet and the bike were nowhere in sight.

'Good morning, Mr Davies. Have you been walking too?' Wyndham asked innocently.

'No, indeed, Mr Jones. I've had places to go and people to see this morning; especially one person who I wanted to make sure is who he says he is.'

'That sounds exciting, Mr Davies. I didn't realise that as well as being a plumber and a deputy sheriff, you are also a spy. Are you working for SMERSH?' Wyndham couldn't help rubbing the man up the wrong way.

'Truth is stranger than fiction, Mr Jones. That is what I've discovered in life. What road did you take to get here?'

'I took the road toward Halfway, Mr Davies, but I expect you already know that. A very pleasant walk too, although there seems to be at least one dangerous motorcyclist in the area; perhaps that's something you could look into. Can I get you a cold drink, Mr Davies? You look a bit red in the face.'

In fact, Dai Sluice looked as though he was about to boil over. It didn't take much to rile him.

'If I want cold drinks, I'll get them myself, thank you. I've warned you to mind your Ps and Qs, I won't tell you again.'

'I heard you the first time, Mr Davies, and I think your warning was unwarranted. I told you that I am simply someone who wants to walk quietly and stay in a nice pub with good food and a warm bed. If that is seditious behaviour, then I'm guilty of it, and so are many other people.'

Dai Sluice looked as though he would explode and he got up and marched away, catching his toe on the kerb and only just retaining his footing. A few minutes later, a motorcycle went past very fast and very noisily, followed by a police car with its siren on.

Wyndham burst out laughing but his mind was whirling. It was now clear that the suspicions about the sheriff and his deputy were on the right road; Dai Sluice had something to hide. Wyndham also had a second serious enemy.

He checked his Blackcurrant. There was a message from Emia to stand by for news and to be very careful. He frowned; something was up but he would have to wait until Emia contacted him again.

Wyndham spent a little time wandering around Llandovery and then he headed south of the town to the old castle. Built about 900 years before by the Anglo-Saxons and captured almost at once by the Welsh, the motte still stood and various other ruined parts still showed proudly on a high mound. He went up to the top of the motte and looked at the river and the trees beyond; it was so tranquil and pretty. Now he had to head for the trees on the same side of the river. As it happened, a fairly large group of people from the campsite was heading in a similar direction so he mingled with them and managed to reach the trees inconspicuously.

The trees were denser than he'd thought and there wasn't much light to see the ground. Several trees around the crime scene had been marked with paint so he set off to find them.

Wyndham soon noticed some silver paint, now flaking, on a couple of trees and looked around for any more signs of the crime scene. At last he found three other trees with the same paint. They formed a semi-circle so he started looking within the semi-circle for anything that might give further clues. The CCSU would have been over the site with a fine tooth comb but he had been lucky at the ditch near Llangadog so it was worth looking.

An hour later, he had found nothing within the semi-circle so he started to move outward. The sun was doing its best to filter through the trees and there was flash above him as a ray of sunlight penetrated the woods. He looked up and, again, as a cloud passed over the sun, there was a flash. He moved over to a tall tree and could see something sticking out of the bark about fifteen feet above the ground. There were a few branches that he could reach but they didn't look strong enough to hold his weight. He thought for a moment and then looked in his bag. He had a length of very light rope but would it be long enough? He took it out of the bag and tied a loop in it, like a lasso. There wasn't much room for manoeuvre in the woods but he'd give it a try. He swung the rope round and threw but it fell to the ground. It took four more tries before he managed to get the rope to hang on whatever was sticking out of the tree. He pulled gently on the rope so that it was holding what must be a knife firmly, then he jerked backwards. Nothing happened. He pulled again and the knife fell to the ground. He put on some latex gloves and ran over to pick it up; the knife point must still be in the tree, it was broken but he had most of the blade and the handle was complete. He returned the rope to his knapsack and took out an evidence bag for the knife. It was very similar to the knife he'd found the previous day. Before putting it into the bag, he photographed it and e-mailed the photo to CI with a message about where it had been found.

Within minutes, a message came back to him with

instructions for dropping off the evidence. He was to go back to Bron Farm and wait by the entrance to the farm, where someone would contact him in twenty-five minutes.

Wyndham set off immediately at a steady pace, avoiding the camping ground. He didn't want to draw attention to himself by walking too quickly and Bron Farm was quite close anyway so he took time to look at the birds of prey circling the fields. He still arrived at the farm a little early but the same man who had waved to him that morning was working close to the entrance, hosing down the yard.

'*Prynhawn da*,' said Wyndham, 'you've got plenty of work on there.'

The young man turned to him and Wyndham was startled to see that it was his friend, Aled; the same Aled who had taken him up the Towy in the motor boat.

Aled replied, 'Aye, always plenty of work on a farm,' and he winked at Wyndham. 'Care to see the new tractor?'

Wyndham followed Aled into the yard and they went to look at the tractor.

'I'll take the evidence bag, Wyndham; then you can feel safer on the way to Myddfai.'

Concealed from the road, behind the tractor, Wyndham removed the evidence from his knapsack and handed it over to Aled with a sense of relief; he wouldn't have liked to encounter either the sheriff or Dai Sluice with the knife in his bag. Aled hid the evidence bag in the tractor and they walked around it, chatting about farming, and back toward the road. Wyndham asked Aled if he would be leaving the farm immediately and Aled said he would but he told Wyndham that the farmer had worked with CI in the past so if Wyndham was really in a jam, he could go there. Wyndham left Aled with a wave and set off back to Myddfai, in no hurry now.

By the time he sauntered back into the village it was almost 3.30pm. There was no sign of Dai Sluice or his superior so Wyndham headed back to the pub and up the steps to his room. Clearly, Mrs Williams had been in there since he left that morning as fresh towels had been put in the bathroom and she had cleaned up the talc from the floor. There was no evidence of anyone else visiting the room; he looked at his bag in the wardrobe and could see that the blond hair he'd left on the bag was still in position.

He put down his bag and took off his jacket. There was a knock on the door and he went to answer. It was Mrs Williams bearing a basket with a kettle, teabags, fresh milk and a small tin of biscuits.

'Hallo, Haydn. I thought you might like some refreshment after your walk; keep these in your room while you're here so you can make tea whenever you want. Thank you for keeping the room so tidy and clean, by the way.'

'Wonderful, Mrs Williams, thank you so much. Some tea is just what I want now. I always try to keep my sleeping quarters tidy, even at home.'

She turned to go, then said, 'Um, Haydn, there's something I should tell you, I think. When I came this morning to clean the room, the sheriff was at the top of the steps and he looked a bit guilty when I spoke to him. He said he was hoping to catch you before you left the village this morning.'

'Thank you for telling me, Mrs Williams. I'll try to speak to him later today.' Haydn didn't tell her that the sheriff had seen him leaving the village that morning as he didn't want to alarm her. 'It's possible that I might stay an extra night, Mrs Williams. I hope that won't be inconvenient. I'll make sure you have more money tomorrow.'

Mrs Williams smiled and said, 'We'll be glad to have you here, Haydn. You are the perfect guest!'

She left the room and Wyndham placed the chair against door again, having locked it. Then he put away his equipment under the floorboard and undressed. He made a cup of tea and sat on the bed to check his messages. There was an urgent message from Emia. She told him about Iori meeting Harri Harris and that someone must know he was in the Myddfai area; she would let him know more when she had news.

This was bad; Wyndham had never encountered Harri but he certainly knew of him and what he knew did not recommend him to that gentleman. Wyndham suddenly felt hunted; he had the sheriff and Dai Sluice on the one hand and Harri on the other. It was a great relief that he had found the murder weapons and the missing hiker so quickly and that the evidence was all safely with CI. At that moment, another message came through to say that the second knife had been received safely from Aled. Wyndham drank his tea, ate a delicious home-made biscuit and, setting his alarm for 6pm, he lay down on the bed and slept.

At about 5pm, Wyndham was woken by a scratching sound at the door. On the alert, in case Dai Sluice was about again, Wyndham looked out of the window nearest the door and could just see the cat's tail. He pulled the chair away from the door and opened it. Hannibal gave him a look that said 'What took you so long?' and sauntered in, making straight for the bed. Wyndham locked the door again and replaced the chair with a smile on his face. He liked this cat's attitude. He fetched a saucer from the table and poured some milk into it, then he held it for the cat who lapped it up and licked his lips appreciatively. Putting the saucer aside, Wyndham climbed back into bed, although Hannibal had managed to take up most of it, and lay down again. Despite Hannibal resenting this intrusion and then washing himself vigorously after his refreshment, Wyndham fell asleep almost immediately and didn't wake again until the alarm.

After switching off the clock, Wyndham lay quietly for a few minutes, going over the past two days in his mind. He'd certainly been successful in his mission to Myddfai but the sheriff and his deputy definitely deserved investigation and he would stay on, unless otherwise instructed. Gently, he got up from the bed, trying not to disturb the cat, and went to take a shower. The walk that day had helped to loosen him up again after the night's exertions and the hot water soothed him. After showering, he washed his underwear and a T-shirt and hung them up to dry in the shower cubicle; they were made from a quick-drying fabric that was perfect for this kind of mission.

He shaved, dressed and tidied the room. All his equipment was safely put away so he could go down to the pub and have his supper. He sat on the bed for a couple of minutes and stroked the cat who had now woken and was enjoying all the attention. Hannibal plucked at the bedclothes with his claws, as though kneading dough.

It was now 6.45pm and Wyndham checked for messages. What he saw alarmed him. The Boss had sent the message personally; she explained about Iori's behaviour, his meeting with Harri Harris and Mr B, and emphasised that they would probably now know Wyndham's whereabouts. She also told him about Aneurin and the clinic and Wyndham was horrified. Attached to the message were pictures of Harri Harris and Mr B, although whether they would approach Wyndham themselves was a moot point. As yet, The Boss could give him no information about whether the sheriff and his sidekick were involved.

A thought came to him and he punched in a message to HQ. A minute or so later, the answer he was looking for came back. It confirmed that Merle Jenkins was the daughter of the local vicar and he was a man who could be trusted. Wyndham felt some relief because he knew instinctively that Merle was going to be important to him.

Having put his Blackcurrant in the zipped inner pocket of his jacket and attached the knife, in its sheath, to his leg, Wyndham opened the door of his room and, looking at the cat who was now stretched out on the bed, he locked the door from the outside and went down to the bar. He would need to be absolutely alert that evening.

Chapter 19

WYNDHAM WENT TO the front entrance of the pub and opened the door. A few people were already supping their pints at the bar and they turned as he went in.

'*Noswaith dda*, Haydn!'

'What have you got up your sleeve for Dai Sluice tonight, Haydn?'

Wyndham grinned and went up to the bar. 'Hope I can have an evening without him tonight; he's not my idea of a supper companion!'

'No, Haydn, but we know who is!'

Everyone laughed and Wyndham blushed a little; he knew they meant Merle.

'I heard that even her cat has given you the seal of approval, Haydn, and you're only the second young gentleman who's had that honour!' said Siôn Williams, the publican, and Wyndham blushed further.

'Hannibal has made himself at home in my room, that's for certain, and sometimes he allows me some space on the bed!'

They all laughed.

He ordered a half of *Cwrw Nadolig* and asked what Mrs Williams had for him to eat that night. Hearing her name, she came out from the kitchen and said, 'Haydn, I've got a lovely roast chicken tonight, from the farm up the road – all free range up there, and vegetables from the garden. How does that sound?'

'Fantastic, Mrs Williams, just what I want. I had a good walk today and only a sandwich for my lunch.'

She told him to go and sit down while she organised his supper and he settled in the same corner, near the fire, to wait.

At that moment the door opened and Dai Sluice looked in; he saw Wyndham sitting in the corner and immediately went out again.

'Looks like you've got him on the run, Haydn,' said one of the drinkers at the bar. 'Any chance of you coming to live in the village?'

At this his companions roared and all agreed that Wyndham's presence would be an asset where Dai Sluice was concerned. Wyndham grinned but he wondered why the deputy sheriff had left so quickly, unless it was to go and check Wyndham's room again. Not that he would find anything incriminating but he might take the opportunity to place something in the room. He frowned but to follow Dai out now would only cause trouble; best to let things lie.

'Here you are, Haydn, a nice supper for you,' Betti Williams's voice broke his train of thought.

'Oh, it looks wonderful, Mrs Williams, thank you.'

She patted his shoulder and left him to eat.

The food was good and he scarcely looked up from his plate as he ate. The other drinkers in the bar nudged each other and whispered that Haydn was liable to become a regular visitor to the village at this rate, what with Merle and Betti Williams's sure hand in the kitchen.

Just as he'd finished eating, the door opened and he looked up to see Merle and a middle-aged man walking in. The man was wearing a dog-collar so he was obviously Merle's father.

Merle saw him in the corner and smiled, nudging her father. Then she went over and asked if she and her father could join Wyndham.

'Of course, Miss Jenkins, I'll be pleased to have your company.'

She went to speak to her father who was buying drinks at the bar and then went back to sit with Wyndham. A moment later, Vicar Jenkins came to sit down too, bringing three half-pints of *Cwrw Nadolig*. Wyndham stood to welcome the vicar who shook his hand vigorously.

The vicar was a strongly-built man a couple of inches shorter than Wyndham. He had thick, greying hair, which must once have been very dark, and kind brown eyes. He studied Wyndham carefully and then he asked what Wyndham's profession was.

'Well, sir, I trained with the Welsh Army and did a couple of tours of duty with them and then I went into the Welsh Civil Service and I'm still there! I suppose I miss the physical part of the Army training and that's why I do these little walking tours every so often. I played rugby for my local side for a time but I had a shoulder problem so I had to give that up, but I try to keep fit in other ways.'

He could feel Merle's eyes on him when he said that and felt a little uncomfortable in front of her father.

'I can see you are a fit young man, Mr Jones,' said the vicar, 'I was in the Welsh Army myself for some years then I found faith and became a priest.'

Merle broke in at this point. 'Dad was an officer when he left, quite grand!'

Her father laughed and said, 'Not so grand, really, I was a major and I didn't really have any ambition beyond that.'

'I'm impressed, Mr Jenkins, I was only a corporal!' He began to feel comfortable with this man.

Mrs Williams interrupted their conversation.

'Haydn, can I get you something for pudding? I've got a nice apple pie, not long out of the oven.'

Wyndham looked at the vicar and Merle. 'Er, perhaps I'd better not, unless Mr Jenkins and Miss Jenkins would like to join me.'

The vicar said, 'Please go ahead, Mr Jones, we had a good lunch so we're only having something light tonight. In the meantime, I'll get us another drink.'

'Not for me, thank you, Mr Jenkins,' said Wyndham, 'but let me get one for you both.'

He went to the bar and got two more halves for Merle and the vicar and sat down again. Mrs Williams brought his apple pie and he ate it with relish.

'It's good to see someone with such an appreciation of food, Mr Jones,' said the vicar with a grin.

'I think Mrs Williams is the best cook I've come across, Mr Jenkins. Please call me Haydn, by the way,' said Wyndham.

They spent a little time speaking of Wyndham's walks and the small villages nearby, until Wyndham had finished eating.

'Haydn, why don't you come up to the vicarage with us for a cup of coffee and a nightcap now – I have some interesting maps of the area which you might enjoy seeing.'

Wyndham was a little taken aback but he could see that the vicar was a man to be trusted and there seemed to be a reason why he'd been invited that was nothing to do with hikers' maps. He nodded and accepted the invitation, then he said, 'Perhaps we ought to take Hannibal with us! He was asleep on my bed when I came down for supper. He spent most of last night with me too.'

Merle looked down at her lap and reddened, thinking how Hannibal must have come straight from his bed to hers; she liked the thought, though.

They all got up and left the pub, waving to Siôn Williams and the other patrons as they went. They went round to the back and Wyndham went up the steps to his room. Instinct told him that someone had been there while he was having supper, although the door was still locked. He opened the door to see Hannibal standing on the bed, as if ready to attack and he said, 'Hannibal, it's only me, your friend, Haydn,' and the cat relaxed, moving toward him and meowing. Wyndham put on the central light and could see a few drops of blood on the bedcover. 'Hannibal, have you hurt yourself?' the cat meowed again. Wyndham went to the door. 'Mr Jenkins, Merle, there's blood on my bed but I don't think Hannibal is hurt.' They both ran up the steps to join him in the room and Merle ran to Hannibal and checked his paws.

'There's some blood on his paws, Dad, but it's not his… I can see that he's all right,' she said. 'Hannibal, sweetheart, what happened?'

Mr Jenkins looked at the bedcover; fortunately, there was very little blood on it but there was more on the floor, several drops leading toward the door. He turned to Wyndham. 'Haydn, someone has been in here and Hannibal must have attacked whoever it was. Do you have any ideas as to who it could have been?' He looked serious.

Wyndham said, 'The only person I can think of is the deputy sheriff, Dai Sluice. He looked in the pub earlier and checked that I was there so my guess is that he came up here, not realising that the cat was here.'

Mr Jenkins gave him a long look and Wyndham said, 'I know that he's been in here before because I'd dropped some talc on the floor, accidentally, and there was as footprint in it when I got back from walking. It wasn't Mrs Williams's print, that's for sure.'

The vicar looked even more serious.

Merle had lifted Hannibal up and was stroking him. He returned the favour by purring and nuzzling in her neck. Wyndham picked up the bedcover and took it to the shower room to rinse the blood out under cold water. Then he hung it on the radiator to dry. Afterwards he wiped up the blood on the floor with some tissues and took them into the bathroom where he put the tissues into a bag and hid it in the bathroom cupboard; he would have the DNA checked as soon as possible. While he was in the bathroom, he sent a quick message to CI telling them of the intrusion and that he would get the bloody tissues to them. In the meantime, Merle was fussing over Hannibal and Mr Jenkins was looking around the room to see if there were any other clues to the intruder's identity, although he took Wyndham's word for it that Dai Sluice was probably the culprit.

Wyndham came out of the bathroom and Mr Jenkins said, 'Let's go to the vicarage; I think it's unlikely the intruder will return this evening. We'll get the hero of the hour, our Hannibal, back to his own home!'

They left the room, ensuring it was locked again, and walked up the road to the vicarage, Merle carrying Hannibal who had no objection to all the fuss that was made of him. It was a chilly evening but Wyndham felt a deeper chill, that of someone walking over his grave. There was danger here and he had to find out what was going on in this tiny country village in Wales.

Chapter 20

THE VICARAGE WAS a fairly small house but warm and welcoming. As they went in the front door, an elderly woman who had to be Merle's grandmother, as Wyndham could see the same dark prettiness in the old woman's face as in Merle's, came to greet them.

'*Croeso*, welcome,' she said to Wyndham, with a smile. 'My granddaughter was hoping you would come home to see us this evening.'

'*Diolch*, thank you,' said Wyndham, 'we've had a nice chat in the pub but it's lovely to be in someone's home like this.'

'Come you in,' said Mrs Jenkins, 'you'll have a nice drink now and a cup of coffee, won't you?'

'That sounds very tempting, thank you,' answered Wyndham, feeling much more comfortable.

Mr Jenkins had stepped into his study for a few minutes and Merle had taken Hannibal to the kitchen to clean up his paws. Wyndham followed Mrs Jenkins into the sitting room, a warm and inviting room with a log fire and old-fashioned, cosy chairs to sit in. Mrs Jenkins already had a pot of coffee on a table by the fire and poured out a cup for Wyndham, offering him milk and sugar.

Shortly afterwards, as Wyndham was sipping the hot coffee, the vicar came in and sat down, accepting a cup from his mother.

'Forgive me, Mr Jenkins, but is your wife not here?' Wyndham asked.

The vicar looked down at his cup and took a few seconds to reply. 'Unfortunately, my wife met with an accident two years ago, a fatal accident. I know that, as a priest, I should feel grateful that she is with the Lord, but it's very difficult for me, as it is for Merle. We are very lucky to have my mother here with us; she has been a great comfort.' He hesitated, 'Please don't feel awkward for having asked, it was only natural for you to enquire.'

Wyndham hung his head. 'I'm very sorry, Mr Jenkins.'

It was difficult to know what to say but, at that moment, Merle came back in, followed closely by Hannibal, who looked very pleased with himself.

'Sorry to keep you,' said Merle cheerfully, 'I had to give my little hero a treat – there'll be no living with him now! Dad, you promised Wyndham a drink as well as coffee. I'll get the whisky. Do you like Penderyn whisky, Haydn?'

'I do, indeed, thank you, that would be a real treat. I hope I won't be the only one having it though!'

'No, you won't, Haydn. Dad and I like a drop although *Mamgu* prefers a sherry.'

She went to the cabinet and poured out generous glasses of whisky and a small glass of sherry. Then they all sat in front of the fire, happily sipping their drinks while Hannibal washed himself contentedly on the hearthrug.

'Well,' said Merle after a few silent minutes, 'all we have to do is keep an eye out for someone with scratches on them.'

Mrs Jenkins looked puzzled and Merle explained what had happened in Wyndham's room. She looked shocked and, to the others' amusement, said, 'I hope it is that terrible Dai Davies, he deserves more than scratching.'

The vehemence of her speech made the others laugh. She

went on: 'He had to unblock Mrs Beer's toilet and he said to her that he wouldn't be doing jobs like that after he'd got an assistant because it was beneath him now that he's deputy to Mr Iwan ap Rhys. He needs a good spanking to bring him back to reality!'

Mr Jenkins looked at her in mock awe. '*Mam*, I hope I never get on the wrong side of you!' Then he said, 'Haydn, come through to the study for a minute and bring your drink; I've got the maps in there. We'll leave the women to raid the drinks cabinet!'

Merle and Mrs Jenkins both gave the vicar a look.

The vicar closed the study door and motioned Haydn to sit in a chair in front of an electric fire. 'Haydn, listen to me for a moment. I know that you are not Haydn Jones but I also know that your reasons for being in Myddfai are legitimate.'

Wyndham looked a little startled but then remembered the message from HQ. The vicar continued, 'You can trust me. The reason I came into the study when we arrived was to make a call and you needn't worry about anyone listening in to my calls as that is taken care of. You didn't see me taking a photo of you this morning but I sent it to my old superior in WARF and he confirmed who you really are and he gave me an inkling of what you are doing here. I understand that you've been successful so far and you've made yourself popular with the people in Myddfai, apart from the sheriff and his sidekick. I also saw someone creeping out of the village in the middle of the night and going toward Llangadog, from my vantage point in the church tower. You can be certain that the sheriff doesn't know about this because he would have reacted by now.'

'Sir, thank you for being honest with me. I will also be honest with you and tell you that I checked you out, too. You know that I can't tell you any more because it would be dangerous for you and your family but I assume that you have some involvement still with the military or intelligence.'

'You assume correctly.' The vicar was matter-of-fact. 'I've been told to stand by as I might have to become involved; WARF couldn't tell me more but it seems that there is more at stake than originally thought. No doubt you have received information from your HQ about other matters, which I won't ask you to elucidate on. Sufficient to say that should you need a place to run to, I am here and you can count on my cooperation.'

'Thank you, sir. I would be reluctant to involve you because of your daughter and mother; I couldn't endanger them in any way.'

'Thank you for that. They are tougher than they look, of course, but I don't want to endanger them either. It was enough that my wife should have become caught up in things.'

Wyndham was shocked. 'Do you mean your wife was killed because of your intelligence work?'

The vicar sighed and said, 'The word "killed" is the operative one; someone mistakenly thought that she was involved in intelligence and arranged an accident. She was never involved; she was a schoolteacher, a wife and a mother, and a thoroughly decent, honest woman.'

Wyndham was horrified at this and felt more determined than ever to get to the bottom of the conspiracy. As he thought about this, the vicar got up and went to a bookshelf, taking down an old book on walks in the area. He handed it to Wyndham and indicated that they should return to the sitting room.

'We were just about to send out a search party,' said Mrs Jenkins. 'Did you find the maps for Haydn?'

'Yes, don't worry, *Mam*,' said the vicar, 'I've persuaded Haydn to abandon Mrs Williams's cooking tomorrow and have lunch with us.'

'I don't want to be any trouble,' said Wyndham, rather looking forward to spending more time with Merle and feeling quite relieved that he had someone to confide in within the village.

'No trouble at all,' said Mrs Jenkins, 'we'll look forward to seeing you at one o'clock tomorrow and make sure you're hungry!'

'*Mamgu*, Haydn's got a big appetite so we'd better cook enough for at least five people!'

Wyndham thought it was time to excuse himself and he thanked them for their hospitality then bent down to stroke Hannibal and thank him for his heroism. Hannibal took this as his due, just as his Punic namesake might have done. Then the vicar took him to the door and said quietly, 'Take good care going back now and keep alert for Dai and the sheriff.'

Wyndham nodded and waved goodbye, then he set off for the pub.

The sky was quite clear that night; the stars and the soft lights from houses along the way lit his path. No one stepped out to challenge him but Wyndham was certain that there was someone following him. There was nowhere he could stop and hide at that point so he carried on at a steady pace, reaching the front of the pub safely. There he pretended to hesitate, as though unable to decide whether to go in or not and he turned around. There was no one behind him. He walked round to the back of the pub where there was a light above the back door illuminating the steps but keeping the door to his room in semi-darkness, and he saw a figure standing outside his room. A voice said quietly, 'Beat you to it, boy; you're slipping!'

Wyndham breathed a sigh of relief and walked up the steps and opened the door to his room. He and his pursuer entered and Wyndham locked the door behind him while his pursuer switched on the light.

'Well, Wyndham, where's this evidence?' said Aled, laughing.

Wyndham fetched the small bag holding the bloody tissues from the bathroom cupboard. 'I couldn't put them into a proper evidence bag because the vicar and Merle were here. And what the hell were you doing following me like that? I could have turned on you and hurt you.'

'Ha! Who won the last four bouts of *llaw gwag*, my friend? Me. You wouldn't have got me, especially as you've had a few drinks. Anyway, I'll stay a few minutes for a chat and you can tell me about this Merle. Seems you're not as innocent as you look, boy. We'll be playing the James Bond theme every time we see you from now on.'

'There's nothing to tell about Merle except that she's a very nice girl and she's the vicar's daughter so there's no hanky panky,' he said ruefully. 'And, what is more, the vicar is one of us.'

He spoke quietly and explained what the vicar had told him; Aled looked astonished at this news.

'Well, that's a turn-up. It'll be useful for you, though – and for us,' said Aled. 'Anyway, I'd best be going now.'

He looked out of the window and could see that the light outside the back door was off so it was a good time to leave.

'What are your plans for tomorrow? You've found the murder weapons and the missing hiker so you'd better just lie low now.'

Wyndham replied, 'I'll see what orders I get from CI. I'm having lunch with the vicar and his family at 1pm but, if there's nothing else on, I'll take a walk to Halfway in the morning and see if the ruins there hide anything.'

Aled nodded and gave him another bear hug before opening the door and running quickly down the steps, the evidence safely inside his jacket. Five minutes later, he was in the small blue van, driven by Walter, and on his way to Carmarthen. Wyndham had locked his door again and placed the chair up against it.

Elsewhere in the village, the sheriff and Dai lay in their respective beds with their respective long-suffering wives, unaware of Aled's visit. Dai Sluice's hand was bandaged and sore; he'd have to tell the sheriff that he'd hurt himself during a plumbing job as Mr Iwan ap Rhys would not be impressed by his deputy being attacked by a cat and Dai was desperate to impress the sheriff.

Hannibal lay on Merle's bed, satisfied with his day. He'd got that nasty Dai Sluice, the man who had once thrown a bucket of water at him. Merle watched as Hannibal's eyes seemed to light up at the memory and wondered what Hannibal's thoughts were, beyond a full food bowl and a comfy bed. He looked up at her and snuggled up with a purr then fell asleep. Soon after, Merle was sleeping too, dreaming of Wyndham also snuggling up to her.

Chapter 21

THE FOLLOWING MORNING, Wyndham woke at 8am, after his first full night's sleep for what seemed like a long time. He luxuriated in being able to lie in for a while. The mission was going well so far but now there were complications. Iori was clearly a liability although CI apparently did not yet know why; Harri Harris could be after Wyndham already so care had to be taken. On the other hand, the sheriff and his henchman, Dai Sluice, were trouble dressed in cowboy boots and the mystery of the underground room in Llangadog was still to be solved.

He checked his Blackcurrant but there was no update except for a message saying that the evidence had been received and the DNA was being checked. Wyndham had no doubt it would be Dai's DNA but he would await confirmation. He felt frustrated that he was in a dangerous situation without any information to help him, but that was really par for the course in his job so he'd just have to be patient.

He got up and showered and shaved. A quick breakfast and a brisk walk to Halfway before lunch would put heart in him. He was down in the kitchen before 9am and Betti Williams presented him with a plate of scrambled eggs and mushrooms with toasted home-made bread. 'There now, Haydn, that should keep you going,' she said with a smile.

He ate the delicious food with pleasure and told her that he had been invited for lunch at the vicarage that day. She chuckled and said, 'You'll be one of the family there before you know it!'

Wyndham laughed and said that the vicar seemed very pleasant.

Betti looked serious. 'He is a good man, Haydn, but being friendly with him won't put you in the sheriff's good books; there's suspicion on the vicar's side and bad feeling on the sheriff's, so it will be another mark against you.'

'I'll risk that, Mrs Williams,' said Wyndham. 'There's nothing I can do to get into the sheriff's good books anyway and the way Dai Sluice looks at me, I think he'd like to see me roasted on a platter.'

'Now he's a small man, Haydn, and he's stupid but that makes him more of a problem in a way.'

'I agree. Keep an eye out for him today though, see if he's bandaged. Hannibal gave him a going over last night!'

Betti Williams grinned broadly at this. 'You've just about made my day already! Seems you've got a real friend in that cat, and in his mistress!' She added, 'Merle's got a reputation as a bit of a flirt and she's had a few boyfriends but really she's a nice girl and only one of those boys had the Hannibal seal of approval so I don't think the others were serious, if you know what I mean. It was a shame about the one serious boy though; he joined the army and he was killed on his first tour.' She sighed and turned to get on with her work.

Wyndham finished his breakfast thoughtfully. Leaving Betti to get on with her cooking, he went up to his room and packed his knapsack for the morning's walk.

Chapter 22

E MIA CONTACTED THE security section again and spoke
to Alun. She didn't want to do any further investigations
in front of Iori so she asked if she could go down to Alun's
office and he agreed immediately. She also asked that someone
would be sent up to keep an eye on Iori, in case he should
turn on The Boss.

'Iori, I'm just going to be out of my office for a while, in
a meeting. Doug is coming up for a briefing with The Boss
any minute now.'

Iori scarcely looked up. 'Okay, Emia.'

As he spoke, Doug came in and nodded to Emia, then
went through to The Boss's office.

Emia looked at Iori for a long moment then took the lift
down to Security. Alun was waiting for her and took her to
a computer where she could look for the young man in the
photos. She scanned the photos she had into the computer
and then set it searching on all databases. In the meantime,
she sat thinking about all the events that had led up to this
moment. After about twenty minutes, the computer buzzed
and the word 'MATCH' flashed on the screen. Alun joined
her at her computer and they both looked at the information
on the screen. The name was Eryl Daniels and he lived on a
farm in Betws. Emia and Alun looked at each other; Eryl had
apparently been arrested on four occasions but never charged;
the arrests had been for minor reasons and the last time had
been just two weeks before. According to the records, he had
been removed from the police station by a solicitor named Mr

Bryn and the police had received instructions from a higher authority to leave Eryl alone. The authority was not named but Emia could take a guess at who Mr Bryn really was.

She printed off the information for herself and e-mailed it to The Boss, then returned to her office. Soon after she returned, Doug came out of The Boss's office, winked at her and left. Iori didn't even glance at them. Emia went into see The Boss who was already on the phone to the Director in Swansea about it. The Director instructed her to leave Eryl to his agents; they would go immediately to Betws to speak to him and verify whether the solicitor, Mr Bryn, was the same person as Mr B.

The Boss gave Emia instructions to keep Wyndham abreast of developments. A few minutes later, she had sent a message to Wyndham's Blackcurrant with the warning to stand by.

Wyndham was well on the road to Halfway when he received the message. As soon as his Blackcurrant vibrated, he got off the road and looked at the pictures and information Emia had sent. The situation seemed to get more complicated by the minute and there was nothing he could do at present. He put the phone away and continued down the road. As he walked, he thought he could hear the revving of a motorbike so, yet again, he hopped over the nearest farm gate and sat behind the hedge, waiting for Dai Sluice to come by.

Chapter 23

'SPECIAL AGENT LEWIS, I have a project for you,' the Director spoke seriously to the agent. 'Delegate two agents to go to this farm in Betws and speak to Eryl Daniels.'

He went on to explain what Emia had found out and told Lewis that he didn't want the agents returning without having spoken to Daniels.

Lewis understood the urgency and nodded, taking the pictures of Eryl Daniels and calling up two reliable agents to get them off to Betws quickly. Then he contacted the police and asked for a description of the solicitor, Mr Bryn, who had had Daniels released. A sergeant whom Lewis knew came on the line and told him that Mr Bryn had been a short, non-descript sort of man, middle-aged and with missing teeth. Lewis thanked him and rang off then went and told the Director.

'That dratted man seems to be in several places at once, Lewis, and we need to keep an eye on him at all times from now on,' said the Director. He picked up the phone and rang The Boss in Carmarthen to tell her of Mr B's other persona. He assured her that his office would be keeping twenty-four hour surveillance on Mr B from then on.

The Boss sighed with frustration. That Mr B seemed to be everywhere but who was he working for? It seemed as though the clinics had come under his control in any case. She had spent time trying to find a link between the clinics, the underground room in Llangadog and the Sheriff of Myddfai and she kept coming back to Mr B each time. If he was the link, then how had he achieved all this without anyone noticing?

As she mulled over these questions, two agents from Swansea were speeding through Pontarddulais toward Betws to find Eryl Daniels. That young man would come to regret the moment of abandonment in Blackpill as much as Iori had but, unlike Iori, he would not be granted the peace of forgetfulness.

Chapter 24

A T LLANFIHANGEL, ANEURIN had been escorted down to lunch by Nurse Jones. He exulted in the knowledge that he would be leaving within two days but he was obliged to appear blankly unconcerned, as though still under hypnosis. He was still not entirely certain of his identity but he felt sure now that Rhodri was not his name. Mr Goronwy Evan Evans still preyed on his mind and that name, Aneurin Ebenezer Hopkins, was so familiar and comfortable that he was prepared to swear that was his real name. Holding on to that, he felt that he could deal with anything that was thrown at him. The instruction to kill still worried him; he knew that he had not been hypnotised into doing anything against his will but how could he warn whoever was the proposed victim? If it was someone at CI, and it was probably someone important, how could he tell them?

Nurse Jones took him to a table by the window in the dining room. A waitress appeared and Nurse Jones told her to bring anything Aneurin wanted. The waitress told him of the day's specials and he asked for the steak with potatoes and salad. A few minutes later, the food arrived and Aneurin did his best to look as though he was enjoying it, although he was simply cutting up the food and pushing it about the plate, only taking small bites occasionally. The Beddgelert tea he simply poured into a nearby pot plant. He managed to put some of the food into a paper napkin so that his plate looked as though he'd eaten most of his lunch. The waitress offered him pudding but he said he was saving himself for supper so she smiled and took away his plate.

For a time he sat, holding his teacup as though sipping from it at times, and looking out of the window. A voice said, 'Well, I hear that you are leaving all of your friends here soon.'

It was the man with the missing teeth, looking cheerful as always. Aneurin had a vague memory of that face being in Dr Owain ap Owain's room so this man was definitely not to be trusted. He answered, 'So I'm told. I've been very comfortable here and I'm sure it's done me good, but we all like to be home, don't we?'

Mr Brynaman looked at him like an old pal. 'Of course we do, Rhodri, of course. Nothing like home, sweet home. But we'll miss your cheerful face and all the jokes, you know.'

'Thank you. It's nice to be missed by someone. I hope I'll live up to everyone's hopes of me once I leave.'

Mr Brynaman smiled, showing the gaps in his teeth. 'Oh, I'm sure you will, Rhodri. Dr Owain ap Owain has a lot of faith in you, I'm told. One of his best patients, so you are honoured.'

With that, he left the dining room to confirm to the good doctor that Aneurin was well and truly duped. Aneurin breathed more easily and got up from the table. Walking slowly and smiling at various people in the dining room, he passed the rubbish trolley and quickly dumped the paper napkin in it as he went. Then he went to the sitting room, hoping to find Mr Goronwy Evan Evans, but there were no other patients there and he went back to his room.

This time, he got some tissues before sitting in his easy chair and had them ready to stuff in his ears if the whispering should start again and he kept his back to the screen. Aneurin was beginning to recover and his situation was bringing out the best in him.

After speaking to Dr Owain ap Owain, Mr Brynaman left the clinic and got in the dark car again, along with Harri Harris. There were things to do before this evening and, now that Aneurin was dealt with, they would bring Iori further under their power. That red-headed boy from CI would need to be seen to of course; he liked the thought of all these little projects.

His meditations were cut short by the driver telling him that there was a call for him. Mr Brynaman picked up the in-car phone and, within moments, his cheeriness changed to fury. He said nothing but just listened for several minutes, then he put the phone down. The driver had seen the change but kept quiet. Mr Brynaman bared those gums in a grimace. 'Take me to Myddfai now. Those fools at Llangadog were found out.' He picked up the phone again and spoke to Dr Owain ap Owain, telling him it was vital to get Aneurin back to Carmarthen as soon as possible, to carry out his task.

The driver swung left to the Nantgaredig road and took the A40 toward Llangadog while Mr Brynaman fumed silently and Harri Harris's small brain tried to work out what was happening.

Chapter 25

WYNDHAM LISTENED AS the motorcycle drew nearer. The hedge was high and should protect him from view but he crouched down for safety. This time, the biker didn't slow down but carried on at the same speed toward Halfway and Wyndham stood up slowly. He hopped back over the gate to the road, and then heard the sound of a car or van coming from the road leading to Bron Farm. He stood still and waited. A Land Rover with a trailer soon appeared and the driver hailed him. He was a man of about 55 and solidly built, from what Wyndham could see.

'*Bore da*, I'm Llew Jones from the farm up there,' he pointed behind him. 'I think I saw you walking past yesterday.'

Wyndham approached the car. 'Yes, I'm staying in Myddfai and I took a walk up to Llandovery. I was planning to walk to Halfway today.'

'Hop in,' said the farmer, 'I'm going to Pentrebach with some machinery, perhaps you'd like to give me a hand.'

Wyndham remembered Aled telling him about the farmer at Bron Farm and thought it would be good idea to get to know him, so he jumped in the passenger seat and they set off. As they went steadily along, a motorbike passed them in the other direction and Wyndham could see that the rider was his enemy, Dai Sluice. Dai failed to notice the passenger in the Land Rover and Wyndham couldn't help smiling.

'Dai Sluice following you, is he?' said Llew. 'You want to watch him. He's stupid and stupid people are often the most dangerous. I know Aled told you about me so you know me now and you know that you have somewhere to go in an emergency.'

Wyndham said, 'Yes, Aled told me and thanks. That's the second time Dai Sluice has followed me but I managed to lose him the last time, too. He's searched my room at the pub once but the last time he tried, he was attacked by Hannibal, the vicarage cat!'

Llew roared with laughter, rocking the car as they went along. 'Good for Hannibal. You probably don't know that Dai threw a bucket of water over him a few months ago. Hannibal has been biding his time to get revenge; that is a cat with character.'

They had reached Pentrebach and Llew turned carefully into a narrow lane leading to a small farm. He pulled up and both of them got out and went to the trailer at the back.

'Don't worry, the stuff's not dirty so you'll be tidy enough for your lunch at the vicarage!'

Wyndham looked at him in surprise and Llew continued, 'The vicar told me about you; don't you concern yourself, you've got friends here.'

Wyndham nodded and helped Llew pick up the metal parts and take them to a shed nearby. After half an hour they were finished and the parts had been left neatly in their shelter. Llew opened a coolbox in the trailer and offered Wyndham a chilled soft drink.

'So, lad, I think you'll find that someone will be on the warpath now about you finding the room at Llangadog but we're not sure who, so keep your eyes peeled.'

'My gut feeling is that the room is linked not only to my mission here but to other strange things that have been happening in the past few days,' said Wyndham, 'only I can't see what the link is yet.'

'I'm sure you're right but we'll have to be patient. What you can be sure of is that the sheriff is involved either directly or indirectly. As for Dai Sluice, he's just an idiot who likes a little bit of power and he's milking his position for all it's worth but he has no influence, I'm certain of that. He's just playing Billy the Kid.'

'Thank heavens he hasn't got a gun then,' said Wyndham, 'because if he had, I think I'd have been shot by now and buried in Boot Hill.'

Llew shifted. 'We've got a bit of time before you have to be back so do you want to stop in Halfway? I can give you a lift back to the turning then. Nothing much to see any more really, it's like a ghost town now, quite sad I suppose.'

They got back in the car and Llew headed back to the road and Halfway. Llew was right; there were still cottages there and an old chapel but the people had long gone and there was an eeriness about the place. They stopped and got out of the Land Rover and Llew joined him in a stroll through the old village where so many people over the years had lived, loved, worshipped and died. Now there was no one. After a few minutes of contemplation, they set off again and Llew dropped Wyndham off at the turning to the farm.

'Don't forget, now, I'll be here if you need anything.'

Wyndham thanked him sincerely and waved as the Land Rover turned towards the farm. Then he walked slowly back to Myddfai, still trying to make sense of everything that had happened.

He arrived back in Myddfai with plenty of time to spare for freshening up before his lunch at the vicarage. Close to the pub, he saw a motorbike parked and he was obliged to pass it, in order to get to his room. He made sure that he didn't touch it though, as it would be like Dai to accuse him of trying to sabotage the bike. He went up the steps to his room and saw, to his surprise, that a padlock had been attached to the outside. Going back down to the pub, he signalled to Siôn behind the bar. The publican obviously realised what was up and gave Wyndham a key.

'Sorry about that, Haydn, but we can't have our guests disturbed by unwanted visitors in their rooms,' and he grinned, indicating that Dai was sitting behind him. 'That should make you feel a bit safer, and there's a bolt now on the other side of the door.'

Dai glowered over his spritzer, this time decorated with cherries, and cradled his sore hand which Wyndham could see was quite heavily bandaged.

'Nice walk, Haydn?' the publican went on.

'Thanks, Mr Williams, for the bolt and padlock. Yes, I had a pleasant walk up to Halfway.'

At this Dai looked perplexed.

'It's a sad little place. Anyway, I've got to get ready for my lunch now. I'll see you later, Mr Williams.'

Dai sat pondering how Wyndham had eluded him yet again. The sheriff would not be happy about this. He looked at his watch and growled; another sink to unblock so he'd better get down to it.

Wyndham went back to his room, grinning. He couldn't help being cheered up by Dai's hopelessness. It took him only a few minutes to freshen up and put on a clean sweater. He remembered to lock the door with the padlock and then sauntered along to the vicarage. He noticed some bunting being put up in the street and what looked like large braziers being lined up at the side of the road. 'Strange,' he thought, 'is it some sort of festival this week?'

Mrs Jenkins was standing in the doorway when he arrived and she welcomed him with a broad smile on her pretty face; the resemblance between her and Merle was even more marked.

'Come into the warm, Haydn. We've all been helping put things ready for the festival tonight so we're glad of the fire.'

Wyndham followed her into the comfortable sitting room and sat opposite her by the fire.

'I seem to have lost track of the days since I've been here, Mrs Jenkins, so what is the festival tonight?'

The vicar answered him: 'This time in March, nearing the Christian Easter, we have the festival of the Goddess Eostre, the Goddess Arianrhod and the return of the Sun God, Llew. We'll be walking up to Llwynywormwood tonight and waiting for the return of Llew at dawn tomorrow. There is nothing new under the sun, Haydn, no pun intended. The rising again of Osiris of the Egyptians, of Llew the Celtic Sun God, the rising of Christ from the grave. We do well to pay attention and respect to all of these. Who is to say that the god of the old religion is not the god of the new?'

'I think you speak wisely, Mr Jenkins. I suppose I hadn't thought of it like that but I can see the truth in what you say. Am I allowed to attend tonight?'

'Of course you are, Haydn,' said Merle, coming into the room with Hannibal following, 'I was hoping you would join us. We go equipped with drinks and snacks to keep us going! We'll be setting off at about 11.30pm so we'll call for you then, at the pub.'

'Thank you, I'll look forward to it. Better dress up warm, I suppose, and see if Mrs Williams will lend me a car rug.'

Hannibal had come up to rub against his legs and Wyndham stroked the cat with affection. 'Are you coming too, Hannibal?' he said.

The cat looked up at him, meowed and seemed to wink. There were plenty of rich pickings in the grounds of Llwynywormwood for a hunting cat like Hannibal so he would be going.

Chapter 26

AFTER A CHAT in the warm Vicarage sitting room, Wyndham sat down to lunch with the Jenkins family at about 1.30pm, the same time that Mr Brynaman was leaving the clinic at Llanfihangel and receiving the bad news on the car telephone. As the vicar, his family and Wyndham ate a delicious fish pie, Mr Brynaman was ordering his driver to take him to take him to Myddfai. Wyndham was still at the vicarage enjoying the meal when a dark car with tinted windows pulled up outside the sheriff's house and a short, non-descript man with missing teeth got out and walked up the path to the sheriff's front door.

A sharp rap at the door brought the sheriff's wife to open it. Mr Brynaman pushed past her into the hall, much to her surprise, and went into the sheriff's study, where Iwan ap Rhys was just finishing his post-prandial coffee. Mrs Rhys scurried after the intruder but her husband waved her away, saying, 'Leave it, I know this man. You can bring us some more coffee and another cup though.' She hurried to the kitchen to make the coffee, sensing that her husband was in one of his moods, and took the tray back to his study, knocking before she went in.

The visitor didn't look at her but she could see that he looked very angry so she backed out quickly after putting the tray down. Her husband ignored her, as he usually did. She went to the front room and looked out at the dark car. There was a very large man, like a bouncer, standing by it, and a uniformed driver. After a moment, she went back to the kitchen and, grabbing her coat on the way, she went out the back door and along the road to the vicarage. A few minutes later, she was in the vicarage dining room telling the vicar all about it. As soon as he heard the description of the car and the visitors, Wyndham realised who they were and whispered to the vicar.

'Mrs Rhys,' said the vicar, 'I'd like you to stay here with my mother and Merle for the time being. Don't alarm yourself but Haydn here and I think we know who this is and you will be wise to keep out of the way.'

Mrs Rhys gave a little cry but Mrs Jenkins took her firmly by the arm and into the sitting room to give her a small brandy.

'Haydn, she'll be all right with my mother and Merle. We had better go and see what's happening but, as they know about you now, we'd better keep a very low profile. I'll be back with you in a minute now, put your jacket on.'

As good as his word, the vicar was back very quickly, dressed casually with a wool cap on his head. He gave Wyndham a woolly hat to wear too and then they left the vicarage.

As they approached the sheriff's house, Wyndham took out his Blackcurrant and took photos of the car, Harri Harris and the driver. Then he and the vicar walked past the car, making small talk and studiously ignoring the visitors. They headed straight for the pub and walked in, signalling to Mr Williams that they needed to speak to him. He took them aside and the vicar briefed him about the newcomers.

The phone rang and Siôn went to answer it. Whatever was said at the other end of the line, Siôn said no more than, 'Right, see you in a few minutes.' He returned to the vicar and Wyndham. 'Call from Llew Jones. Merle rang him and he's coming straight away. Sit you down now and I'll get you a couple of drinks, better make them St Clement's or something because we need to keep our wits about us.'

The vicar and Wyndham nodded and went to sit in a corner.

'Mr Jenkins, how did Merle know to ring Llew Jones?' Wyndham asked.

'I asked her to do it, before we left. But she knows anyway – it was no surprise to her. And, in case you're worried, Mrs Rhys will be safe with my mother. She is Rhian Jenkins, a heroine of the Welsh Resistance, and I still wouldn't take her on in a *llaw gwag* contest, even at her age!'

The vicar laughed and Wyndham looked at him in astonishment. Rhian Jenkins was an icon of the Welsh Resistance and Wyndham could scarcely believe that the pretty, cosy old lady with whom he'd just lunched was famous for hand-to-hand fighting and resistance work.

'Is everyone in the village involved?' asked Wyndham.

The vicar shook his head. 'No, but Siôn and Betti came here because of my mother and there are several villagers we know we can rely on in an emergency. Hannibal is an honorary member now, of course!'

Mr Williams brought their drinks and went back to the bar and Betti waved to them from the kitchen door, giving them the thumbs up.

They sat, sipping their drinks and talking in low voices for a time. Then the door opened and a regular customer, whose face Wyndham knew, came in and looked around. Seeing the vicar in the corner, he went up and said quietly, 'They're still there. Toff is keeping an eye out at the moment but we'll change around again soon and keep you briefed.'

He left them and they found themselves looking at Llew Jones. 'Hallo boys, can I join you for a drink?'

'Siôn, Mr Jones will have a drink with us, please,' said the vicar, and Mr Williams brought over another soft drink.

Wyndham said quietly, 'I'll just go to the gents and send the photos through to HQ.'

The other two men nodded and carried on talking as Wyndham went through to the men's room and sent his message. He explained that the vicar, Llew and Mr Williams were helping and that they were all at the pub. He went back to the table and sat down and, two minutes later, the phone vibrated and a message from The Boss appeared on the screen to stand by and expect someone from Swansea to arrive soon. Wyndham spoke quietly to the other two men and told them he didn't know the people in Swansea but the vicar reassured him that he and Llew did know some people there.

Every so often, someone would come in and give them the message that the car and the visitors were still there. After about forty minutes, they heard a car draw up outside and a tall, good-looking man with expensively-cut grey hair and a light tan walked in, wearing casual clothes and carrying a flat cap. The vicar looked a little surprised and said, 'They've sent the big gun, this is our man.' He walked over to the bar and stood next to the grey-haired man, the Director from Swansea.

The Director spoke to Mr Williams. '*Prynhawn da*, I think you have a room for me. I spoke to your wife earlier.'

Mr Williams calmly said, 'Oh yes; she'll take you up now.'

Mrs Williams appeared from the kitchen and took the Director through to the stairs and showed him up to his room. Her husband came to clear the vicar's table and said, very quietly, 'Go round to the back door and Betti will take you up to the Director's room so you can talk in private.' He went back to the bar with the empty glasses.

Llew Jones said in a low voice, 'I'll get in my Land Rover and drive it around the corner, then I'll come to the back door. You go ahead because we don't all want to leave at the same time.' Then he said in a normal voice, 'Right boys, I'd better get going – see you soon.'

He left the pub and they heard him rev up the Land Rover and drive off. The vicar and Wyndham got up and went to the door, waving to Mr Williams who nodded at them. Llew was already in the kitchen when they went around the back and Betti took them all upstairs to the Director.

'Well, tell me all about it,' said the Director.

There were two chairs in the room; he sat in one and the vicar took the other, while Llew and Wyndham sat on the bed. The Director looked toward Wyndham and said, 'I've been kept up to date with all of your exploits, young man, and I'm very impressed with your work. We're in unknown territory here but we can be sure that whatever is happening at the sheriff's now is linked to what you have discovered and to whatever is happening to Iori at your office and to Aneurin at the clinic.'

Wyndham took out his Blackcurrant and showed Llew and the vicar the photos of Mr B and Harri Harris. They both looked very serious.

'I had some dealings with Mr B about twenty years ago, Director,' said Llew, 'and that is definitely him in the photos. So that is the man at the sheriff's house now too.'

The Director nodded towards Wyndham again and said, 'The vicar and Llew may know most of what you've done but I'd be grateful if you'd go through it all again.'

Wyndham started at the beginning, from the kidnap of Aneurin, and gave the whole story. When he'd finished, Llew looked at him in admiration and slapped him on the back. 'Good lad,' he said.

The Director's phone buzzed at that moment and he answered it. 'Keep up with them. I want to know where they're going now – 24-hour surveillance and you'd better not lose them.' He turned to the others, 'They're on the move, gone towards Llandovery by the look of it.'

'What's the next step, please, sir,' asked Wyndham. He felt more at ease now that he had so many people with him but he was also anxious to get into action.

'It's a waiting game, lad,' said the Director, 'I'm going to keep this room for tonight at least. Llew better go back to the farm but please keep on standby. The vicar will be nearby anyway, and the Williams pair on the spot.'

Llew said, 'I'll be back down here tonight, because it's the festival. There'll be people wandering around all night so the sheriff and Dai will be occupied with that, I should think.'

'You've given me an idea, Llew,' said the Director. 'Do you think you could organise one or two of the villagers to create a diversion to keep the sheriff and Dai busy tonight?'

Llew grinned, 'No problem at all, Director. There's nothing like causing trouble for those two and there'll be people pleased to do it. What time were you thinking?'

'I think we'll say 2am. While they are kept busy, I'll go to the sheriff's house myself and have a look at what is going on there,' said the Director.

'Will you take me along, Director?' asked Wyndham eagerly.

The Director looked at him, seeing his keenness, but he shook his head. 'No, not this time. I don't want disappoint you but I want you to carry on keeping a low profile for the time being, until we know where we stand. I'll have someone with me but I want you and the vicar to do whatever you were planning this evening. We'll be in constant touch though. I suggest that everyone gets a bit of rest this afternoon as we're likely to have a very busy night.'

Wyndham did look disappointed but he had to follow orders. The vicar told the Director what the arrangements for that night's festival were and then he, Wyndham and Llew left the Director. Llew went to fetch his Land Rover and drove back to his farm. The vicar asked Wyndham to go back to the vicarage with him and they set off, passing the sheriff's house again.

Merle came to the door to meet them and hugged her father. Wyndham would have liked her to hug him too but she just smiled and they all trooped through to the sitting room, where Mrs Rhys sat in a chair by the fire, dozing, and Mrs Jenkins sat opposite her, quietly crocheting. Wyndham marvelled at this; Mrs Jenkins's hands had probably injured, if not killed, a number of people in the Battle for Wales but now they were crocheting something pretty. He was in awe of her. Hannibal lay on the hearthrug, gazing at them all as if he knew their secrets, and purring as he plucked at the rug.

Mrs Jenkins spoke softly, 'The poor woman is exhausted from running around after that awful man, and she's had a shock today, so we'll leave her alone for a bit.'

They brought Merle and Mrs Jenkins up to date although they didn't say anything about the Director's plan for the night at that point.

The vicar turned to Wyndham. 'We'll keep Mrs Rhys here for as long as we think it's wise. It's unlikely that the sheriff has even given a thought to her anyway. You go back to the pub and to your room now and get some rest before tonight. I'll call for you at 11.30, as arranged, but I'll contact you beforehand if anything comes up.'

Wyndham nodded and got up. Mrs Rhys was still asleep so he tiptoed out.

Merle came after him, saying, 'Haydn, you didn't have any pudding because you had to rush off, so here's a nice bit of fruit cake for you to eat in your room. And we'll be together all night, Haydn!'

He grinned and left the vicarage. A few minutes later, he was back in his room safely. He bolted the door and undressed to his underwear and then checked his messages. There was one stating that the hiker was recovering slowly and would be available for questioning by the following day. That was good news. The next message told him that Mr B and Harri had been followed to Llandovery, where they had booked into a hotel and were still under surveillance; Wyndham would be alerted if they returned to Myddfai.

He allowed himself a few minutes to think about Vicar Jenkins's family. A mother who was a national heroine and a daughter who was clearly unfazed by her father being involved in Intelligence. He really liked Merle. He fell asleep thinking about her, having set his alarm for 8pm.

Chapter 27

ANEURIN HAD SPENT the afternoon in his room. Once again, the screen had descended from the ceiling and the whispering had started. He sat in the chair, facing away from the screen and keeping tissues stuffed in his ears. After fifteen minutes, he looked and could see the screen ascending again. So he threw away the tissues and lay down on his bed, in case the orderlies came again. Dr Owain ap Owain had said that he wouldn't see Aneurin again before he left but he couldn't take any risks.

No one came and eventually he fell asleep. At about 6.30pm, Nurse Jones came into the room and put her hand on his shoulder.

'Rhodri, wake up!'

She spoke gently and he opened his eyes.

'Is it supper time already, Nurse?' he asked, rubbing his eyes.

'Yes, Rhodri, so come now and have your supper, because you're leaving earlier than expected. Once you've eaten, you'll be going home. I'll pack for you while you're eating and I'll put some of that cream in the bag, for your face.'

'Okay. I'll just use the bathroom before I go down then.'

When he came out of the shower room, Nurse Jones was packing his bag for him and he thanked her and went down to the dining room. He was hungry, having eaten so little of his lunch, and he'd only drunk tap water since, hoping that it wasn't drugged. Certainly he felt more alert than he had done since his arrival at the clinic, however long ago that had been. Only one more meal to get through and he'd be free. His heart was thumping with nervousness; it seemed so loud to him that everyone could hear it, but of course no one took any more notice of him than usual.

The dining room was quite full of people but he managed to get a table by the window and could just see in the darkness the lights in the harbour, although there was no harbour there. He wondered how they did it. He asked for boiled eggs, thinking that it would be difficult to drug them. A few minutes later, the waitress brought the eggs and some bread and butter for him, along with the ubiquitous Beddgelert green tea. One day, Aneurin would find out whether there was really any tea grown in North Wales, but that would have to wait.

He tapped the first egg and looked at the yolk and white inside. He poured salt on the yolk and noticed that it turned a rather odd colour so, taking a piece of bread, he scraped the yolk and white onto it and pretended to be making a sandwich of it. Then he cut up the sandwich into small pieces and made a play of eating it in small amounts, whereas he was actually transferring it to his napkin as far as possible. He did the same with the second egg and the bread. The waitress came to take away the plates and asked him if he'd like anything else but he told her he would just enjoy his tea and thanked her politely.

He managed to pour some of the tea into the pot plant by his table and got up casually, walked past the rubbish trolley and dropped in the napkin, as he had at lunchtime. By the time he reached the dining room door, he felt quite shaky.

'Rhodri!' a voice called and Aneurin nearly jumped in the air. He turned and the waitress came up to him. 'I've been told you're leaving, Rhodri, so I just wanted to say goodbye and good luck. You've always been so polite.'

'Oh, thank you very much. I'm sure I'll need some luck.'

As he walked to the stairs, Nurse Jones was coming down with his bag.

'Am I leaving immediately then, Nurse?'

'Yes, Rhodri. The car will be out the front in two minutes. Let's go and wait in the porch. Here, put your jacket on as it's a bit cold this evening; the sea air doesn't help!'

They walked to the porch; it was dark outside so Aneurin couldn't see far. A car arrived and an orderly jumped out. He took Aneurin's bag and put it in the car and motioned for Aneurin to get in too. Before doing so, Aneurin kissed Nurse Jones on the cheek and thanked her. Without looking back, he got in the car and sat down with his bag at his feet. The car windows were so dark that he couldn't see out; he supposed that they didn't want him to see that he was in Llanfihangel. The orderly closed the door and got in the front seat, next to the driver. Red lights on the doors showed that they locked; in any case, if Aneurin wanted to find out what was really happening, he would have to go along with this charade. He also wanted to be in a position to save the person he was supposed to shoot.

The car sped off from the clinic and Aneurin sat back, thinking. Suddenly, he smelled gas. There was nothing he could do and, within seconds, he was unconscious.

Chapter 28

IN AN INTERVIEW room at WBI HQ in Swansea, a slight young man from Betws was sitting, sweating with nervousness.

Eryl Daniels had been picked up from his parents' farm earlier that day and had been interrogated by two agents. Special Agent Lewis entered the room, carrying a cup of tea and some cigarettes.

'I thought you might like some refreshment, Eryl. It's really a no-smoking building here but we'll make an exception today, just for you.'

The other two agents stood back and went to lean against the wall as Lewis sat down in front of the shaking farmer's son. Eryl took a cigarette, his hand trembling, and Lewis lit it for him.

'Drink the tea, it'll relax you,' Lewis advised. 'Now, Eryl, let's have a little chat. It's very simple really; you received a visit from someone asking you about a little incident in Blackpill which took place some years ago. All we'd like you to do is to take us through the conversation that you had with the person concerned.'

Eryl coughed and croaked, 'I don't know who they were but they said they'd make sure that something would happen to my parents if I didn't tell them about Iori.'

He was almost in tears and the two agents standing near him looked at each other with raised eyebrows.

He coughed again, 'There were two of them. One was

short and old-ish and he had missing teeth; the other one was massive and he didn't speak, only grunted, but the short one called him Harri.'

'So far, so good, Eryl. Keep going.'

'Promise me that nothing will happen to my mum and dad because of this,' he said, sounding desperate.

'I promise, Eryl. There's a team of agents up at the farm looking after them now,' said Lewis. 'Now, carry on and you'll be able to go back to your mum and dad all the sooner.'

'This short man told me that he knew something about me and Iori and he wanted all the details. I didn't want to hurt Iori but that Harri picked me up and started to twist my arm behind me. I don't pretend to be brave and I knew that he wouldn't think twice about breaking my arm, so I told them. It all happened so long ago now and it was only the one time. We'd finished college then and I never saw Iori after that. It's the twenty-first century; surely these things don't matter much any more?'

Lewis spoke, 'Unfortunately, Eryl, they do if the person concerned has not told his employers of his leanings. It wouldn't have mattered otherwise and the men you've told me about would have had no leverage.' He sat for a moment and then said, 'All right, Eryl, these gentlemen will take you to have a shower. Then you can eat something and have a rest before we decide on the next step.'

'But I thought that if I told you, I could go home,' Eryl whined. He looked with fear at the other two agents.

'Don't worry, Eryl, you'll go home but I need to speak to someone first and you'll be treated well, I promise.'

Lewis got up and left the room, leaving Eryl looking at the other two agents in trepidation. They merely indicated that he should get up and go with them. They took him to a shower room and waited while he washed, gave him a prisoner's uniform to wear while his clothes were cleaned and showed him into a cell where he could lie down. Someone brought him a meal on a tray and he ate the food, despite his shaking hands.

In the meantime, Lewis contacted the Director in Myddfai and told him what Eryl had revealed. The Director instructed Lewis to ensure that Iori was never out of sight of the surveillance officers. He told Lewis about the arrangements for that night and asked him to stand by.

Lewis returned to his desk on the top floor and called The Boss in Carmarthen with Emia listening in. They were shocked. They knew that Mr B and Harri were now in Llandovery and were relieved that Wyndham was not now on his own in Myddfai. Lewis instructed them to stay in Carmarthen and not interfere.

As soon as he'd put the phone down, it buzzed and an agent following Aneurin's car from the clinic told Lewis that it was on the way to Carmarthen. He rang The Boss again, 'Ma'am, I have to tell you that Aneurin has been let out of the clinic early and the car is bringing him back to Carmarthen. Someone is following them so as soon as we know where they put him, I'll let you know.'

The Boss breathed a sigh of relief that Aneurin was being brought home. She called Emia in to the office. 'Emia, Aneurin is coming back to Carmarthen. Special Agent Lewis has just phoned.'

Emia was also relieved. 'Poor Aneurin; I wonder what he's gone through in that terrible place?'

'We'll have to be patient, Emia. Now, I'm afraid that if

you had arrangements for tonight, they'll have to be cancelled. We've got a long night ahead of us. There are so many strands to this case that we've got to keep our wits about us.'

'I didn't arrange anything for tonight, Boss, with everything that's been happening. But have I got time to go home, have a shower and change? I can do all of that in an hour.'

The Boss gave her permission to leave, with the proviso that she came back with some food for them both. She watched Emia leave and thought, 'At last, something is really happening and perhaps we can get Sir Geraint out of Llanfihangel now.'

Chapter 29

WHEN IORI FINISHED work two evenings after his encounter with Mr B and Harri Harris at his flat, he was back in self-satisfied mode. The encounter had been wiped from his memory by the hypnosis the previous night and he was completely unaware of his betrayal of Wyndham and CI. He had spent the day happily checking the CI expenses although he had been a little bewildered by Emia bringing him coffee and asking him about Bonnie Tyler, and then even asking him about the Welsh Home Stores café. So unlike her.

He did some food shopping before the market closed and managed to get some pic'n'mix from Woolworths before they shut their doors so his evening was something to look forward to. He'd even treated himself to a couple of cans of shandy.

He walked quite breezily up Hall Street to his front door and let himself in. The following evening he had the Irish Harp Club meeting so he'd spend a bit of time that night practising. In the hallway he found two envelopes on the mat. One letter was from his book club but the other looked like a fancy invitation, not something Iori would usually receive. He went upstairs, unlocked the door to his little studio flat and went in. He opened the large envelope; it really was an invitation and for that night: the opening of a new music club, invited guests only, in Little Bridge Street. He hesitated; perhaps it would be better to stay home. But, on the other hand, he didn't get invited anywhere very often and this sounded rather snazzy. The dress code said, 'Gentlemen in smart jackets, no trainers,' as if he would wear trainers. He was tempted. 'Why not,' he thought, 'something to talk about at the office and I'll bet no one else there has had an invitation like this.' The opening was at 9pm so he had plenty of time to eat and do a bit of harp practice; perhaps there would be someone there who appreciated the Irish harp. It would be an opportunity to impress people.

He cooked a light meal and even drank a glass of shandy in celebration. He spent about an hour practising on the harp and then showered. Best to look as smart as possible but a tie probably wasn't needed and, as it was close by his flat, he wouldn't bother with a coat, just put on a vest underneath his shirt. He wouldn't arrive on time as he'd read that it was fashionable to arrive a bit late so he didn't leave home until 9.15pm. It was a mild night and he was still warm from the shower so he felt comfortable walking past the Angel Vaults and down to Little Bridge Street.

As Iori left home, a man standing outside the estate agents in Nott Square spoke quietly into his sleeve and followed as Iori walked to the club.

Bridge Street and Little Bridge Street were both busy; the shops were closed but the smart bistros and the shady clubs with their anonymous frontages were doing good business. Anyone unaware of Carmarthen's darker side would never have realised that the respectable façades of the buildings in the area concealed places where the criminal fraternity and gamblers gathered.

Iori found the club and was immediately impressed by the entrance, which was guarded by men in commissionaires' uniforms and a man with a clipboard and earpiece. Elegant bronze torches with gas flames burned at either side of the doorway. For a moment, Iori felt a little shy but he forced himself to walk forward and handed over his invitation to the man with the clipboard who took it, ticked a name on his list and smiled as Iori entered the building.

A young man in what seemed like uncomfortably tight trousers and a bow tie, worn without a shirt, offered Iori a glass of champagne from a tray. The champagne had a raspberry in it and Iori thought that was so chic that he took the glass and walked through another door into a large room with some rather elegant-looking men and women in it. The lighting was quite dim and there was one of those mirror-balls on the ceiling, which distorted things a little, but there were comfortable sofas and chairs to sit in so Iori was reassured. A jazz band played on a small stage and he felt pleased that he'd come.

The man who had followed Iori from Nott Square watched from the darkness of a doorway and spoke again into his sleeve; he couldn't go into the club so he would have to wait outside. Someone would have to check if there was another entrance to the club and cover it.

More people arrived, the men smartly dressed and the women in cocktail outfits. Every so often, the watcher would take pictures on his camera phone and e-mail them. Eventually, he received a message through his earpiece that there was another entrance at the rear of the building and that someone was keeping an eye on it. He was afraid it would be a long night.

Iori stood near a wall, sipping his champagne, and found that his glass kept being refilled by passing young men wearing the same outfit as the lad in the reception. There didn't seem to be any food so, despite his supper earlier on that evening, he began to feel more than a little relaxed.

The jazz band played some smoochy music and a young woman, quite tall and brunette, and wearing a slinky, black, sequined dress came up to him, taking his hand. He hadn't danced with anyone since his student days and he felt awkward but the woman and effect of the champagne carried him forward to the dance floor and he put his arm around her.

They spent some time swaying to the music, the woman hanging on Iori's neck and nuzzling his ear. He felt as though he was in a dream and floating above the dance floor. Then she whispered in his ear and led him to a staircase at the end of the room. At the top of the stairs he hesitated, but she smiled and caressed his face. He followed her into a private room, in which there was a large divan. A bottle of champagne stood in an ice bucket on a small table and the woman poured out two glasses then sat on the divan and pulled Iori toward her. Almost before he knew what was happening, she was undressing him. Then he found himself lying on the divan while she held the champagne glass to his lips and he sipped. He lay back and closed his eyes, giving himself up to her.

Chapter 30

'GOLD! GOLD!'
    Everyone in the room turned and looked at the girl. She looked around excitedly, 'I've finally found out what's been happening in that room in Llangadog! It's all about gold.'

Her colleagues in the Welsh Bureau of Investigation's computer analysis lab gathered around with interest. While they all looked at her screen, she telephoned Special Agent Lewis and told him of the breakthrough. She pushed away her colleagues and e-mailed through to Lewis all the details she had found.

On the top floor of Swansea's only skyscraper, Special Agent Lewis gazed at the screen in astonishment. Here were maps and plans of potential gold mines in the Towy Valley. Another message came through from the lab; the attachment showed messages sent to and from Anglo-Saxons over the border and in several of them a certain Mr B was mentioned.

Lewis sorted the messages and sent several examples to the Director's laptop in Myddfai. This was a huge step forward; they had the motive for the murders, the kidnap, Aneurin's incarceration in Llanfihangel and Iori's hypnosis. It also established the reason for the link between the sheriff in Myddfai and Mr B. Undoubtedly, the sheriff had offshore accounts and could be of use to whoever was hoping to do a deal with the Angles.

His phone buzzed. 'Lewis, thanks for that, it explains nearly everything. But I can see from these messages between the Angles and the conspirators that this is not just about selling and buying gold, it's about a complete takeover. You can bet your life that this will not be confined to the Towy Valley but spread throughout Wales. My guess is that whoever is behind this will dismiss the Senate and take over the country. Lewis, we are fighting for our country here. Send me everything else you've got and keep me updated if anything is found.'

Lewis was horrified. He sent all the other plans and messages through to the Director and instructed the lab to work twice as hard to see what was on the other hard drives confiscated from Llangadog.

In Myddfai, the Director phoned the vicar on his mobile and told him of the new development. The vicar was shocked; in all his military and Intelligence career he had never heard of anything like this. As a man of integrity, he could scarcely believe that any Welsh person would so betray their own country.

'There's no question in my mind that Mr B is not the top man in this,' said the Director, 'but finding the person who is... well, I'll have to think about that. The lab is working on the e-mail address to see who sent the messages, but I've no doubt they'll be deeply encrypted.'

'Keep me updated, Director. I'm assuming we are to carry on with the plan as before, though?'

'Yes, no change at present. Get some rest before you go out and, much as I don't like to ask a man of God to arm himself, I'm afraid I must ask you, for your own and your family's safety, to carry a weapon tonight. Our young agency man will have one secreted somewhere too.'

The vicar agreed and rang off, leaving the Director deep in

thought and very troubled. He picked up his phone again and rang CIHQ. Emia had returned to the office, dressed casually to be comfortable, and had brought some food. She and The Boss were eating when the phone rang.

'I have news for you,' he said to The Boss. 'We've found the motive for all these different problems we've been dealing with over the past few days. The short answer is gold. At the moment I'm guessing, but I believe that there is an Anglo-Saxon cabal working with Welsh traitors not only to set up gold mines in Wales, specifically the Towy Valley at present, but to make a political and social coup which would effectively destroy everything we've worked so hard to build up over the past century. I'm talking about the dismissal of the Senate, the wiping of our language and culture from the map and the completion of the Anglo-Saxon plan for total domination, which they have hitherto failed to carry out over one and a half millennia.'

The Boss pulled herself together and said, 'So we don't yet know all our enemies, Director? We know Mr B and his henchman, we know the Sheriff of Myddfai, Dr Owain ap Owain and the staff at the clinics, but who is on the Anglo side?'

'You are correct to say that we know many of those on our side. The lab is still working on the computer hard drives from Llangadog, hoping to find clues to the identity of the person or people sending the messages, but the other way we can find out is to ask Mr B; my guess is that the sheriff is only partially informed, they need him for the financial side but they probably haven't told him the full story,' answered the Director.

'Rather you than me, if you don't mind my saying so, Director, but if that is what it takes, I will volunteer to approach him. We would have to get rid of Harri beforehand though.'

'Thank you for your courage in volunteering, but I shall not ask you to do that. You are, of course, right that Harri will have to be dealt with first and I have an idea about that. I'll get back to you.' He rang off.

The Boss and Emia looked at each other in amazement. The enormity of what they had just heard was difficult to cope with. It had been 43 years since the Battle for Wales and, since then, so much had been achieved with the country having its own Senate and the ancient Welsh language having reclaimed its position from the invaders' own Anglo-Saxon tongue after a desperate struggle. Surely they could now sit back and enjoy the fruits of all the sacrifices made by the Welsh people during those fearful days almost half a century ago. But it seemed that it was not to be.

Chapter 31

A NEURIN'S EYELIDS FLICKERED. He listened but there was no sound around him and there was no movement so he couldn't be in the car still.

He opened his eyes. He was lying on a sofa in a familiar room; a table lamp was lit to his left. It was his own sitting room in Carmarthen! Oh, wait a moment, if they could convince him he was in Porthgain when he was really in Llanfihangel, perhaps they were trying to convince him he was in Carmarthen when he was really somewhere else. He got up, went out of his first-floor flat down to the street door and opened it quickly. A passerby looked at him with surprise and Aneurin just raised his hand and smiled weakly. He was in Little Water Street, Carmarthen.

Aneurin could have wept with relief. The strain of his stay at the clinic suddenly left his legs weak and he clutched at the door frame. Closing the door, he went back to the sitting room upstairs and looked around, then he went into the other rooms in his small home. He discovered that the fridge had food in it, fresh food; he could have sworn he'd bought some of that stuff recently himself. His bedroom was neat, as always. Everything looked normal.

There was a clatter as something fell through the letterbox downstairs and he dashed down again; it was the local free paper. When he looked at the date, he could see that only a few days had passed since he was taken to the clinic. He hadn't been there for weeks after all. What was going on? And who did they want him to shoot?

One thing was for sure: they would be back. And were they monitoring him now? He had to be careful in that case. He went to the kitchen again and looked in the fridge. Would they have drugged his food here? He ran the cold tap and had a glass of water to help him think. There were some frozen meals in the freezer; it would have been difficult to drug those. He took out a frozen fish pie and opened the pack; it was still sealed so he had to take a chance. It would only take a few minutes in the microwave. He went back to the bathroom and opened the cupboard where he saw a piece of paper on one of the shelves with a message that read:

YOU ARE ANEURIN EBENEZER HOPKINS

YOU WORK FOR CARMARTHEN INTELLIGENCE

YOU ARE UNDER SURVEILLANCE BY PERSONS UNKNOWN IN THE LIVING ROOM, KITCHEN AND HALL

CARMARTHEN INTELLIGENCE HAS HACKED INTO THE SURVEILLANCE AND WILL MONITOR YOUR SAFETY

So, he was being watched – there must be cameras in the house. It was good to know that someone was looking out for him though. He left the note in the cupboard, returned to the kitchen and set the table for his meal. He still felt shaky after his ride from Llanfihangel and from the lack of nourishment that day. A meal would make him feel stronger and more confident, he told himself. If only he could contact CI and tell them about the instructions to kill someone. He had to find a way.

At Swansea and at CI, screens revealed that Aneurin had

been brought home by clinic staff and, after depositing him in his home, the staff left quickly. The camera in the living room showed Aneurin waking up and the one in the kitchen showed him cooking a meal for himself. They were certain he had been to the bathroom and hoped that he had seen the note and not been brainwashed completely.

Aneurin's old instincts started to kick in now but he was physically and mentally drained after the past few days. He would find a way to contact CI but first he had to get some rest. Watching the TV was out of the question as they might have rigged it up to hypnotise him again. He'd put some earplugs in before going to bed, in case that whispering started in the night. Having secured the front door with a chain and bolt, he went to the bathroom and took a shower, changed into pyjamas and went to bed, keeping a bedside lamp on. Although it was still only about 9pm, he was asleep within minutes.

At CIHQ, The Boss was informed that Aneurin had gone to bed and would be under constant watch that night. She sighed, at least that was one thing being slowly cleared up although Aneurin might still be in danger. She and Emia sat in the office, looking through the computer files, trying to think who else could be involved. For the next few hours, they racked their brains about it.

At 11.30pm The Boss said, 'Wyndham and his friends in Myddfai will be going to that festival about now. I wish I could be there to see what's happening. The Director has a plan for tonight but he hasn't told me what it is, beyond hoping to get into the sheriff's house to look around.'

Her phone rang. 'Ma'am, our surveillance team in Little Bridge Street has just checked in and said that Iori has not yet come out of the club so they'll stay with it and keep checking in every hour.' Lewis rang off.

'And that's another thing,' said The Boss, 'there's that damned Iori to deal with too. I know that Swansea is taking care of the surveillance but I feel responsible for the little idiot. How often does he get invitations to anything, let alone something in a posh club in Little Bridge Street? No, there's something very strange going on and it's got to be linked to the blackmail and Mr B.'

'Can't we get into the club then?' asked Emia. 'I know we are supposed to leave to Swansea to deal with it, but it seems pretty feeble not to be able to get in there to see what's going on. I'm willing to go in, if you let me.'

'Emia, I'm very grateful to you for volunteering to do that but it would be dangerous for you on your own. No, our place is here and I'm afraid we just have to leave it to Swansea.'

Emia nodded; she had to accept her boss's decision and she didn't really know what she would have done, even if she'd managed to get into the club. She wasn't a trained agent, after all.

'If we could get Sir Geraint out of the clinic then he might be able to tell us something, if he hasn't been brainwashed.'

While the two women sat in their office pondering these questions, Aneurin slept in his own bed in Little Water Street and Iori slept on a velvet-covered divan in a club in Little Bridge Street, naked barring his socks.

Chapter 32

WYNDHAM HAD SLEPT deeply until the alarm went off at 8pm. Unhurriedly, he showered, dressed warmly, ensuring that his sheathed knife was safely fastened around his leg. Getting out his knapsack, he put into it all the things he thought he might need that night, including a large hip flask which had belonged to his father and grandfather before him. The latter had carried it throughout the Battle for Wales and it was a bit battered but, for Wyndham, it was a proud possession and his good luck charm. Putting the entire knapsack back under the floorboards for safety, he went down to the pub for some supper.

Betti Williams welcomed him with a smile and whispered that she had a car rug for him to take that evening, big enough to share if he wanted! He grinned and asked if he could have some supper. Mr Williams offered him a glass of St Clement's and Wyndham went to sit down in his usual corner.

A few minutes later, Betti brought him a big plate of local sausages and mash with carrots and gravy and Wyndham tucked in. He'd be glad of a hot meal inside him, to keep him going for the rest of the night.

'Not very busy at the moment, Mr Williams?' said Wyndham.

'Oh, it will be busy enough for the hour or so before closing time. Then everyone will go up to Llwynywormwood for the festival rites. We'll be rushed off our feet by 10pm, Haydn.'

Wyndham nodded. No doubt, the sheriff and Dai would

be kept occupied during that period and during the arrival of people at the festival site. Wyndham planned to go up to the tower at Llwynywormwood during the festival, if he could get away safely. There was no sign of the Director, but when Betti came to collect his plate she told him that the Director was eating in his room and wanted Wyndham to go up to see him at 10.30pm. She brought Wyndham some rhubarb fool as pudding and he ate with enjoyment.

A few regulars came in and chatted to Wyndham from the bar for a time, then he excused himself, telling them he'd see them up at the festival, and went into the kitchen. They called after him, teasingly, that he would have eyes for only one person by then.

Having praised Mrs Williams for the delicious supper, he settled his outstanding bill and went up to the Director's room.

'Sir, you wanted to see me?' said Wyndham, after the Director had answered his door.

'Wyndham, I've got a lot to tell you before we go out so make yourself as comfortable as possible.'

The Director looked very serious and Wyndham frowned as he sat down. There must have been further developments.

'First, Wyndham, I'll give you some good news. Aneurin is back in Carmarthen, at his own house. However, he is under surveillance there by our enemy and CI have had to hack into the surveillance equipment to ensure Aneurin's safety, and, hopefully, find out what has happened to him. Apparently, he's gone to bed and all is quiet there. What we have to work out is how to contact him without letting the enemy know that we are on to them. That is the good news. Now for the bad, and I'm afraid it's really bad. The computers that you found at Llangadog were used for research into potential gold mines in the Towy Valley and it seems that there are several in the region with the possibility of huge returns; there's evidence that they were also looking at other areas of Wales. It's not just the gold though. The messages we found in the hard drives make it clear that there is a political coup underway; we can expect the complete ruination of everything we have strived for over several decades. There are hints of assassination plans too.

'The messages were passing to and from the Anglo-Saxons and traitors here in Wales, including, of course, Mr B. As I told the vicar, I believe that the sheriff is being kept in the dark about the political aspects and is being used as a money-laundering service as he has offshore accounts; he's probably been promised a large share of the gold too.'

While the Director spoke, Wyndham's face showed more and more astonishment, then horror, at this plan. How could these people betray their country?

'Sir, I'm shocked at what you've said but I can see now why the hikers must have been killed and the last one was kept prisoner. They must have seen something. The first two presumably managed to get away but someone caught up with them, the last one was just unlucky that he happened to be interested in the castle and stumbled on the hidden room. He was fortunate that it was only those two computer geeks that found him though. But, from what you've said about the clinics, I don't really see where those link up with the plan, although I agree that they must.'

The Director shifted in his chair. 'We have to conclude that the people being held at the clinics, including Sir Geraint Williams-Jones, are to some extent people who still have influence and who might be dangerous to the cabal. As far as

Aneurin is concerned, I fear that he is the one marked down to do the assassinations. He is a crack shot and his weakness for the beer was a gift to the plotters.'

Wyndham pondered this and nodded. 'I see, sir, you are quite right I'm sure. Then we must find out if Aneurin is completely under their influence, mustn't we? And try to rescue Sir Geraint and the others from the clinics. But what about Iori?'

'Iori is also under surveillance but I'm a bit concerned as he was apparently invited to the opening of a club this evening, in Carmarthen.'

Wyndham snorted at this and the Director looked at him quizzically.

'Sir, Iori doesn't get invited anywhere. He's not a social animal and his only evenings out are to harp practice. He's not a popular person, I'm afraid.'

The Director looked worried and picked up his phone. 'Excuse me a moment, Wyndham, while I phone HQ.' He waited for a moment and then spoke into the phone: 'Lewis, what is the situation with Iori in Carmarthen?'

The Director listened for a few moments and Wyndham sat forward impatiently.

'Lewis, get someone into that club somehow. This is far more urgent than we'd realised. I don't care how you do it as long as you don't give us away, just get someone in there.'

'Iori went in at about 9.20pm and hasn't come out. I told them that they shouldn't lose sight of him but they didn't follow him in.'

The Director was angry.

There was a knock at the door and Wyndham went to answer it. The vicar stood there with his mother and Merle and the Director called for them all to go in. No sooner had they all gone into the room than there was another knock and Wyndham went to answer once again. This time it was Llew Jones. The vicar had informed Llew of developments and he was a picture of fury. The Director said to him, 'So Llew, you know about the plot now, at least as much as we know.'

He nodded, scarcely able to contain himself. 'Those Anglo-Saxons. Give them an inch and they take a country. They did pretty well for themselves over fifteen hundred years ago but we've managed to hold them off since then. Now they're taking the sneaky route.' He took a deep breath. 'Just wait until I see that Mr B.'

Wyndham couldn't help smiling at Llew's fervour; with people like him on their side, they would sort out the enemy. Mrs Jenkins patted Llew's hand and he put his other hand on top of hers gently.

'Now,' said the Director, 'we are all angry and want to get down to some action but we must deal with this professionally. Is that clear?'

They all nodded.

'Tonight, at 2am, I shall go to the sheriff's house to see what I can find. I take it Mrs Rhys is still at the vicarage, Mrs Jenkins?'

She nodded and explained that a friend of theirs was watching over Mrs Rhys and could be relied upon to keep her safe.

The Director carried on: 'Llew has arranged for a diversion to keep the sheriff and Dai at the festival site while I go and do the business. I'm being kept appraised of Mr B's movements and it seems he hasn't shifted from Llandovery yet. Well, it's 11.25pm now and we might as well make a start to the site.

Ladies and gentlemen, you can treat this as the second Battle for Wales.'

With this dramatic statement, he got up and led them from the room.

Chapter 33

E MIA AND THE Boss felt both frustrated and helpless at CIHQ in Carmarthen. They had sat for hours, looking at the evidence and then looking again, until neither of them was able to make sense of anything. Both of them were dozing in their chairs when the group in Myddfai set off for the festival.

The Boss's phone rang and she leapt up from the chair in surprise. 'CIHQ, is that Special Agent Lewis?' She listened for a few minutes and then put the phone down. 'All right, Emia, let's get going to Swansea. Lewis suggests we'd be better off waiting there, in the centre of things. I don't know if he's right but we certainly aren't getting any further here.'

Emia went to fetch her things and shortly afterwards they were in the lift to the fifth floor down and the express train to Swansea. Again there was a young woman, dressed in a plaid skirt, white blouse and buckled shoes to serve them refreshments. Emia took a cup of tea but The Boss declined. Twenty minutes later they were in Swansea, beneath the glittering skyscraper, and an agent came to take them up to the top floor again. Special Agent Lewis, looking rather tired, was there to meet them.

'Ma'am, Miss Glas, I was told to ask you to come here by the Director. Please make yourselves comfortable. There haven't been any developments since we last spoke.'

Emia and The Boss nodded and thanked him. Another agent offered them drinks and they felt justified in taking something stronger than water after a very fraught day. The agent also brought them small sandwiches and olives.

As they sat, Lewis's phone rang and he answered it. His face fell. 'All right, get all three of them up to Swansea and please make sure that they are dressed before they leave the club,' he said with some irritation.

Emia and The Boss looked at each other with raised eyebrows.

Lewis came over and sat with them. 'It seems that Iori is in trouble again; the invitation to the club was just a ruse of course. Our men have found him in a room with a transvestite and a photographer; they'd given him that date-rape drug by the looks of it. All three are being brought in now.'

Emia was stunned by this news. The Boss said, 'I thought that Iori wasn't supposed to be let out of sight?'

Lewis said, 'That was the plan but the men on surveillance didn't go into the club, only waited outside. They'll be disciplined.'

The Boss sat forward, her head in her hands. 'For heaven's sake! Poor Iori. I don't like the man, Special Agent Lewis, but I do feel some pity for him; he's such a pathetic character. His career is in ruins now because your men didn't do what they were supposed to do; in fact his life is in ruins as he has almost nothing else.'

Emia hung her head; she had almost wanted to laugh when she heard about Iori's circumstances and now she felt rather ashamed. She sipped her gin and tonic and stared at her feet. Lewis also hung his head; it wasn't his fault but he felt some responsibility, nonetheless.

'Oh, well, there's nothing to be done as we can't change what's already happened,' said The Boss. 'I don't mean to blame you, Special Agent Lewis, it's not down to you personally. I just can't help being angry about it.'

'I understand, Ma'am. We'll deal with it as sensitively as we can. In any case, Iori has to be given time to recover before anything else; I'll have him taken to the infirmary here. We'll find out who paid the transvestite and the photographer in the meantime, which might help us; perhaps you would like to be involved in the interrogation?'

The Boss nodded and gave Lewis a weak smile, which he returned. While they waited for the car to arrive from Carmarthen, they sat quietly and finished their drinks without speaking. All conversation seemed redundant.

Chapter 34

THE LARGE GROUP of people leaving the pub that night split up into smaller groups so as not to excite the suspicions of the sheriff and his deputy. The Director and Llew walked together ahead of the rest, followed by Wyndham and Merle. The vicar and Rhian Jenkins took up the rear. As they walked, more people joined them and chattered happily, nudging each other at Wyndham and Merle being together. Mr and Mrs Williams were due to follow on, after clearing up the pub.

At the entrance to Llwynywormwood, they could see the sheriff standing guard. As Wyndham approached, the sheriff put out his hand to stop him. 'Now, my lad, you are new to our festival and I'll tell you that we are taking a zero tolerance view on any bad behaviour, so watch your step.'

Wyndham looked at him in astonishment. 'Mr Iwan ap Rhys, I am, as you can see, accompanying the vicar's daughter this evening and will be with her family. I will act accordingly, I can assure you.'

The sheriff looked at him through narrowed eyes and leaned forward, saying in a whisper, 'You might be with the vicar but I don't trust him any more than I trust you, so watch it.'

If Mr Iwan ap Rhys had thought that this would scare Wyndham, he was sadly mistaken. Wyndham merely walked past the sheriff, grasping Merle's elbow, and went into the grounds. They could see Dai Sluice patrolling the grounds ahead of them. Merle was shaking with fury beside Wyndham and he put his arm around her shoulders gently to calm her. She looked up at him and smiled, 'I'll be good, Haydn, I promise. Even though I could easily do that man some damage!'

Some of the other villagers saw Wyndham's gesture and chattered excitedly about this development.

People were spreading out rugs and settling themselves on the ground, many with picnic baskets and cool bags. The vicar had a large bag with him and Llew was carrying the rugs for them to sit on. Wyndham was surprised to see Rhian Jenkins walk away from them and go to a small tent near the ruins but Merle touched his arm and said, 'Wait and see what *Mamgu* does!'

Now that people were sitting, Wyndham could see what looked like a large cauldron and, to the north of it by some yards, a stone table. By the table was a massive candle and, at regular intervals, seeming to create a circle, there were three other candles; each of these candles had a smaller one at its base. A woman in a long robe carried a flaming torch around the circle and lit the smaller candles.

Everyone was silent and then there was the sound of a harp being played. A second woman, wearing a floor-length red robe and what looked like a long chiffon scarf on her head approached the north-east of the circle and entered it, carrying a long stick. She walked with dignity toward the eastern candle and then moved slowly around the circle, marking it with the rod, three times. At last, she placed the rod at the base of the stone table, which Wyndham now realised must be an altar.

The woman, whose face was covered by the chiffon veil, then picked something up from the altar and again walked around the perimeter of the circle three times, casting something on the ground and speaking in the ancient tongue.

189

Having done that, she went to the southern candle and took the smaller one from its base, again walking three times around the circle and chanting some words. Handing the candle to a minion, she picked up a jug from the altar and walked around the circle three times, casting water on the perimeter and chanting.

Wyndham was spellbound. It seemed to him that the woman grew taller each time she walked around the perimeter; the atmosphere was electric.

Having returned the jug to its place, she took incense and, yet again, walked around the circle three times, casting it on the ground.

Lastly, she took the flaming torch and went to two candles on the altar. She spoke the prayers to the goddess Ceridwen and the god Cernunnos.

A young woman, accompanied by someone holding a candle arrived at the north-east gate of the circle and the priestess challenged them; Wyndham couldn't understand the words but he understood what was happening at that stage. Words were exchanged between the two women and the priestess then kissed the young woman on the cheek, welcoming her in. Other people arrived and received a similar welcome, until there were half a dozen people in the circle with the priestess and the candle-bearer.

Everyone in the circle then faced east and the young woman rang a bell three times. The priestess hit the ground three times with the rod and raised her arms, making a sign with the rod. Then she spoke in the ancient tongue but the last words were in modern Welsh and Wyndham could finally understand her: '*The children of light bid you to join us at this holy sabbat in the sacred grove of the wise.*'

She lit the eastern great candle and hit the ground again with the rod, three times. Then Wyndham was surprised that everyone around him, as well as in the circle, said, '*So must it be.*'

Moving to the southern great candle, again she spoke in the ancient tongue although, to Wyndham's ears, she seemed to be calling to someone different. However, she ended with the same words in modern Welsh: '*The children of light bid you to join us at this holy sabbat in the sacred grove of the wise.*'

After she hit the ground three times with the rod, everyone around Wyndham spoke the response: '*So must it be.*'

At the western great candle and the northern great candle, the rite was again observed and the call made to the god. Wyndham found himself joining in the response.

The priestess returned to the altar and placed the rod in front of it and the young woman handed the flaming torch to the priestess who took it to the cauldron and lit the wood beneath it. Everyone in the circle stood around the cauldron, holding their hands out with the palms down and, led by the priestess, they chanted.

Turning to face the west, they called out the name of the goddess Ceridwen. After this, the priestess moved back to the altar where the moon was invoked in the ancient tongue, the last words again being in modern Welsh: '*Within this sacred grove will our goddess dance among us.*'

And everyone answered: '*So must it be.*'

Wyndham realised that he'd been sitting staring at the circle and had not noticed that the Director had already left. Llew saw Wyndham's gaze and gave him the thumbs up sign and mouthed, 'Keep cool, no need to do anything just yet.'

Wyndham looked quickly around and could see that the

sheriff and Dai had disappeared; he looked back at Llew who just grinned.

Now the priestess, having invoked the moon, turned to the west along with all the others in the circle and spoke for some time in the ancient tongue. Even though he couldn't understand the language, Wyndham was riveted. At last, she spoke in modern Welsh: '*I have been with you from the beginning, and I have been with you from the beginning, and I am that which is attained at the end of desire.*'

Everyone called out: '*Blessed be, blessed be.*'

Further rituals took place with responses from the people sitting around the circle. Other gods and goddesses were invoked and everyone seemed caught up in the moment, in the extraordinary atmosphere. Salt, meal and honey were consecrated and offered to the deities. Wyndham glanced at the vicar who sat as enthralled as everyone else. At last, signs were made by the priestess and, slowly, she walked around the circle with the young woman, who extinguished the candles one by one. This time she spoke in modern Welsh only:

'*By the holy flame*
This circle disappears
And can be found no more
All things are as they were
From the beginning of time
Except the magic worked herein
By ritual and rhyme.'

The priestess and her minions left the circle and went to the tent. The meal, honey, salt and other offerings were sprinkled around the circle for the birds to eat and there was a silence.

Suddenly, as if given a signal, everyone began to speak and

unpack their picnic baskets and cool bags. It took Wyndham a moment to get back to normal. When he looked at his watch, he couldn't believe that it was 4am. The Director was sitting on his rug, as though he had never left, chatting to Llew.

Merle spoke to him, 'Haydn, will you help me unpack the cool bag please?'

He moved to help her and for the next few minutes was kept busy with setting out food and drink for everyone. Llew had brought a bag too and put his offerings out with Merle's. There was plenty to eat and two bottles of Penderyn whisky, along with a half-bottle of sherry and some Welsh sparkling wine.

'Merle, where is your grandmother? I was so caught up in the ritual that I never realised she hadn't come back.'

Merle laughed, 'Didn't you recognise *Mamgu*, Haydn? She was the priestess!'

Wyndham looked stunned and just gaped as Rhian Jenkins returned to them, wearing her warm trousers and waxed jacket, and looking quite normal. She saw his look and patted his shoulder gently, saying, 'I'm hungry now and I could do with a nice drop of sherry, please.'

Merle poured out a cup of sherry for her and handed her a sandwich. Mrs Jenkins sat, ate and drank and made conversation quite normally, as though she had never invoked the gods at a sabbat in her life.

'Haydn, come back to the land of the living!' said Merle. 'Have something to eat and drink. Look, here's some whisky for you and a smoked salmon sandwich.'

He took them from her and touched her hand gently. She looked down, embarrassed, and then took his hand in her own for a moment. The gesture did not go unseen by the vicar and he smiled. During that moment of bliss, Wyndham didn't notice that his sandwich was being stolen; a certain cat had smelled the smoked salmon and was now having a feast next to him. When Wyndham turned around, Hannibal was looking up at him in all innocence, albeit with a few buttery crumbs on his whiskers, and, like Oliver Twist, asking for more.

Chapter 35

A T THE SWANSEA HQ of the WBI, Emia and The Boss lay on separate sofas, dozing. Even Lewis had given in to his exhaustion and sat with his feet up in a large chair.

At last, at about 3.30am, there was a buzzing sound and Lewis leapt up from his chair, dazed and scarcely knowing where he was. The sound was coming from his computer bank and he ran over to it. In the meantime, Emia and The Boss sat up, rubbing their eyes.

Special Agent Lewis looked at his personal screen and saw photographs coming through. His phone rang at the same time and he picked it up awkwardly, still almost too tired to coordinate. He listened to the voice at the other end of the line, while watching the photographs on his screen. 'Yes sir, I've got them coming through... Yes sir, they'll be on their way within five minutes... Yes sir, I've got all that.'

The Boss and Emia made their way over to him and he showed them the pictures on the screen. While they looked at the photographs, he made a phone call: 'The Director wants you in Myddfai as quickly as possible. Go to the pub, *Y Ceffyl Du*, in the village and knock on the back door; you'll be met by Siôn Williams who will brief you. I'll mail a picture of him to you in the meantime. Be absolutely discreet as there are traitors in the village.' He put the phone down again and looked at the two women. 'I think you can see what's been happening from those photos. The Director couldn't take anything from the sheriff's house so he photographed everything. He's also downloaded everything from the sheriff's computer and we're getting that even as we speak.'

Indeed, as he was telling them this, more was coming through on another screen and the scope of the sheriff's involvement was becoming clear.

He turned away from them, went to another screen and called up details for Siôn Williams. He mailed the picture of the publican to the agents who were already on their way to Myddfai.

To keep herself occupied while all the information was downloaded at Swansea, Emia went to the small kitchen behind the bar and made a large pot of coffee. She found some biscuits in the cupboard and took everything to a table in the middle of the room. Having poured coffee for Lewis, she took it over to him with a couple of biscuits and he looked at her gratefully.

They all sat, sipping hot coffee, and looked at the information coming through. It was clear that the sheriff was already making money from the plot; there were details of his offshore accounts and of amounts that had already gone through them.

Lewis picked up his phone again and dialled a number.

'Gareth, I'm going to send you some bank account numbers, offshore of course, and I want them frozen before trading this morning. The instructions must appear to be from the account owner, Mr Iwan ap Rhys of Myddfai. You know the sort of thing I mean, don't you?' The response from the other end of the line was clearly in the affirmative so Lewis put the down phone with a sigh. 'Now, I think this will be the beginning of the end, if we're lucky.' He looked at The Boss and Emia. 'Once the sheriff thinks someone has been interfering with his accounts, he's going to contact Mr B, and

Mr B is more than likely to contact Mr Big, whoever he may be. Our communications department has already managed to find out what phone numbers Mr B is using and we'll go from there.'

Emia and The Boss looked at Lewis in admiration as he sent the account information to Gareth.

'You've done a very good job, Special Agent Lewis,' said The Boss.

He shrugged and printed out the information the Director had sent so that Emia and The Boss could sit and study it. His phone rang again.

'No, we're not ready to interview them yet. Iori will have to recover in the infirmary first and the other two can stew for a while in separate cells. The head of CI will be coming with me to interrogate them at 9am; don't let them sleep too much before then.'

He turned to Emia and The Boss and told them that the transvestite and photographer from the club in Carmarthen had been causing trouble since they arrived but had been given mild sedation to calm them. Iori was still in the infirmary and unlikely to be fully recovered until mid-morning. Until then, he suggested that they all get some proper sleep. He rang for another agent and a woman came into the room, Special Agent Bowen. She offered to show them somewhere more comfortable to freshen up and then sleep for a few hours. The Boss asked, 'What about you, Special Agent Lewis? I hope you will get some rest too.' He nodded but stayed at his desk, drinking coffee.

The women all went out of the room and he went to lie down on a sofa. Pulling a woollen throw over him, he fell asleep immediately. Emia and The Boss were shown to a room with a couple of narrow beds and a small shower room. They took it in turns to freshen up and then lay on their respective beds and they too were very quickly asleep.

Also asleep in the Swansea HQ were the two computer geeks from Llangadog. Thankful to be alive, they had not caused any trouble at WARF or after their transfer to Swansea but sat in their separate cells, grateful for the food and drink they were given; they realised how much worse their fate might have been. Iori slept on in the infirmary, totally unaware of what had happened to him or where he was.

A dark figure crossed a rooftop in Little Water Street, Carmarthen, and quietly climbed down a light rope ladder to a window. With great patience, he removed one of the small panes and unlocked the window. Opening it, he climbed in and tiptoed across the room. He did not wake the sleeping man but left a note on the bedside table, next to the alarm clock. Then he turned and left the same way, replacing the small window pane, and climbed back on to the roof. A few minutes later, he was back in his car in St Peter's car park. Aled grinned, he'd enjoyed that.

Chapter 36

THE GOD LLEW, as opposed to the farmer Llew, had begun to make his appearance in the eastern sky by the time the revellers returned to the village from the festival rites and picnic. Wyndham had not had the opportunity to visit the ruined tower at Llwynywormwood but it had not been necessary after all.

The vicar, his daughter, his mother, Llew and Wyndham were all agog to find out what the Director had discovered at the sheriff's house. They all trooped back down the hill and went into the pub kitchen, where Betti Williams had set out some food and a large pot of tea. Sitting themselves down around the table, they learned from the Director that, as he had suspected, the sheriff had a number of offshore accounts and there had been suspicious activity in these recently. He told them that WBI were freezing the accounts before trading that morning; that would keep the sheriff busy for a time. His landline would be tapped for any phone calls to Mr B or anyone else and they would be able to track any mobile calls too. Mr B's room phone at the hotel had also been tapped but there was nothing to go on, as far as finding the Mr Big was concerned.

The Director was also able to tell them that Aneurin was safely back in Carmarthen, albeit under surveillance. He told them that someone had managed to enter Aneurin's home during the night without being seen and leave a note with instructions. As for Iori, the Director held back the full details of his humiliation and was content to tell them that the CI employee was in the WBI infirmary for the moment.

Llew said, 'This is good progress but we must now deal with Harri Harris, if we are to make Mr B feel vulnerable.'

The Director replied, 'You're right, Llew. Mr B also has two more henchmen with him now; they are not as big as Harri and they're likely to be more intelligent. Any ideas about how to tackle him will be gratefully received.'

Rhian Jenkins spoke up, 'I don't know if you can use this information at all but I happen to know that both Mr B and Harri have a weakness for sweets. Harri is known to like those triangular sweets from Quality Street, the ones wrapped in green paper.' She sipped her tea and looked around the table at the others' expressions.

The vicar said, 'Now that is a very good way of getting to them, don't you think? If it were possible to inject some sort of drug into the sweets, we could catch Harri much more easily.'

Wyndham laughed and said, 'It's going to need a ton of whatever drug you use, he's so huge.'

The Director said, 'It's worth a try, I think. Thank you Mrs Jenkins, for that. It could very well work. What about if the hotel, as it's quite a smart one, were to leave a bowl of sweets in the room, with compliments?'

They all nodded and the decision was made. The Director rang his office immediately and asked for someone to go out that morning and buy some sweets from Woolworths or a confectionery shop, making sure that they bought a very large number of the triangular ones. Then he rang Lewis, who was still deeply asleep on his sofa on the top floor of the WBI building, and told him about the arrangement, asking him to ensure that all the triangles were injected with a strong but tasteless sedative and that a few of the other sweets should be injected too. Lewis blinked at this request but assured his boss that it would be carried out.

All the group in the pub kitchen agreed to reconvene at midday in the Director's room at the pub and they parted company. Wyndham went out the back door and up the steps to his room; Hannibal sat at the top of the steps, waiting for him. Merle, following Wyndham out of the kitchen door, noticed Hannibal and said, 'Oh, am I not good enough for you now, you naughty cat?' Wyndham opened his door and Hannibal rubbed against his legs but did not stay; he was happy to go home with his beloved Merle. Wyndham stood at the top of the steps as the Jenkins family, and cat, walked away to the vicarage. Merle turned back and smiled at him, standing still for a few moments, and Hannibal stood with her until she was ready to go home.

Llew was now standing at the bottom of the steps and noticed the connection between Merle and Wyndham. He thought that was a good pairing but they had a job to do first and they all had to keep their minds clear of romance until it was done. Wyndham saw Llew watching him and reddened. With a wave to Llew, he went into his room, locking the door behind him. He too knew that it was impossible to think about a relationship until the job was finished but he also knew that Merle was the girl for him. Sighing, he undressed and went to bed, setting his alarm for 11am. He was asleep in a moment.

The Director went to his room, where two men from the WBI were waiting, already briefed by Siôn Williams. The Director gave them instructions and they left him to get some sleep.

Back in the vicarage, Merle hugged her father and

grandmother and went up to her room. Mrs Rhys was apparently still asleep and the friend watching her agreed to stay on while Mrs Jenkins and the vicar got some rest.

Hannibal was already in Merle's bed and purring. She undressed quickly and got under the covers. 'So, wicked one, you like him, don't you? So do I. But he's got to finish the job first, before anything else. I think he likes me though!'

Hannibal meowed approvingly and moved up the bed until his head was next to hers.

The entire village was quiet that morning, until trading time started and a loud cry emanated from the house occupied by Mr Iwan ap Rhys.

Chapter 37

A T THE SMALL but smart hotel in Llandovery, Mr
Brynaman sat in his room, eating his breakfast. His sweet
tooth, of those teeth left to him, demanded plenty of jam for
his toast and a sugary cereal. These had been provided and Mr
Brynaman had shown himself to be both friendly and grateful
to the serving staff, who had nothing but good to say of him.
Harri was having his breakfast in the dining room, where he
was stared at by sundry small children and dogs. He never
ate breakfast with Mr Brynaman, at least not since Mr B had
watched him eat a fried egg sandwich rather squelchily one
morning and had felt a little unwell for the rest of the day.
The other two men also sat in the dining room, but well away
from Harri. Mr Harris took no umbrage at this; it would not
have occurred to him.

Despite the Llangadog fiasco, Mr Brynaman was quite
satisfied with progress. The two computer geeks had gone
missing but there had apparently been no fallout from this
and he had no doubt his men would eventually catch up with
them and dispose of them in a suitable fashion. Iori had been
successfully seduced but could be left to stew for the moment
as he was just an insurance policy in case anything went wrong
with the plan in Carmarthen. Aneurin had been hypnotised
and could be put to work in the very near future, to carry out
that nasty little task at Carmarthen Intelligence. The Sheriff
of Myddfai was, of course, a bit of a nuisance but a necessary
one. However, once he outlived his usefulness, he could be
disposed of without any trouble. That sidekick plumber was

just an idiot and could easily be dealt with. They had still not been able to catch up with that red-headed young man from CI, but he didn't seem to be causing trouble at the moment so that would happen all in good time. Oh, yes, life wasn't bad the moment and there were so many good things to come in the future. Not that Mr Brynaman was politically motivated, or even politically interested. No, he had always had a little dream of a pretty villa in the South of France, or even Italy, with a few vines and olive trees and a view of the sea. That sort of dream tended to cost money, that was the problem for Mr B. But now it was almost in his grasp.

His room phone rang and, irritated at his dreaming being interrupted, he barked, 'Yes, what is it?'

A voice at the other end, barely comprehensible and raving, yelled at him, 'You've closed them down, frozen them.'

Mr Brynaman said, 'Shut up and ring me back on my mobile phone.' He put the receiver down angrily and his mobile phone started to ring almost immediately. 'Before you start ranting, calm yourself and then tell me what this is all about,' said Mr Brynaman.

The person at the other end of the line took a deep breath and then said, 'You must know what this is all about. This morning I discovered that my offshore accounts have been frozen and all the banks concerned say that I gave the instruction. Who else knew about the accounts except your lot?'

'Mr Rhys, I can assure you that I haven't touched your accounts. I've always left the management of the money side to you. I wouldn't even know how to contact those banks. You must have done something yourself, on the internet perhaps.'

'Don't be an idiot, man. I know when I've given

instructions to my bank or not. Find out what's happening or else your retirement plans are going up in smoke.'

Mr Iwan ap Rhys rang off and Mr Brynaman's eyes narrowed with fury. He picked up his mobile phone again and dialled a number in Hay-on-Wye, across the border. A phone was picked up at the other end and Mr Brynaman said, 'This is Llewellyn's son, I need to speak to him urgently.'

The person at the other end put down the phone and Mr Brynaman put his down too. A moment later, it rang and a voice said, 'What now? Something else gone wrong? If I knew how incompetent you people were, I'd have done this another way.'

Mr Brynaman calmed himself. 'Our banking friend, the sheriff, just rang and told me all his accounts are being frozen. Is this something to do with you?'

'Ha! Why on earth would we freeze the very accounts we need for this deal? Find out what's happening… no, don't, because your lot can't get anything right. I'll look into it and get back to you. Don't leave the hotel today, in case you trip over a kerb and get run down by a pram.'

The line went dead.

Mr Brynaman knew that the sheriff was right; if this plan went down the Swanee, he could forget about France, olive trees and sea views. He'd be lucky to get sheltered housing in the Valleys, with a vista of the old pits.

His breakfast was as ashes in his mouth and he gave up eating it. After about fifteen minutes, Harri knocked on the door and went in. Mr Brynaman looked at him, empty-eyed. 'We can't leave the hotel today; go to your room for the moment, while I think. Send the others up to see me though.'

Harri went to find the other men and give them the message. Then he went to his room and sat on the bed, putting on the television for the children's programmes, of which he was very fond. He was disappointed as Mr B had told him he could go to buy sweets that day. Even as he was thinking about this, there was a light knock on his door and a voice called his name. He went to answer and a porter stood in the corridor bearing a basket full of sweets, in particular a large number of his favourite triangles from Quality Street.

'Umph,' he said and took the basket, closing the door in the porter's face.

Harri found a note on the basket saying, 'With the compliments of the hotel management.' He threw it in the waste paper basket and sat down on the bed to watch his favourite cartoon and eat his green-wrapped triangles. Life was sweet after all and he forgot completely about Mr Brynaman.

Chapter 38

A NEURIN HAD HAD his first undisturbed night of sleep that week. He was still coming to terms with his kidnap, being hypnotised into believing he had been at the clinic for several weeks and the duplicity of the clinic staff, but he was now feeling more in control. He woke up and looked at his alarm clock with half-closed eyes. Something else on the bedside table registered in his mind and he sat up awkwardly. An envelope? How had that got there? He'd locked and bolted the front door the previous night so no one could have entered that way. Carefully, he opened the envelope and took out the folded sheet of paper and a small roll of tape. It was a message from CI with a code at the top of the paper to show its authenticity:

'Aneurin – This message is to assure you that we are still keeping you in our sights. We don't want to give away the fact that we know you are under surveillance so please follow our instructions. If you can remember anything of what happened at the clinic, please write it down and put it into the same envelope, then leave it taped to the outside of your bedroom window tonight. It will be taken by an operative. Whenever you need to contact us, you can use this method and your window will be checked every night at midnight. If you need to contact us urgently and at another time, please go to the kitchen or living room and sing *Ar Lan y Môr*. We are still hacking into the enemy's surveillance cameras so we'll see you immediately and we'll send someone to fetch the message from the window.'

The message was signed by the acting head of CI, in The Boss's absence. Immediately, Aneurin looked for a pen and began to write on the reverse of the sheet of paper. He explained, as succinctly as possible, what had happened and that he was due to kill someone, a woman, at CI and that the trigger words would be 'Macsen's sword'. He also mentioned a non-descript man with missing teeth who had seemed suspicious, and a Mr Goronwy Evan Evans, along with the Beddgelert green tea. There was nothing more he could do at that point so he put the paper back into the envelope and, using the roll of tape, he stuck the envelope securely to the outside of the window. Believing that the sooner CI knew about the proposed assassination the better, he then wandered into the kitchen looking dozy and sang the first few lines of *Ar Lan y Môr* as he put the kettle on to make tea. At both CIHQ and at Swansea, there was hurried discussion and, at Carmarthen, Aled was sent for and instructed to collect the message.

Aneurin made sure that for the next hour or so, he stayed within range of the cameras. He cooked breakfast, ate it slowly and washed the dishes. While he did so, Aled was able to take the envelope from the window by the simple expedient of pretending to be a window cleaner. The house next door got its windows cleaned for nothing as part of the ruse but, within forty minutes, Aled had got the message back to CIHQ and they had passed on the information to Swansea.

Aneurin was relieved to see that the envelope had gone when he returned to the bedroom. He showered, shaved and dressed and then went to sit in the living room with an old paperback to keep him occupied. He was still reluctant to look at the television, in case it was going to be used to hypnotise him again.

Mr Brynaman's minions, keeping surveillance on Aneurin from a distance, became rather bored with the lack of action but they knew enough of Mr Brynaman's temper not to lose concentration. Word was that things were going wrong for him anyway but they would have to stick it out for the time being.

Chapter 39

WHILE ANEURIN STARTED his day, The Boss, Emia and Special Agent Lewis were about to begin their interrogation of the transvestite and the photographer at Swansea.

The Boss and Emia had managed to get a few hours sleep and felt a little more refreshed. Special Agent Lewis had slept only intermittently but had managed to change into fresh clothes. Soon after 9am, they all trooped into an interview room to meet the transvestite.

The man, with the unlikely name of Wayne, was now wearing a prisoner's jumpsuit and had his hair tied back. His face was bare of cosmetics although Emia had to admit to herself that he had good skin and a feminine face. He looked frightened when he saw three people entering the room.

'Good morning, Wayne. I hope you got some sleep as we need you to be bright-eyed and bushy-tailed today,' said Special Agent Lewis in a not-unfriendly way. He opened proceedings formally by announcing that it was 09.08am and that he, The Boss and Emia Glas would be interviewing the suspect. The conversation would be taped for both voice and video and he explained this to Wayne before they started.

Wayne looked around the room for the cameras and Lewis had to call for his attention.

'Would you please give your full name and address for the record.'

'Wayne Broderick, Cwmycendy House, Carmarthen.'

'And what is your occupation, Wayne?' asked Lewis.

'I'm a waiter at the Cheeky Cherubs bar in Little Bridge Street, Carmarthen.'

'Please state for the record what you were doing last night from 9pm onwards,' said Lewis.

'I was at the opening of the new club in Little Bridge Street.'

'Were you instructed to be there and paid for being there?' asked The Boss.

'Yes, both.' Wayne could see that there was no point in prevaricating. 'I was told that if I spent the evening there and managed to get a certain person upstairs to a private room, I would be paid £500.'

'Were you given instructions as to who that person would be?' Emia asked.

'Yes, I was given a photograph of him and told to seduce him. They gave me £150 upfront to buy a dress and shoes suitable for the venue.'

'What was to happen in the private room, Wayne?' asked The Boss.

'I was to take it as far as I had to, to get him to drink the champagne.'

'Did you take the champagne up to the room?'

'No, I was told there would be a bottle up there but that I shouldn't drink it, only make sure that the man drank.'

'Were you aware that the champagne had been drugged?'

'They didn't tell me that but I guessed when they told me not drink any.'

'What about the photographer? Had they warned you that someone would be there to take pictures?'

'Yes. And I knew the photographer anyway so it was easy.'

'What reason did you suppose these people who instructed you had for doing all this?'

'I didn't think it was my business. I was getting paid and I got a new dress and shoes out of it too, so I wasn't bothered.'

At this he did begin to look a little ashamed. He was also exhausted from not being allowed to sleep during his incarceration.

Lewis shifted in his chair and quite calmly said, 'Wayne, if I told you that your involvement makes you an accessory to murder and treason, what would you say?'

At this, Wayne became ashen. 'But I didn't kill the bloke. He isn't dead, is he?'

'No, Wayne, he isn't dead, but others are. Not directly by your hand but by the hands of those who employed you. You are mixed up in something very dangerous. For the time being, here, you are safe and we can protect you, but we can't guarantee your safety in the outside world. Particularly when they discover that you weren't entirely successful.'

Wayne looked at them all in horror. 'What can I do? Can I stay here until you've got them?'

Special Agent Lewis looked at The Boss and Emia and then said, 'Interview halted at 9.35am, to be resumed in due course.'

All three rose from their seats and, without saying any more to Wayne, left the room. Wayne stayed in his chair, observed by a guard, and shivered with fright.

All three interrogators then headed for the interview room occupied by the photographer. He had a more ebullient attitude than Wayne and fancied himself as a bit of a jack-the-lad.

Again, all three seated themselves and Special Agent Lewis made the formal introduction to the interview. He asked the photographer to state his name and address.

'Lyn Knighton, 508 King Edward Road, Swansea.'

'Lyn, would you please tell us where you were from 9pm last night.'

'I was at the new bar opening in Little Bridge Street, Carmarthen. I don't know why you're asking me when you already know.'

'Lyn, this is a formal interview. I've already explained that. We need you make these statements.'

'All right, all right. I was at that bar.'

'Had you been instructed to go to that bar last night?'

'Yes, I was paid to go. They gave me £250 to do it.'

'And what were the full instructions, Lyn?'

'I had to go there, like, take photos of people, just like I always do at these openings. Then I had to watch out for Wayne and a bloke going upstairs and follow them up.'

'And what were you to do then?'

'Wayne was going to tell me when to go into the room and take photos. I didn't know the bloke or who he was but I supposed he was someone important who they wanted to blackmail.'

'Didn't you have any qualms about this?'

'No skin off my nose; if people get into those situations, it's their own fault.'

'You're all heart, Lyn. So, you took the photos.'

'You know I did, you've got them. Not bad either!' he chuckled.

Special Agent Lewis had a look of disgust on his face at this but he said nothing.

'Look, mate,' said Lyn, 'no disrespect, like, but you've got the photos so there's no harm done and you can let me go. I've got places to go and people to see, like.'

'I'm sorry, Lyn, but leaving here won't be possible for the time being.'

Lyn's face fell at this. He was tired and he just wanted to get home.

'You see, Lyn, there's a question of your being an accessory in murder and treason.'

Lyn's jaw dropped but he recovered and said, 'Nah... you're just having me on, trying to put the wind up me. Look, just let me go now and we'll say no more about it. How's that? In any case, I'm supposed to get a solicitor now, aren't I? You can't just hold me here, like, for as long as you want.'

'Oh, Lyn, I'm sorry to tell you that we can hold you for as long as we want and that a solicitor is out of the question for as long as we say so.'

Again, Lewis called a halt to the interview and all three interrogators left the room, leaving Lyn gaping at the closing door. For once, he was speechless.

Lewis returned to Wayne's cell, along with Emia and The Boss. Wayne was still very pale and the guard in the cell raised an eyebrow when the interrogators returned and gave them a half-smile.

'09.50 hours. Special Agent Lewis, Miss Glas and CI Boss return to interrogate Wayne Broderick. Now Wayne, tell us what you remember of the people who made the arrangements for last night.'

Wayne cleared his throat and looked at Emia, hoping to find some sympathy in her eyes. He failed. 'Well, these men came into the Cheeky Cherubs bar on Friday night, last week. I was just finishing my shift and they followed me out. I tried to run up the road because they frightened me but there was another one, as big as a bungalow, and he stopped me. I was so scared that I just froze. The first two came up to me and said they'd take me home; I had no choice. When we got there, they told me what to do and they said they'd be watching me so I couldn't get out of it. In any case, they gave me some money, the money to buy the dress and shoes, and half the rest of it... £250. They said that so long as I was successful, I'd get another £250 today. Then they left. I know that they called the really big bloke Harri but I don't know the names of the other two.'

'Thank you, Wayne. Did you at any time see a shorter man, in his fifties and with missing teeth?'

He thought for a time, 'Not that night, no. But, now you mention it, I saw a man like that a few nights before at the club, the Cheeky Cherubs I mean. I noticed him because he didn't seem like our usual customers.'

'Excellent, thank you. You've done well, Wayne.'

'Can I go home, please? I promise I won't run away. I've got my job to go to as well.'

Lewis picked up his files and stood up. 'Sorry, Wayne. You won't be safe out of here. We'll let the club know that you've been taken ill and have to be off work for a few nights. So long as you are kept here, those men won't be able to get to you. As soon as everything is dealt with, we'll see what we can do. In the meantime, you'll be well looked after so don't worry.'

'What about the money they gave me? Do I have to give it back?' Wayne was clearly agitated.

'No, Wayne. I'd keep it if I were you, along with the dress and shoes. They'll be returned to you, by the way, although I don't suppose you'll want to wear them while you're here!'

Lewis, Emia and The Boss left the room and Wayne was taken back to his cell. Then they returned to Lyn Knighton in the other interrogation room. He was definitely more cowed than previously.

'10.20 hours, resumption of interrogation of Lyn Knighton by Special Agent Lewis, Miss Glas and CI Boss.' Lewis looked at Lyn Knighton with some dislike. 'Now, Mr Knighton, who approached you to take the photographs at the club last night?'

Knighton stared at the floor and replied, 'Don't know their names. Two big blokes came to the office at Wind Street to tell me what to do. They handed over £150, like, and told me that I'd have the rest today, when they'd got the photos. I didn't like the look of them but money is money and it was an easy gig, like. They didn't look like the type you could argue with anyway. And there was a bigger bloke outside, huge. Didn't fancy being taken on by any of them.'

'Did you at any time see another man? He would have short-ish, in his fifties and with missing teeth.'

Knighton bit his lower lip and thought for a while. 'Might have seen someone like that last week looking through the window from the street. Haven't spoken to anyone like that though, not recently.'

Lewis looked at the guard and nodded to him to return Knighton to his cell. As he stood up, Knighton said, 'Look, how long do you think I'll be here? I've got a job to do and

I can't afford to stay here all the time.'

Lewis answered him, 'Knighton, you should think yourself lucky that you are somewhere safe. If you were on the outside, your life wouldn't be worth tuppence right now. The men that you've been mixing with are very dangerous and they'd think nothing of killing you. Be grateful that we've got you and take the time you'll spend here to consider how you got yourself into this situation.'

Knighton was taken away looking somewhat chastened but Lewis doubted that he would change character, however long he was held at the WBI HQ.

'Well, Ma'am, Miss Glas, I think we should have some breakfast while I send this information to the Director and we wait for the computer lab to come up with something. There's not a lot more we can do.'

'I'm impressed by your interviewing technique,' said The Boss with a smile, 'yes, let's have some breakfast and go through everything again so we can see if we've missed anything that could tell us who might be in the Anglo-Saxon cabal.'

Yet again, they headed up to the top floor. Emia was still impressed by both the room and the view but wished she could see them in happier circumstances. When they returned to the room, Special Agent Bowen was laying out tea, coffee and *bara brith tyfolau,* a type of Welsh croissant.

The Boss privately wondered if she could call RSJ Williams from the WBI; she hadn't seen him that week because of the current situation and had scarcely spoken to him. She also wondered, rather moodily, if it was worth continuing the relationship and RSJ was always on the move somewhere when he wasn't at the *Cymanfa,* and she herself was in a position of importance and couldn't just drop everything to see him when it was convenient for him. Over the past few months, they had seen less and less of each other and she thought it was probably wise to call it a day. Her thoughts were interrupted by Emia offering her a cup of tea and a *tyfol*. She thanked Emia and took her breakfast over to the window where she tried her mobile phone. There were no private messages from RSJ. She decided to send him a text message, did so and then returned to sit with the others and eat her breakfast.

Across the border a mobile phone rang. A tall, good-looking and well-dressed man picked it up and looked at the text message. At that moment he was definitely not in the mood for responding and he sighed, putting the phone down. He'd get back to the caller later that day. He went to the window of his hotel room and looked out at the streets. He had always liked it there, roaming around the bookshops, but now he was beginning to loathe Hay-on-Wye.

He went back to the table and picked up his phone again, then he dialled a number in Llandovery. It was time to tackle Mr Brynaman.

Chapter 40

A VERY LARGE man stood at the top of the fire escape outside a hotel in Llandovery. He wore combat gear with three stripes on the arms and a red beret bearing a small leek motif. In his right hand he held a hefty night-stick and he wore a revolver in a holster under his arm. He waited, expressionless, as two more very large men, similarly attired, came up the fire escape to join him, one of them carrying a stretcher.

'*Bore da*, butty, what's the job this morning?' asked one of the men climbing the steps.

'Harri Harris; we've got to get him out of his room and away without anyone seeing.'

The sergeant's face remained unanimated.

'Phew, don't want much, do you?' said the second sergeant. 'What if he doesn't want to go?' He chuckled and the corporal carrying the stretcher, large as he was, looked rather shaken at the idea.

'He's not going to know; he should be out of it by now... drugged,' said the first sergeant.

'Hope they gave him a few gallons of it then,' answered the second sergeant. 'Still, waiting here isn't getting anything done. Let's go.'

They eased open the fire escape door and found the corridor empty. All three walked surprisingly lightly down to Harri's room, the first sergeant taking out the master key from his pocket. Quietly, he opened the door and looked in the room, then pulled the door shut again quickly. Even he looked rather disquieted. The others looked at him and he opened the door again. Harri was sitting up on the bed, rigid and staring at Spot the Dog on the television. The first sergeant approached the bed but Harri remained rigid. Quickly, he poked Harri with the night-stick and jumped back but Harri continued to sit and stare.

The corporal whispered, 'Is he dead?' with some hope in his voice.

The second sergeant tried Harri's pulse and replied, 'No, the bugger's still alive! Better get this done quick then but let's close his eyes first, they're giving me the ab-dabs.'

As quickly as they could, given Harri's enormous weight, they laid him flat and moved him onto the stretcher, which bent alarmingly when they lifted it. The first sergeant checked the corridor then they moved as swiftly as their burden would allow to the fire escape door. Hearing the lift doors open, they hurried out, having to hold Harri almost upright as they did so. Five awkward and exhausting minutes later, they had Harri tethered in the back of a truck and three further soldiers guarded him as they left the hotel.

In a Jeep behind the truck, the two sergeants and the corporal rubbed their aching arms and breathed a sigh of relief.

'Well, butty, how did they get the drug into him?' asked the second sergeant.

'Sweets. I went with one of the WBI agents to a sweet shop early this morning. Had to wake up the owner, he nearly filled his pants when he saw us! Told him it was national security and all that and we needed those Quality Street triangles. Got a load of those and some other sweets and the agent had them injected with some sedative or something. It was daft; there were four of them injecting stuff into sweets in the back of the truck! Then they put them in a basket and had them delivered to the room. It worked though, I have to admit.'

The other two gave long, low whistles at this tale.

'I thought I'd heard it all before,' said the second sergeant, 'but that beats everything.'

The truck and the Jeep made their way to the WARF camp nearby and Harri was removed, still rigid, and placed in the infirmary where his right leg and left arm were put in plaster.

Back at the hotel, a maid let herself into Harri's room, cleaned up all the sweet papers and tidied the room. Then she packed Harri's belongings, not that there were many, and took them out of the room, leaving everything neat. The bag containing his belongings was taken to the back door of the hotel and handed over to a WBI agent who took them away with him. It was as if Harri had never been in the hotel, indeed as if he had never existed.

One hour later, Mr Brynaman's two henchmen knocked on Harri's door and then used a key to open it. They were surprised to see the room empty and checked the bathroom. One of them rang reception and asked if Harri had gone out but the receptionist and porter claimed not to have seen him. Leaving the room hurriedly, they went to see Mr Brynaman and told him that Harri had disappeared.

'Find him, you idiots!' yelled Mr Brynaman. 'No, we'll all go in the car to Hay-on-Wye. What the hell is going on?'

He picked up some papers from the table, stuffed them into a briefcase and they all left the hotel. As they headed for the Brecon road, a pale blue van followed them, the driver of which spoke hurriedly into his mobile phone. Walter was on the trail.

Chapter 41

NURSE MAIR BEYNON finished her shift at the clinic in Llanfihangel-ar-Arth, left the building with a wave to a fellow nurse and walked down the drive to the road.

It was a fine day and she was glad to be out in the fresh air. As she wondered how much longer she could manage to do the job at the clinic, and how she could get early retirement, she felt a strong arm grasp her around the shoulders and she gasped. A tall man in combat dress stood by her side, holding her firmly against him. Terrified, she stood stock still and looked around to see several other soldiers, all armed. She was by no means comforted to hear a friendly voice say, 'Nurse Beynon, there's no need to panic, you will not be hurt in any way. Now please go with the gentleman at your side and he will take you somewhere safe.'

Still unable to utter a word, Nurse Beynon staggered a little then walked away with the soldier. Having placed her in a car hidden behind some trees, the soldier stood aside as a woman, also in combat dress, approached.

'Nurse Beynon, thank you for being cooperative. I am Commander Angharad Bleddyn of the Welsh Assault and Rescue Force and you are quite safe with my brigade.'

'But what's happening, please?' asked Nurse Beynon. 'I don't understand why you're here.'

'Nurse Beynon, you don't need to understand at this moment. Please take my word for it that you will come to no harm if you stay here with the brigade. If you try to leave, then I cannot answer for your safety.'

The commander walked away, leaving Nurse Beynon feeling even more nervous. She had no intention of trying to get away and believed what the commander had told her. Another woman soldier came with some water for her and a car rug to keep her warm.

In the meantime, Commander Bleddyn was speaking to her officers and, shortly afterwards, a group of soldiers in combat dress ran down the drive and around the back of the building, out of sight of the surveillance cameras. Several military ambulances drove up to the front of the building where they released another group of armed soldiers who ran into the building.

It was a tightly-run operation and, within the space of twenty minutes, Dr Owain ap Owain and all his staff had been rounded up, relieved of mobile phones and lined up in the front drive. Military nursing staff took over the clinic and reassured the patients that all was well.

Another truck arrived with a group of agents from the WBI; their job was to go over the entire building and look for surveillance equipment used on the patients and remove it.

Commander Bleddyn entered the hospital and went to speak to the patients, all of whom had been gathered in the patients' sitting room.

'Ladies and gentlemen,' she began, 'I apologise to you all for the disturbance today and I'd like to reassure you that you are all safe here. It will take us a little time to get organised but we have plenty of nurses and doctors to take over from Dr Owain ap Owain's staff and if you have any queries about medication, please direct them to the new nursing staff. Now, many or all of you may believe that you are at the clinic in Porthgain; this is clearly something that Dr Owain wanted you to believe. I am sorry to tell you that you are not at Porthgain but at Llanfihangel-ar-Arth.'

At this, the patients looked at each other in bewilderment and disbelief. One man spoke rather faintly, 'But we can see the sea from this building.'

Commander Bleddyn spoke, 'Yes, sir, I know you can see the sea but it is all an illusion created by Dr Owain and his staff. I'll be happy to take you outside to show you, if you wish. From what we've been able to learn about Dr Owain's operation, none of you is seriously ill and most of you probably do not need the medication you've been given. We intend to get all of that sorted out for you by the end of the day. Hopefully, many of you will be able to go home in the very near future although we would like to debrief as many of you as can manage our questions today and tomorrow. Now, is there a gentleman here known as Mr Goronwy Evan Evans, please? I would particularly like to talk to him now, if possible.'

Some of the patients looked over their shoulders and one or two pointed to an elderly man sitting near the window. The commander went over to him, while her brigade started to take the names of all the patients and give them assurance.

'Mr Goronwy Evan Evans, I am Commander Bleddyn and I've been asked to look out for you particularly, on behalf of the boss of Carmarthen Intelligence.'

He looked at her with weary eyes and said, 'I'm told that I'm Goronwy Evan Evans but I have never really believed it.'

'You were right not to believe it, sir. You are Sir Geraint Williams-Jones and I am honoured to meet you.'

The commander took his hand gently and held it. The old

man wept silently, 'Forgive me, Commander, but it's such a relief and I'm so tired.'

They sat for a time without moving as the commander's brigade did its work and the WBI agents removed the film of Porthgain and revealed the gardens of the Llanfihangel clinic beyond the windows.

Chapter 42

I N SWANSEA, THE Boss waited in vain for a response from RSJ Williams. She felt helpless sitting in the top room of the skyscraper but there was nothing practical that she could do at that stage. She heard a telephone ring and Special Agent Lewis, who had been talking to Emia, went to answer. Several minutes later, most of which Lewis had spent listening, rather than talking, he put down the phone and went over to The Boss.

'Ma'am, I've just heard from the Director. Aneurin is clearly recovering from his ordeal and he's informed us that Dr Owain ap Owain tried to hypnotise him into assassinating someone at CI. We believe that the proposed victim is yourself although Aneurin wasn't given the identity of the person, only told that it would be a woman.'

Emia gasped in shock but The Boss simply looked glassily at Special Agent Lewis. The agent continued, 'The good news is that the Llanfihangel clinic is now under our control, Dr Owain ap Owain is in custody along with his staff, and Mr Brynaman is being followed at this moment. Harri Harris is in WARF's custody and still heavily drugged. However, ma'am, neither the Director nor I feel it is wise for you to leave here for the present. If you would like some clothes brought from your home, I can arrange that for you, as well as a safe and comfortable place for you to stay until the all clear is given.'

Emia said, 'I can go and fetch some things for you, Boss, if you like.'

Lewis held up his hand to stop her. 'Thank you for

offering, Miss Glas, but I don't think it's safe for you to leave either at the moment as you might be followed. If you both note down the things you need, I'll send a female officer to your respective homes to fetch them. Alternatively, someone could go to the shops here in Swansea and get you some basics for the present.'

The Boss finally spoke. 'Thank you, Special Agent Lewis. You are correct to say that I should stay here, however frustrating it is for me. Also, you are right to say that it would be unsafe for Emia to go anywhere at the moment. If we could speak to one of the female agents, then I'm sure we can come up with a list of things available here in Swansea.'

Emia nodded and picked up a pad and pen from the table.

Lewis went over to The Boss and touched her arm. 'I have more good news for you though. Sir Geraint Williams-Jones is alive. The Director asked me to tell you that Sir Geraint should be fine after some good care from the nursing staff at WARF.'

She smiled gratefully at him and went over to Emia to help her with the list.

Again the telephone rang and Lewis ran to answer it. After a few moments, he put down the phone and told the women that Mr Brynaman was heading for the border and being followed by CI and WBI agents. It was likely that he was going to meet a member of the cabal. Emia and The Boss looked a great deal more cheerful after that and, having finished making up a list of requirements, went back to looking at the maps of potential gold mines. A female agent came and took away the list after having a few words with the two women.

'Special Agent Lewis, do you know what the Director and

Wyndham are planning at the moment?' asked The Boss.

'As far as I know, ma'am, they're planning on visiting the great Sheriff of Myddfai today. He'll be tearing his hair out by now as all his accounts have been frozen!'

That thought cheered them up and they all settled to looking at the maps and other papers from the sheriff's house and the Llangadog underground room.

Chapter 43

O N THE DAY following the festival, it was traditional for the pub to stay closed at lunchtime, giving Siôn and Betti Williams time to recover. Wyndham had set his alarm for 11am, to give him time to get ready slowly and gather his thoughts. He looked out of the window and saw it was another fine day; he also saw Dai Sluice leaning against a post opposite the pub, chewing gum and looking up at Wyndham's window. 'That man is getting more ridiculous every day,' Wyndham thought to himself. Stretching, he went to take a shower and shave; the hair dye was holding up well so anyone looking for a red-headed man would not look at Wyndham.

As soon as he'd dressed, he made his bed neatly and lay down again for a few minutes, only to fall asleep. It was 11.55am when he awoke and he sat up sharply, hearing noises below.

When he left his room, Dai Sluice had disappeared and Wyndham let himself into the kitchen where he found Llew Jones sitting with a large mug of tea, talking to the vicar. Betti appeared and gave Wyndham a mug of tea and a biscuit, then they all trooped upstairs to the Director's room.

For a man who had been up most of the night and had done some housebreaking, the Director was in remarkable shape. He looked immaculate in casual clothing.

'*Bore da*, everyone. Hope you all got some sleep as we've got another busy day ahead of us, by the looks of things. First, I'll bring you up to date. Make yourselves comfortable.' He looked around at them cheerfully. 'Lots of good news and some bad so I'll get started. The bad news is that Aneurin has informed us that he is to assassinate a woman at CI; we've concluded the victim must be your boss, Haydn.'

Wyndham was shocked but he just nodded at the Director to carry on.

'Of course, Aneurin only pretended to be hypnotised but, for the moment, we are letting him carry on pretending for the benefit of Brynaman. Aneurin has turned out to be a good man, just as we always thought. The good news is that the CI Boss and Miss Glas are safely at Swansea HQ and will stay there until we can guarantee their safety. Next, we've taken control of the clinics at Porthgain and, more importantly, at Llanfihangel. Dr Owain ap Owain is in custody now, along with the clinic staff, all of whom will be questioned. Harri Harris has been removed from the hotel in Llandovery and is in the infirmary at the WARF camp where, when he wakes up, he'll believe that he's broken a leg and an arm! Yes, he's in plaster!'

At this they all laughed.

The Director continued, 'Special Agent Lewis, Haydn's boss and Miss Glas interrogated the transvestite and the photographer this morning and they all recognised photos of Brynaman and Harri Harris although they were both approached by other men regarding Iori. The latter is of course still in the infirmary and is apparently still unable to answer questions but that is a minor issue for us at the moment.'

The vicar spoke, 'Presumably, Mr Brynaman is aware of the sheriff's account problems by now?'

The Director said, 'He certainly is. He's already crossed the border and, I'm told, is just sitting in his car in Hay-on-Wye, waiting for something. We've got a large team of agents keeping an eye on him and they'll contact me as soon as anything happens.'

Llew asked, 'So what do we do now, here in Myddfai? I'm sure you have a plan for us!'

The Director answered, 'I certainly do. I've got a couple of men watching the sheriff's house right now and I'm going to ring them as soon as we are walking from the pub to get one of them round the back of the sheriff's house. Then we are all going to have a chat with the sheriff and scare him right out of his cowboy boots!'

They all got up and went down to the kitchen, leaving their mugs on the table. Betti wished them luck and locked the kitchen door after them.

The village was very quiet after the excitement of the previous night and the weather was cool but fine. The three men walked up the road as the Director made a quick call to give instructions to one of the men watching the sheriff's house. They arrived very quickly at the front door and the Director knocked loudly. They heard footsteps in the hallway and the sound of a bolt being drawn back.

'Yes, what is it?'

The sheriff was not at his best; he was barefoot, the famous cowboy boots were not to be seen. His hair stood up on end, his shirt was half hanging out of his trousers and he'd forgotten to put in those Hollywood-white teeth. He gaped at his visitors, his mouth an empty hole. For all Wyndham's experiences as a soldier and an agent, one thing he found repulsive was the sight of someone without their false teeth; it turned his stomach.

The Director spoke harshly: 'Rhys, we've come to discuss your offshore accounts and what you intended to do with them.'

The sheriff was so dazed that he just stood back from the

doorway and they followed him into his study. The room was in a mess, with papers all over the floor. At last, the sheriff managed to speak again.

'You're too late, I don't know what's happened to my accounts. I can't get into them and the banks have told me that I told them to freeze the accounts, even though I didn't.' He continued, 'I rang everyone but no one knows what happened… all that money.' He looked ready to cry but none of his visitors felt any sympathy.

The Director looked at him and said, 'We'll see what we can do, Sheriff, if you come across with some information for us.'

The sheriff brightened a little.

'Tell us, Rhys, who is in the money-laundering business with you.'

The sheriff looked slyly at the Director. 'What laundering? My accounts are just private, nothing to do with anyone else.'

'Indeed? Then Mr Brynaman was merely paying a social visit to you? Forget trying to lie your way out of this, Rhys, because we know about Brynaman and he's under surveillance at this very moment in Hay-on-Wye. Your days are numbered, Sheriff Iwan ap Rhys, and I'm sure you know it. I'm also sure that you were not told the full extent of the operation in which you were involved but that is neither here nor there because you are an accessory to treason, murder and attempted murder. I'm sure we can find another few charges to throw at you too and the Revenue service will be interested to see all your accounts.'

The Director stared at the sheriff who seemed to shrink into his chair.

'Brynaman only wanted to use my accounts to send some money out of the country, that's all I know. I don't even know where the money was coming from but he said I'd be paid generously. I haven't met anyone else involved, even if there is someone else.' He appeared to be telling the truth. Looking at Wyndham, he said, 'I knew I was right about you, from the beginning.' The heart seemed to go out him and he stared at his feet, as though not recognising them.

The front doorbell rang and they all looked up. The Director nodded to Wyndham to answer the door. Wyndham checked through the glass pane before opening the door and saw the Director's man, along with a woman. He opened up and, before the agent could say anything, Mrs Dai Davies said, 'Oh, I'm looking for my husband. He went to unblock a customer's sink but no one's seen him since. Does Mr Iwan ap Rhys know where he is?'

The agent raised his eyebrows to Wyndham and Wyndham said that Dai wasn't there with them but he would phone the vicarage to see if they'd seen Dai. Mrs Davies nodded and walked away.

Wyndham returned to the study and asked the vicar what the vicarage number was. The vicar dialled it for him and Mrs Jenkins answered.

'Mrs Jenkins, this is Haydn. Can you tell me if you've seen Dai Davies since about eleven this morning, please? Mrs Davies seems to be worried about him.'

As Mrs Jenkins responded, a smile broke out on Wyndham's face and, by the time she had finished speaking, he was grinning broadly.

The others had listened with interest, including the sheriff.

'Well?' said the vicar.

'It seems that Mr Dai Davies, Deputy Sheriff of Myddfai and plumber extraordinaire, is doing some involuntary underground exploration at the vicarage, courtesy of Mrs Jenkins,' said Wyndham. 'In other words, she's shut him in a large drain.'

Llew gave a great roar of laughter and the vicar and Director were hard put to it to keep a straight face. The sheriff was not amused but he had almost ceased to care about anything by then.

'Haydn, would you go up and get the sheriff some clean clothes and some shoes, toiletries and so on as he's going on an extended visit to WARF. Thank you.'

Wyndham went upstairs and found the marital bedroom. Refusing even to consider the cowboy boots, he looked in the wardrobe for shoes and found some loafers. These he added to a couple of pairs of jeans, some T-shirts and denim shirts, underpants and toiletries. He also found the sheriff's false teeth in a glass of water in the bathroom. He couldn't bring himself to touch them and carried the glass down along with the bag.

Going back to the study, the sheriff was being tidied up by Llew although Llew seemed to think that tidying up also meant slapping the sheriff about a bit. The Director didn't say anything and was secretly amused. After a few minutes, the sheriff looked more like himself although he clearly regretted the cowboy boots which Wyndham had not provided. With his teeth in once again, he looked more normal, which was a relief to Wyndham.

The vicar went to the back door and brought in the agent who had been guarding the rear of the house. The sheriff was handcuffed behind his back and he and his bag were taken out. The Director gave instructions for him to be taken to the WARF camp and kept in seclusion for the time being.

After the agents had taken the sheriff away, the four men began to look through the papers in the study and try to put them in some sort of order. The Director rang Lewis and asked him to send a team up to Myddfai to take away all the information and sort through it.

No sooner had he finished the call to Lewis than his phone rang again. As the call went on, the Director looked more and more serious and then very angry. The other men looked at each other and then back at the Director. Finally, the call was over and the Director turned to them.

'I've just been informed who Mr Brynaman is meeting in Hay-on-Wye. It's even worse that we thought. As soon as the team arrives here to take over these premises, we're going up to Hay, that is if Llew and the vicar can come with us.'

Both men nodded their assent. The Director put his hand on Wyndham's shoulder and said quietly, 'I don't know how I'm going to tell your boss about this.'

Wyndham, Llew and the vicar were all bewildered but knew they would have to wait until the Director was ready to tell them what was going on.

They all sat in the study until the team from Swansea arrived. The Director gave them instructions to leave the house tidy and to treat Mrs Rhys's things with respect but to make sure they had searched everywhere before they left. Then the four men returned to the pub, where the Director's driver was waiting for him. Wyndham asked if he was going to need a gun but the Director shook his head; there would be plenty of weaponry on site without that. Bidding Betti

Williams goodbye, they all got into the Director's car and sped off to Hay.

Chapter 44

M R Brynaman was sitting in the lounge of the hotel in Hay-on-Wye. His henchmen also waited, one in the car and one in the foyer of the hotel.

All of Mr Brynaman's dreams were swiftly disappearing into the blue yonder, something that Mr Brynaman himself would have liked to have done at that moment. His villa in the South of France, or Italy, would remain a dream unless they could retrieve something from this mess. All the planning over the past two years would come to nothing if they couldn't get the sheriff's accounts back on track again.

And what had happened to Harri? The big man didn't have the intelligence to do anything on his own, without instructions. Mr Brynaman wished he was a little boy again and that his mother would take care of everything.

A member of the hotel staff approached him and informed him that he was expected in room 113 immediately. Mr Brynaman sighed and braced himself for the coming encounter. Stopping in the foyer, he told his henchman that he was going up to room 113 and couldn't say how long he would be.

His legs wouldn't support him up the stairs so he took the lift and slowly walked to the hotel suite. He knocked on the door and said, 'It's Llewellyn's son.' The door opened and a hard-faced young man nodded for him to enter, closed the door behind Mr Brynaman and stood guarding it.

Mr Brynaman walked over to the window, to reassure himself that his driver was outside, then waited. The door of the bedroom adjoining this sitting room opened and a tall, good-looking man in a very smart suit came in.

'So, Brynaman, you were told not to come here until instructed. What's happened now?'

Mr Brynaman cleared his throat and his words tumbled out. 'The bank accounts have all definitely been frozen and the sheriff doesn't know how to unfreeze them. Harri has disappeared and we've sent Aneurin home under surveillance.'

He hoped that the man would allow him to sit down as his legs were feeling unsteady but the man simply looked at him in disgust.

'Two years of preparation, Mr Brynaman. Two patient years and, at the last minute, everything falls apart and it all comes back to you somehow. What do you have to say to that?'

Mr Brynaman stuttered, 'But I don't know how it happened. Everything was going just fine. We had Aneurin hypnotised, Iori onside, the offshore accounts. Then the boys in Llangadog were found, all because they wanted to go and have a night out, probably. It's their fault really.'

The man just shrugged. 'Whoever's fault it is hardly matters now as the whole scheme will have to be abandoned. My contacts are not going to be pleased after all they've invested in the plan and all they hoped to gain. But I'm telling you, Mr Brynaman, I am not taking the blame for this fiasco. And don't think that you'll be able to get away anywhere because you will be watched from now on. Any plans you have for the future will now involve a council flat in Tonyrefail at best. You had better get back to your little flat in Whitland and hope that you can hold on to it; you won't be needing drivers and sidekicks from now on.'

Mr Brynaman's face fell and he clutched at a chair to stop himself fainting. The man and his guard looked at him without sympathy. Then the good–looking man returned to the bedroom and closed the door, effectively ending their discussion. The guard stepped away from the suite door and indicated to Mr Brynaman that it was time to leave. He did so, with dragging feet, and the door closed behind him.

He stood in the corridor for a few moments, unable to move. Then he walked slowly to the lift and went downstairs. There was no one in the foyer so he went out to the car and got in the back, where two men grabbed him and handcuffed him. The car drove away quickly and headed back over the border to the WARF camp.

Back at the hotel, a woman approached room 113 and knocked at the door, saying, 'Chambermaid service, sir.' The door opened and the woman kicked it in, simultaneously shooting a dart into the guard to sedate him. The guard dropped to the floor and the woman ran into the room, followed by uniformed WARF personnel. The bedroom door opened and the woman could see a gun pointed at her; she immediately shot another dart at the hand holding the gun and the gun dropped to the ground. The soldiers rushed into the bedroom, grabbed the gunman, who had only been grazed by the dart, and dragged him into the sitting room, placing him roughly in a chair and holding him down.

'Handcuff him now,' said the woman and they did so.

The man sneered at her. 'Do you know who I am? You can't just break into a hotel room and handcuff me.'

'I can, and I have. From here on in, you're going to remember this as the best part of today. Robert Steffan John

Williams, I am arresting you under the Welsh Treason Act, as amended, for treason against the Welsh nation and its people, and conspiracy to murder.'

RSJ Williams, Deputy Speaker of the *Cymanfa*, showed no emotion and said nothing in response.

Four more people walked into the room but RSJ Williams continued to look at the floor and say nothing. The Director introduced himself to the woman and soldiers and then introduced the vicar, Llew and Wyndham. He turned to RSJ Williams and said, 'Mr Williams, you have been formally arrested and will be taken to the WARF camp for interrogation. Words fail me at the moment. Your actions are so heinous that my friends and I cannot comprehend how you could have sunk so low. You have betrayed your country and your people and have even conspired to murder your own girlfriend, a woman of honour and integrity.'

RSJ Williams continued to look at the floor. He showed no reaction to the Director's speech so the Director simply said, 'Take him away.'

Four soldiers took away the Deputy Speaker and his guard and the remaining troops, with their female commander, stayed to look around the room and pack up RSJ Williams's belongings. Together with the Director, Wyndham, Llew and the vicar, they went over the suite with a fine tooth comb. The mobile telephone was clearly going to be the biggest help in finding the remaining members of the cabal, along with the laptop computer.

An hour later, they had finished searching and all the Deputy Speaker's belongings, as well as his guard's, had been packed up and taken to the WARF camp. The brigade commander and her men had left.

The hotel manager came up to the room and asked about

payment, whether he would be able to charge anything to the guest's card. The Director asked him to make up the bill and give it to him to deal with and the manager rushed off. Llew, Wyndham, the vicar and the Director all sat down, still in a state of shock at RSJ Williams's betrayal of Wales.

Wyndham spoke, 'Director, was this what you meant about not knowing what to say to my boss?'

The Director nodded sadly. 'Yes. I'm afraid this is going to be a real blow to her. There was a text message on his mobile phone from her, saying that she wanted to talk about the relationship. I'm afraid there'll be a lot more to talk about before she's finished with him.'

Llew asked, 'What about the other members of the cabal? What plans do you have to find them now? Looks like RSJ is keeping his mouth shut at the moment.'

The Director replied, 'He may be keeping quiet now but he'll spill the beans before long, if I know WARF's methods.'

The vicar nodded sagely; he knew WARF's methods very well and there were few that could withstand them.

The manager returned with the bill and a credit card machine. The Director paid the bill, only commenting that some people knew to how live. Then they all left the room and the Director returned the key to the manager who bowed several times as he left them. The four men returned to their car with heavy hearts and drove to the WARF camp.

Chapter 45

Back at Swansea, The Boss and Emia were still studying the maps of potential goldmines with fascination when Lewis's telephone rang. He spent several minutes on the phone and, when the call was over, went over to the two women.

'Ma'am, Miss Glas, I have news for you. Mr B has been taken to the WARF camp for interrogation. They've also arrested his contact at Hay-on-Wye so now we are really getting somewhere. The Director wants you both to stay here though, at present, because the attempted shooting might still be going ahead and we need to find out about that first.'

'Special Agent Lewis, did the Director say who the contact at Hay was?' asked The Boss.

'He said he would discuss that with you personally, ma'am; he didn't tell me who it was.'

Lewis looked his usual imperturbable self and The Boss didn't guess that he was lying.

'Well,' said Emia, 'at last we seem to be getting somewhere. Surely it's only a matter of time now before everything is resolved?'

'I think we can relax a little bit now that we know the patients at the clinics are safe and the conspirators that we know about are behind bars,' said The Boss. 'I don't know about you but I feel hungry now!'

Lewis said, 'Yes, we can relax a little. I'll see what's available for lunch; we haven't eaten a proper meal for a time so I'll check what meals are available and we can have the food sent up.'

Emia looked at him with gratitude; she had come to admire Lewis's professionalism and liked his cool good looks and smartness. 'I'm hungry too,' she said, and Lewis was struck by her husky voice. He hurried away to speak to someone about getting a late lunch sent up, thinking that when all of this was over he might ask Miss Glas to go out with him. He thought it was a good idea for The Boss to get a good meal before the shock that awaited her. The Director wouldn't return to Swansea for a few hours so there was time for them to eat and for them all to get some more rest.

The two women had been brought some extra clothes from the local shops and went to freshen up and change before eating. By the time they returned to the top floor, a meal had been laid out for them and they all sat down together to make the most of it. An hour later, Lewis, The Boss and Emia were all sitting with their feet up and dozing.

At the WARF camp, the Director and his companions sat down with the commander of the camp and discussed the procedure for interrogation. The Director explained to the commander that there were other people involved, Anglo-Saxons, and that they needed to identify everyone in the cabal. The commander nodded and assured the Director that they would do their utmost to find out who those people were. He told them that they had no further intelligence regarding the proposed assassination but they were still working on it.

The Director suggested that he, Llew, the vicar and Wyndham should all return to Myddfai; he would leave his companions there and go back to HQ in Swansea to speak to The Boss. None of the others envied him this undertaking.

They arrived in Myddfai at about 4.30pm. The Director paid Betti Williams for his stay, packed up and left in his official car, leaving the other men at the pub. He told his companions that they could tell Siôn and Betti the bare bones of the story. They decided not to reveal the name of the contact at Hay but just said that they'd caught Mr B and his crony.

Llew said, 'I don't know about you but I'd be glad of a drink right now, even if the pub isn't open!'

Siôn immediately went to the bar and brought drinks back to the kitchen, including one for himself and for Betti. 'On the house, lads,' he said. 'You deserve it.'

They all raised their glasses to him and drank gratefully.

Finishing his drink, the vicar said, 'Well, I'd better get back to the vicarage and tell my two women all about it. They'll be climbing the walls with impatience by now! I'll see you later, Haydn. Get some rest now.'

Llew offered to drop him off as it was on his way and Wyndham was left alone in the kitchen with Betti Williams. Suddenly, he felt exhausted.

'Mrs Williams, I didn't have any lunch but I'm suddenly so tired that I've got to go to bed for a while.'

She nodded and said, 'You go now and have a good sleep. I'll keep a hot supper for you, as late as you want.'

'You're very good, Mrs Williams, thank you. I'll set my alarm for 9pm and come straight down.'

He left by the kitchen door. At the top of the steps sat Hannibal, waiting patiently for his friend to return. Wyndham bent to stroke him and groaned as he stood up, 'Oh, Hannibal, I need to lie down and have a good rest. Come in now.'

The cat followed him in and jumped onto the bed.

Wyndham managed to lock the door securely and strip off his clothes. He set the alarm for 9pm, plugged in his Blackcurrant and got under the covers. In seconds, he was asleep and Hannibal kept watch while Wyndham slept, eventually closing his own eyes and joining his human companion in rest.

Chapter 46

THE DIRECTOR REACHED Swansea HQ early that evening and went to his office. There he checked details sent by WARF from RSJ Williams's mobile phone and laptop. E-mails had been sent by a roundabout route, via several other countries, and they were still looking into who had sent them to the Deputy Speaker.

He sat for a while, wondering how to break the news to The Boss. There was nothing for it, he would just have to be straight with her. He picked up the phone and rang Lewis, asking him to bring The Boss down to see him.

Lewis went over to The Boss and woke her gently, explaining that the Director had returned. She got up, stretching, and went to wake Emia but Lewis stopped her and told her that the Director expressly wished to see her alone. A little surprised, she followed Lewis out of the room and then took the lift to the Director's floor.

Lewis left her and the Director together and returned to the top floor. The Director poured The Boss a drink and set it in front of her.

'I hope you've been looked after well and given something to eat today,' he said.

'Special Agent Lewis has looked after us very well, as have other members of your staff. Naturally, Emia and I would prefer to be in our own homes but I can see that it would not be wise at present. I've been thinking, though, that the easiest way to find out who has involved Aneurin in this would be for me to appear in public and draw them out.'

'We may have to come to that eventually, depending on what happens at WARF, but let's leave that subject for a few moments. Lewis has probably told you that Mr B and his contact in Hay have been arrested today. However, he did not tell you who the contact was.'

The Director went and stood by The Boss and looked down at her sympathetically. She looked puzzled at his expression.

'I'm sorry to tell you that the contact was RSJ Williams, the Deputy Speaker of the *Cymanfa*.'

The Boss went white and placed her drink on the Director's desk with a shaking hand. She didn't speak for several minutes and the Director waited patiently for her to recover.

'That explains why he didn't reply to my text message,' she said quietly. 'Did he say anything when he was arrested? Did he make any denials?'

'No, he made no denials. He said nothing.'

'Then he is one of the people who want me dead. Clearly my text message about wanting to discuss our relationship was redundant.' She was icily calm as she spoke. 'I wonder how long this has been going on.'

'From what I can gather, they must have been planning this for at least eighteen months, probably more like two years, but the initial idea must have been mooted a long time before that, given that Sir Geraint Williams-Jones has been incarcerated for several years.'

'RSJ and I have been seeing each other for two and a half years, Director, yet I never suspected anything. Does that make me bad at my job?'

'Not at all. Why should you have suspected him? He was Deputy Speaker of the Senate, sworn to defend his country and his people.'

'I still feel I should have seen something. Granted, we haven't seen very much of each other over the past few months but I should have seen *something*. Of course, I shall resign once all this is cleared up.'

'Nonsense. I won't hear of it. The least you can do is allow yourself time to take all this in, finish the job properly and then get your bearings. You are too good at your job and have come too far to allow this to destroy all you've worked for. Please, I'm asking you to put these thoughts aside until the job is finished and then think again.'

She picked up her drink again and sipped at it thoughtfully. 'Very well. I'll take your advice for the present and I thank you for your kind words. I'm surprised, though, that no one has thought me to be involved, given my relationship with RSJ.'

'We all know you too well for that. We'll sit for a little while and finish our drinks and then you can go upstairs to speak to Emia; it's up to you how much you tell her.'

'I'll tell her everything, of course. She's been a faithful employee.'

They sat for a time, saying nothing. The Boss managed to maintain a calm façade but inside she was raging and desperate to weep and yell.

When they had finished their drinks, the Director took her to the lift and left her to make her way back to the top floor. He sighed, returned to his office and to the fray.

Chapter 47

At Llanfihangel and Porthgain, the teams investigating the clinics had taken samples from food and drink, including the famous Beddgelert green tea, and found everything clear; however, they had also found capsules of strong sedative in the kitchens which must have been used to drug individual dishes and drinks.

Nursing staff at both clinics had taken blood samples from all the inmates, to establish whether any of them were suffering from physical illness and to see what medication they had been given. It was clear that most of the patients did not require medication of any kind and many had been kept mildly sedated for no reason other than Dr Owain ap Owain's involvement in the plans of RSJ Williams.

While the investigation was taking place, all the inmates were asked to stay at the clinics and take their meals as normal, but they were served by WARF staff. The TV screens were reprogrammed to show only regular television programmes and there was no more hypnotherapy.

The patients slowly became more animated and discussed the latest developments between themselves. At Llanfihangel, Commander Bleddyn took some of them outside to prove to them that they were in the countryside, not at the sea. Some of the more elderly patients were so shocked that they had to receive medical treatment, but soon recovered.

The slow process of questioning each patient had begun. As this was part of a larger operation to catch the cabal, the commander could not contact the patients' families at that stage. Everything had to remain secret. She and her team explained this to each individual patient and assured them that they would go home as soon as everything had been resolved.

Sir Geraint Williams-Jones was being cared for in his room. His ordeal over the four-year period he had been held had left him frail. The commander had spent time in his room, telling him of the recent developments although she held back the information about the Deputy Speaker, feeling that would be too much of a blow for the old man.

Doctors had examined Sir Geraint and pronounced him in reasonable health; the small scar on his temple was checked but, if anything had been planted in his head, it had since been removed. A new diet was prescribed to build up his strength and the doctors ordered that he should be kept in a calm environment.

In the meantime, close to the Anglo-Saxon border, the WARF camp was humming with activity. The cells were filled with miscreants and there was an air of excitement over the camp.

Major Amy Madoc-Griffiths, who had led the raid at Hay-on-Wye, was now supervising the interrogation of Mr Brynaman, his henchmen and driver. All four men had been taken to the cells after being stripped, searched, showered and given prison jumpsuits. RSJ Williams and his guard had been given the same treatment. All now sat in their individual cells, stripped not just of their clothing but of any power that they had wielded.

The Deputy Speaker had remained silent although the guard, despite his hard face and demeanour, had been surprisingly forthcoming already; he had told them that no one else at the *Cymanfa*, to his knowledge, was involved. All the others in the cabal were Anglo-Saxons but he didn't know their real names.

The camp commander had contacted the Director again and asked him to inform the Speaker of the *Cymanfa* that he would be requiring a new deputy. The Director felt that a personal visit to the Senate would be necessary for that and arranged to go the following day.

At the camp, rumour was spreading about who was being held and what they had done. The computer lab was busy with experts trying to trace the incoming e-mails to RSJ Williams's laptop. Messages were routed via central Europe and Scandinavia so there was difficulty in finding the origin. After about two hours of searching, a shout went up from one of the experts and the Major was called. She arrived quickly and the technician showed her where some of the messages were coming from; she was disgusted but not wholly surprised. Ordering the other technicians to keep working, the messages were printed out and she went to see the camp commander.

In the camp commander's office, the Major handed her superior the printed messages and told him of their origin.

'So,' he said, 'we should have guessed this was coming from the top, or near it anyway. As soon as you get anything on the other messages, let me know. I'll speak to the Director at Swansea about this. Good work by you and your team, Major. Keep it up now.'

The Major saluted and left the commander's office.

The Director had gone home to his loft apartment by the time the Commander rang him, but the call was automatically transferred from the WBI HQ and the Director, just out of the shower, answered quickly. Having heard the latest news, he asked the Commander to have the messages e-mailed to him immediately. Dressing in casual clothes, he pondered what he'd been told, thinking that the person who had sent those messages hadn't the nous to think up such a scheme so it would be interesting to see who else was involved. He went to his study, still drying his hair with a towel, and sat at his desk. The messages were coming in now and he sat for a time, reading them.

Chapter 48

BACK AT WBI HQ, Lewis had temporarily been replaced by the agent Anni Bowen as Lewis had not been home for some time. She ensured that Emia and The Boss had somewhere more comfortable to sleep and ordered some supper for them.

Special Agent Bowen sat apart from the two other women and The Boss, having been very quiet since her visit to the Director's office, eventually spoke to Emia.

'Emia, I have something to tell you. It's been quite a dreadful shock to me, after all the shocking things that have happened this week, and it's personal.'

Emia sat up and looked alarmed.

'Emia, the person that was arrested in Hay-on-Wye was RSJ Williams, the Deputy Speaker of the Senate.' She stood and walked over to the window, unable to face Emia in case she burst into tears.

Emia said, 'I'm so sorry that you've had to deal with this, after everything this week.' It was difficult to think of anything else to say. Emia got up and went over to her boss, putting her hand on the older woman's shoulder. Knowing that The Boss would be embarrassed to cry in front of her, Emia retreated and went to the drinks cabinet to pour a whisky for her superior, then left the glass on the table near her. She poured a gin and tonic for herself and went to sit again. Her boss was clearly struggling with her emotions but Emia knew that it was best to leave her alone while she did so.

Special Agent Bowen said nothing but took in the scene

and returned to reading her book. Her phone rang and she listened to the caller, just said, 'Yes, sir,' and ended the call. Going over to Emia, she said quietly, 'I've just had a call from the Director.'

The Boss turned and said, 'Yes, Special Agent Bowen, what is happening?'

The agent said, 'The Director has just told me that some of the e-mails on Mr Williams's laptop have been sent to him. They were originally sent from the House of Commons in London.'

She went on to tell them who the person who had sent them was and Emia looked at her boss without surprise. 'That's par for the course, from a man like that,' she said.

The Boss replied, 'Yes, but he's not bright enough to have thought it up himself so we'll have to wait to find out who the others are.' She turned to Agent Bowen, 'Do we know whether anyone else at the *Cymanfa* is involved?'

The agent told her that, as far as they knew, all the others in the cabal were Anglo-Saxons. Both the other women nodded as though they expected that. The agent also told them that the Director would be going to Cardiff the following day to see the Speaker.

Both women were exhausted and decided to take an early night. This time, separate rooms had been laid on for them and they wished each other goodnight. Agent Bowen continued to sit in the top floor room, gazing out at the glittering scene below. The lights of Swansea Bay glistened and were reflected in the water; in the streets far beneath her, people were heading out for dinner or to clubs and cinemas, unaware of how close their country had come to complete breakdown and domination by its neighbour.

Chapter 49

THE FOLLOWING DAY, in Myddfai, Wyndham woke up and realised that he had nothing to do that day, at least until instructions were sent to him. He luxuriated in being able to lie in for once.

The previous night, he had got up at 9pm, as promised to Betti Williams, pulled on some clothes and gone downstairs to the kitchen, accompanied by Hannibal. Reluctant to get into conversation with the villagers, he had asked to eat in the kitchen and Betti had given him a good meal, though not heavy enough to disturb his sleep. Hannibal had claimed his share of the fish Wyndham had eaten and then trotted off home, much to Betti's amusement. Wyndham had gone back to his room, undressed again and, having checked his messages, he fell into a deep sleep.

He lay back on the pillow and stretched. Then there was a knock at the door and he got up reluctantly to answer it. First he peeked out of the window and could see Hannibal's tail but nothing else so he drew back the bolt and turned the key, pulling back the door. Merle was standing on the step, holding a basket with some fresh milk, warm bread and butter. Hannibal went straight into the room and jumped on the tumbled bed, rolling on the white sheets with his legs in the air.

Suddenly realising that he was naked, Wyndham said, 'Excuse me a second,' and ran to the shower room. Merle, unperturbed, went into the room, put the basket down on the table and tested the kettle to see if there was water in it. Finding that there was, she put the kettle on and put a teabag in one of the mugs on the table. Then she shifted Hannibal over and sat on the bed with him, tickling his belly. Wyndham came back into the room, holding a towel around his waist and looking a little embarrassed.

'Um, Merle, I think you're sitting on my clothes. I took them off quickly last night because I was so tired.'

She smiled cheekily at him and pulled the clothes out from under her, handing them over to him. 'Don't worry about dressing in front of me, I'm broad-minded, Haydn.'

Feeling that he was bright red from head to foot, Wyndham retreated to the shower room and emerged thirty seconds later in his jeans and T-shirt. She looked him up and down and went to pour water on to the teabag.

'Will you have some tea with me, Merle?' Wyndham asked.

She took another teabag out of the caddy and made herself a cup, handed him his steaming brew and then sat down on the bed again. Wyndham decided to sit in the easy chair. Hannibal lay watching them both lazily.

'Dad wanted me to tell you that Dai Sluice was released from the drain yesterday evening, told that the sheriff had been arrested and sent home to behave himself. Mrs Davies was told to keep an eye on him and let Dad know if he did anything unusual.'

'Didn't she think that was a bit odd, Merle?' asked Wyndham.

'She's willing to do anything to keep some control over her husband. She can see how pathetic he is really, for all his bluster. I think she was quite pleased to be told the sheriff had gone; he was a bad influence on Dai.'

'That's true. What about Mrs Rhys? Is she upset about her husband being arrested?'

'I think she's quite relieved really. Dad said that the Director would organise something with the sheriff's ordinary Welsh bank about letting her use the account, even though he'll never be able to touch it again probably. As for the other accounts, someone is working out which of them are legal and which aren't so she won't be destitute. He is a nasty man and he didn't treat her very nicely. Anyway, she's been taken home now and the neighbours are being good to her.'

'So, things are beginning to come together now. I feel sorry for my boss though; she was seeing RSJ Williams and I think she was quite keen on him.'

'That's a shame for her. What a rotten person he must be, though she's better off without him.' She looked at him shyly, 'Er, Haydn, are you seeing anyone at the moment? Not that it's my business, of course.'

He looked at her, feeling equally shy. 'No, I'm not seeing anyone, Merle. Perhaps it is your business, though, because I like you very much and we get on well, don't we?'

'Yes, we do. I think we suit each other quite well. But I know you've got a job to do here so perhaps you'd better take some time to think about it after you've completed what you're doing.'

She busied herself with stroking Hannibal who purred with appreciation.

'I don't need to think about it, Merle, I already know. First of all though, I should tell you that my name is not Haydn Jones but, for your own safety, I won't tell you my real name for the moment. What's more, I'm not blond! I'd better warn you that my hair is really quite red!'

'Well, Person Who Is Not Haydn Jones, and Person Who Is Not Blond, you can't put me off you!'

She finished her tea, got up and went over to him. Kissing him lightly on the mouth, she opened the door and left the room, leaving him flushed and dizzy with delight. Hannibal watched all these proceedings with interest, jumped off the bed and also went up to Wyndham. He put his front paws up on Wyndham's knees and meowed softly then dropped down again, turned and left the room.

Merle skipped along the road, startling an elderly villager who was just opening his gate. Betti Williams was standing at the front door of the pub and she grinned when she saw Merle dancing along the street, Hannibal hurrying to catch up with her. She closed the pub door and went to find Siôn, giving him a smacking kiss on the cheek. He looked at her in surprise.

'What's that for, then, *cariad*? Have I done something good?'

'It's just for being here, *bach*. Love is in the air, or at least in one of the rooms upstairs!'

'You don't mean… '

'No, not *that*. I've just seen Merle skipping along the street after taking Haydn his breakfast. They must have come to an understanding.'

'Oh, that's all right then. Good show. They'll suit each very well, those two, and I think the vicar will be pleased.'

'Yes, he likes Haydn. He's a good young man, I think. I'll have to start thinking about what to wear to the wedding!'

Siôn shook his head as his wife went off to the kitchen; women and their wedding outfits! Still, he was pleased for Merle and he liked Haydn. It was good news if it was true.

Wyndham's thoughts were disturbed by his Blackcurrant ringing. He found a message from The Boss, telling him to take a rest day as things were getting under control and there was nothing for him to do at present. He felt pity for her but knew that she was a true professional and would force herself to get over it.

He wondered if he should retrieve his gear from Llwynywormwood but the game was not yet over so he decided to leave it for the time being and just keep his knife with him. A walk up to Bron Farm would stretch his legs without tiring him. He took his time getting ready and left the room, locking it securely behind him.

As Wyndham walked along the street, heading for the Llandovery road, the vicar watched him on the camera obscura. He'd seen Merle dancing along the road earlier and concluded that the young people had declared themselves. He was pleased; he knew that people talked a bit about Merle but she was a good girl really and just needed to settle down with a decent young man. He was certain that this young intelligence agent was the right one for his daughter. It would be a popular pairing in the village and Mrs Jenkins would be happy.

The village might have already had Merle and Wyndham settled down in a marital home, at least in their minds, but there was still work to do before that could come about. This morning, though, Wyndham was free for a while and he whistled cheerfully as he walked to Llew's farm, safe in the knowledge that he would not be followed by either the sheriff or Dai Sluice for once.

Chapter 50

THE DIRECTOR WAS early for his meeting with the Speaker and the Leader of the Senate so he took a stroll down to the front of the *Cymanfa* and looked out at the bay. To his right, in the distance, was the elegant, curved roof of the St David's Hotel and to his left, the old Norwegian church. It was a crisp, cold day but the sun sparkled on the water and the air was fresh.

Two young women walked nearby deep in conversation: 'So I said to him, "Where's it to then?" and he just looked at me and said, "Warr?" He's too thick to live, he is.' Her companion nodded with a world-weary air more suited to someone twice her age and they passed along the quayside. The Director wondered how they managed to keep warm in such skimpy clothing and then ticked himself off for being such an old fogey. Surely it hadn't been that long since his own youth? Perhaps it had. He envied their lack of responsibility. But now it was time to see the Leader and the Speaker. He turned back to the impressive glass frontage of the Senate building, revealing the magnificent wooden interior, and went up the steps.

At the WARF camp, Mr Brynaman had made a play at brazening things out initially, but the sight of the very large gentleman with a grim face entering the interrogation room had suddenly given him a near-photographic memory. It became clear that he had only been told enough to tempt him into becoming involved. He had no idea about the remainder of the cabal as RSJ Williams had been his only contact. To his relief, he was allowed to return to his cell and he didn't allow himself to think about where his next home would be or he would have wept.

RSJ Williams had no such relief. Allowed only ten minutes of sleep at a time since his arrest, his interrogators kept waking him and questioning him until he broke down, at which they left him and allowed him to sleep for half an hour. They resumed questioning until he finally gave the name of his contact at the House of Commons. Exhausted and frightened, he was allowed to sleep for another half an hour and given a small amount of food and water.

As soon as the name of the House of Commons contact was revealed, agents in the Anglo-Saxon capital were deployed. One was apparently a lobbyist at the House and another a Parliamentary Private Secretary. The contact was at his office in the House that day, preparing for a Commons vote. The lobbyist and the PPS met outside his office; a secretary greeted them as they walked in but the lobbyist shot her with a sedation dart, leaving her slumped in her chair. They walked straight through to the contact's office to find him standing at the window, speaking on his mobile phone and laughing. Seconds later, the mobile phone had been taken from his hand and switched off and he was handcuffed to the lobbyist. A gun held to his temple persuaded him that the best course of action was to do as his captors said; they left the office and locked the door.

A few minutes later, a porter was surprised to see the Secretary of State for Education walking rather stiffly out of the House of Commons, accompanied by two men. All three went to a large car with tinted windows, the door of which was held open by a tall, very broad-shouldered man with hands like shovels. Minutes after they had left the Secretary of State's office, they were finding their way through the Westminster traffic and making their way toward the M4, the captive now handcuffed to a chain within the car and looking very frightened. His captors waited until they were on the motorway before peeling latex masks off their faces; they were WBI agents who had disguised themselves as the lobbyist and PPS. They said nothing to their captive and barely talked among themselves. Two hours later they had crossed the border and entered the WARF camp where it was found that the Secretary of State for Education had wet himself.

Chapter 51

WYNDHAM ENJOYED HIS walk over to Bron Farm; the weather still kept fine and spring flowers were blooming in the hedgerows and gardens along the way. By the time he arrived at the farm, he felt quite warm and was pleased to see Llew Jones in the yard, knocking back a cold drink.

'Haydn, boy *bach*, good to see you. Hope you had some rest after the excitement yesterday. I'm out of practice with these late nights and long days so I slept like a log. Come and have a cold drink.'

Wyndham followed him into the big farmhouse and into the kitchen. It was a wonderful old room with a long settle against the wall and a huge kitchen table. A couple of hams hung over the old stove and there were strings of onions and garlic hanging from hooks in the ceiling, along with drying herbs. The scents of all these things made Wyndham feel hungry, even though he hadn't long had breakfast.

.'Sit down, now, Haydn. Make yourself comfortable and I'll get us a nice, long cold drink. You'll want to put on the television too; switch it to the satellite channel news. Won't be a minute, I've got some home-made lemonade in the pantry.'

Wyndham did as he was told and switched on the TV, pressing the buttons until he'd found the round-the-clock news. Rock musicians being arrested for drug use and royal conspiracy theories made up the usual fare, then there was a 'breaking news' item and Wyndham really paid attention.

The news was coming from Westminster, where the correspondent said that the Secretary of State for Education had been kidnapped by a lobbyist and a PPS, identified by a porter at the House of Commons and the now-recovered office secretary. Both the lobbyist and the PPS had since been arrested but both protested their innocence and ignorance of the event. Each claimed to have been in meetings at the time of the kidnap and other people were able to verify their claims. Police were now checking surveillance camera tapes. No contact had been made by the kidnappers and the Prime Minister, the Secretary of State's wife and the House of Commons staff could think of no reason why this had happened. Back in the studio, political pundits discussed whether it might be something to do with recent changes in A-level requirements. Then the cameras returned to the House of Commons where the correspondent was able to reveal that two junior ministers in the Transport Secretary's department had also gone missing, although no one had witnessed their departure.

Llew returned with the lemonade and some ice and poured some out for Wyndham and for himself. He nodded toward the TV and grinned at Wyndham.

'Llew, is all of this because of what we've discovered?'

'This is only the start of it, boy *bach*. You can bet that there'll be more later today as the news travels around the constituencies.'

They both sat riveted by the news programme and drank their lemonade thirstily. They didn't notice the time go by. Wyndham was suddenly called back to reality by his Blackcurrant ringing. There was a message from the Director telling him that he'd spoken to the Leader and the Speaker of the Senate, who were shocked by the revelation that RSJ

Williams was a traitor. The Director had asked them to keep it under wraps for the time being, until everyone involved had been caught. He told Wyndham that there was nothing for him to do at present but that he should stand by.

Wyndham told Llew about the message and Llew just grunted; he still hadn't made up his mind about the Senate anyway, having little time for politicians of any colour.

After various less momentous news items, the news channel returned to the House of Commons correspondent who revealed that the Prime Minister had called a special meeting of the Cabinet. At Downing Street, cars arrived carrying the various Cabinet members who hurried into Number 10 without acknowledging the waiting cameras and journalists.

The Chancellor of the Exchequer, Alexander Sweety, was expected to arrive for the meeting via the connecting door to Number 11 but there was no sign of him. The Prime Minister's staff telephoned through to Number 11 but the Chancellor's staff said that Sweety had already gone into Number 10; a search of both buildings revealed that he disappeared. Security men and police were called in but Sweety had gone, simply vanished.

Panic set in at Downing Street. The Prime Minister failed to contain the situation and the Lord Chancellor jumped up and down on the spot with his fists clenched, yelling repeatedly, 'What the hell is going on?'

The leaders of the Opposition party and the Liberal Democrats were interviewed and both sang similar tunes. They said that this was typical of the cack-handed incompetence displayed by the government over the previous decade; not only could they not run the country, they couldn't find their own Cabinet ministers. As for the Chancellor of the

Exchequer, he couldn't even find his way from Number 11 Downing Street to Number 10, so what hope was there for the economy? Playing hide and seek in Downing Street was not what the electorate expected of the Cabinet; you wouldn't have found Mrs Thatcher playing hopscotch during the Falklands Crisis, or Churchill skipping during the evacuation of Dunkirk.

Members were recalled from their constituencies and ordered to attend the House the following day, without fail. Former members of previous Cabinets, many of whom most people had thought to be dead, and some of whom looked as though they were dead, were brought in as talking heads. Lord Plum of Chumley, a now-forgotten figure from Callaghan's government, was wheeled in to give his opinion and, getting the wrong end of the stick, as he had always done in government, confused the issue by saying that he had always been fond of sweeties and hoped there would be no VAT on them. He was quickly wheeled out again, still muttering about Liquorice Allsorts and Pontefract Cakes.

At Llew's farm, Wyndham and his host were almost breathless with laughter. Although it was, of course, a serious situation, they felt the tension of the past few days ease and they felt some relief at the antics recorded by the news programme.

Wyndham managed to catch his breath and leaned back in the chair, looking at Llew. 'Does this mean that the Chancellor of the Exchequer is one of the cabal, Llew?'

Llew shrugged, 'Looks like it, Haydn. Just goes to show what a bunch of stupid shysters that lot are.'

The news switched to a visit by the Queen and the Duke of Edinburgh to the Scottish Parliament building. Both royal personages appeared to be in stitches and wiping their eyes, along with various members of the Parliament, several of whom, ignoring protocol, were leaning on each for support as they laughed.

At a luxury villa in Barbados, the Prime Minister's predecessor was seen to be lying on the beach with his wife and their guru; all three of them were rolling on the sand and laughing, kicking their legs in the air. That was yet another photo opportunity that the former PM's wife would later regret.

Llew looked at his watch and said, '*Diawl*, look at the time, Haydn! Let's have something to eat, then you can help me with some things outside before you go back to the pub.'

Llew's son, Lloyd, arrived back a few minutes later from his work at Llandovery College, and Llew introduced him to Wyndham. They switched off the TV and had a good lunch of cold ham, potato salad and beetroot with fresh bread. Wyndham asked who did the cooking at the farm and Llew admitted that he did most of it and enjoyed doing it. His wife had died of a long illness a few years before and he had got used to looking after himself.

After lunch, Wyndham went out to help the two men with some work outside. It was enjoyable doing manual work, free of worry for a change. At 4pm, they stopped for a cup of tea and then Wyndham went back to the pub, taking his time and making the most of his freedom.

When he got back to his room, he rang The Boss and was relieved to hear her speak in her normal professional manner. He told her that he had seen the news and asked if the Chancellor was definitely one of the cabal. She told him that WBI had confirmed it and that the Chancellor was now spending a little time at WBI HQ in Swansea. She advised him to keep watching the news and explained that she and Emia would be staying at WBI HQ themselves until it was safe for them to leave. Wyndham was to keep standing by, in case he was needed urgently.

He put the phone down and plugged it in to recharge. He thought he might as well have a lie down and catch up on some more sleep. As he was undressing, he heard a meowing sound outside and opened the door; his friend, Hannibal, was at the top of the steps. 'All right, come on in then. I suppose you'll want some milk now, too.' He put his clothes on the chair and went to pour some milk into a saucer for the cat. Lying down on the bed, he watched Hannibal lap up his treat, lick his lips and wash his face. Then Wyndham fell asleep and Hannibal jumped up beside him and stretched out.

Merle was up in the church tower, at the camera obscura. She'd seen Wyndham walking back from the Llandovery road and noticed how Hannibal had followed him up to his room. There would be no problem with Hannibal accepting this new man in her life, the three of them would be happy together. She wondered what sort of home they would have in Carmarthen and what kind of work she could do there. Plenty of time to think about all that, though.

She went down the stairs from the tower and out of the church. Hesitating for a moment, tempted by the thought of seeing the man she loved, she stood at the church gate. Then she shook her head and walked slowly home to her father and grandmother.

Chapter 52

THE FOLLOWING DAY, the House of Commons was packed and the public gallery was heaving with people; security men were mopping their brows, having failed to keep out members of the public wanting to see what would happen next. The Lord Chancellor had a rubber ring under him, on top of his Woolsack, as he had an attack of piles, and he had hurt a toe the previous day when he was jumping up and down, so he was not in a good mood. He sat glowering beneath his wig, which was on inside out anyway.

The Prime Minister finally arrived, looking more ramshackle than ever and as though he'd slept in his suit. He sat in his place on the front bench, even glummer than usual. Opposition backbenchers called out insults and no one took any notice of the Speaker when he arrived in all his pomp.

The Speaker had brought his extra large, special gavel just for the occasion and had taken a few throat sweets beforehand to strengthen his voice. 'Order, order. The House will come to order.' He was obliged to keep yelling for several minutes before he obtained near-silence, by which time his voice was hoarse again. 'The Prime Minister will speak,' he croaked. Giggles erupted in the Opposition back benches and calls of 'Sshhh'.

The Prime Minister stood and cleared his throat, looking behind him for some support from his Cabinet, or what remained of it. The Lord Chancellor looked round at him and mouthed, 'Get on with it, you fool.'

'Honourable Members,' he began. There was an outburst

of laughter from the Liberal Democrats and the Prime Minister looked as though he wanted to cry. He tried again, 'Honourable Members, it is my duty to give you messages from the Chancellor of the Exchequer, the Secretary of State for Education, the Honourable Member for Edley South and the Honourable Member for Scrumley North. All four have family matters that will require their full attention for some time to come and I have accepted letters of resignation from all of them. I am very sorry to lose such valuable members of our party and I am sure you will all join with me in wishing them well.' He sat.

There was a cry from the gallery of 'Is that it, you berk?' This was followed by a woman shouting, 'Yes, tell us why they've really resigned, you liar.' The gallery was so crowded that the security men could not remove the hecklers and their cries were taken up by the Opposition and the Liberal Democrats. 'Yes, tell us, you moron.'

The Prime Minister shrank into his seat and sucked his thumb. The Opposition Leader stood and leaned on the Despatch Box; the Prime Minister hated that cool air of social ease that his opposite number exuded and glared at him. The Opposition Leader merely smirked and said, 'Isn't it a fact, Prime Minister, that you have not received letters of resignation from any of the people named? The truth is that you don't know where any of them actually are. The truth is that all four of them were involved in criminal activity initiated by a foreign power. Prime Minister, the people in this House and the people of this country deserve an honest answer.' He sat down to applause from his side of the House and from the gallery.

The Prime Minister sat and looked around in panic, until the Home Secretary poked him in the bum and told him to stand up and say something. Reluctantly, he went to the Despatch Box and opened his mouth but nothing came out. The Lord Chancellor was inwardly cursing his piles and his toe and just stared ahead of him as if all this was nothing to do with him. The TV cameras were concentrated on the Prime Minister, who stood there, opening and closing his mouth like a carp. There was absolute silence in the House as the Opposition Leader looked across to the Prime Minister smugly.

Eventually, a squeak emerged from the Prime Minister's throat; he looked at the Lord Chancellor, whose rubber ring was slowly deflating, giving him the appearance of a sinking tugboat, and then he looked at the Speaker who glared back at him in astonishment and waggled his gavel at him.

'This isn't fair and I don't want to be Prime Minister any more; I waited for all that time and now all I've got is a big mess. I'm going home.'

With that, he turned and left the chamber, leaving everyone staring at the gap where he had been standing. There was uproar in the House and the Speaker gave up shouting 'Order, order' after a few minutes and took himself and his gavel back to his rooms where he locked the door and opened a large bottle of Scotch, wishing he had never left Dundee.

The President of the United States and his aides were watching the proceedings from the White House with amazement; in Paris, the French President sat on his wife's knee nuzzling her neck and giggling wildly at the antics of Les Rosbifs. In Rome, the Italian President (actually there were two that day but the first one had got back into power by the end of the TV broadcast) threw up his hands and declared a holiday so that everyone could have a laugh at the British Prime Minister.

Much further east and a good bit further north, in an onion-domed building, a man with a very hard face snapped out orders to an underling and looked at his TV set with a sneer. Within one hour, a private jet was on its way to Biggin Hill from Eastern Europe.

In Carmarthen, Aneurin was unaware of what had happened as he was afraid to turn on his TV. Frustrated by not knowing what was going on, he went into the living room and sang a snatch of *Ar Lan y Môr* and, after about ten minutes, went into his bedroom and sat on the bed. Shortly afterwards, Aled arrived, having climbed over the roof again. Aneurin opened the window for him and said, 'I'm going crazy in here, just waiting.' Aled jumped into the room and, very quietly, rang for instructions, explaining Aneurin's frustration. After a few minutes' conversation, he told Aneurin to pack a small bag, preferably a backpack, and dress warmly. That done, they both climbed out of the window and up the light rope ladder to the roof. Aneurin was a little out of practice after his ordeal but he managed quite well and Aled grinned at him. Minutes later, they were both in a WBI car being taken to Swansea. Aled told him all about the past couple of days' events and Aneurin was astonished.

Chapter 53

THAT EVENING, WYNDHAM went downstairs to the pub and was not surprised that all the conversation was about the day's events in Westminster. There was a great deal of laughter despite the seriousness of the charges the Opposition Leader had made. He had received an update from the WBI Director telling him that Sweety, the two junior ministers and the Transport Secretary were all singing like canaries at the WBI and WARF camp; what was more, Sweety had given them the name of Mr Big who had financed the entire scheme for Sweety to become Prime Minister and a very rich man into the bargain. And, following the ridiculous display at the House of Commons, it seemed that a plane had arrived at Biggin Hill from Eastern Europe and the people on that plane had been collected by a diplomatic car and had gone straight to Cardiff. They had been followed, of course, and the car went to RSJ Williams's house, which was empty. The East Europeans were now staying at the St David's Hotel and had taken an entire floor. WBI agents and some of their counterparts from CI had taken the place of hotel staff serving that floor and were keeping a watching brief.

Wyndham had phoned the Director after receiving the message, worried about Aneurin, but the Director assured him that Aneurin had been taken to a place of safety. The Carmarthen Intelligence building was on red alert and the underground trains were ready to evacuate everyone if necessary. All the former patients at Porthgain and Llanfihangel were safely guarded by WARF.

Wyndham ordered some supper from Betti Williams and took a half pint of the new Twm Tomkins spring beer to a corner table. No sooner had he sat down than the vicar came in.

'*Noswaith dda*, Haydn. When Hannibal came home a few minutes ago, I thought to myself that you would be up and about now!'

'*Noswaith dda*, Mr Jenkins. I should have put a note under Hannibal's collar; he'd be better than the pigeon post! I hope you've had some rest since yesterday.'

The vicar looked relaxed. 'I had a sermon to write and the events of the past few days gave me some inspiration. I think my congregation will be a bit surprised at what I have to say. Anyway, the Director has sent me an update so I probably know what you know. This East European development sounds a bit tricky though.'

Wyndham got up to buy the vicar a drink. 'Do you want the new spring beer, Mr Jenkins? Or a whisky?'

'The spring beer will be lovely, thank you, Haydn. I don't know if Merle will join us; she's been round to see Mrs Rhys today and she hadn't come back when I left.'

As he spoke, the pub door opened and Merle and Mrs Jenkins came in. Various regulars at the bar turned and smiled at each other when they saw Merle and one said, 'Won't be long now!'

Both men stood to greet the women and found them chairs. Wyndham took their orders and went to the bar to fetch another half of spring beer and a glass of dry sherry. Betti looked into the bar and said she'd hold back his supper for a short time.

'Here you are,' said Wyndham, putting down the drinks,

'now, who would like to join me in something to eat, too?'

They all looked enthusiastic and Wyndham went to the kitchen to ask Betti if she had enough food for four people.

'Don't you worry, Haydn, I'll get something nice out for all of you now,' and she set to work.

The four sat chatting until Betti brought out plates and bowls of steaming food. They all had hearty appetites, including Mrs Jenkins, and enjoyed the meal. When all the plates had been cleared away, Wyndham got some more drinks and they settled to talk seriously about the past few days. The evening flew and, before they knew it, Siôn was calling time and the pub was emptying. A few of the regulars came over to say goodnight to Wyndham and his companions and one or two of the villagers clapped Wyndham on the shoulder and looked at Merle.

Mrs Jenkins turned to him as she left, 'Haydn, you're invited to lunch at the vicarage tomorrow and I hope that you'll join us in church at 9.30am.'

He thanked her and promised that he would. Rested and relaxed, he offered to help Siôn and Betti with the clearing up and they accepted. With the three of them working, it took very little time to get the pub cleaned up and then Wyndham headed for his room, via the kitchen. As he went out of the door, there was a sound, like a footstep, and he stood absolutely still. Could be Aled playing silly buggers again so he waited. Nothing. He tested the kitchen door and found it was still unlocked. Going back in, he locked the door securely and went back into the bar, where Betti was hanging cloths over the beer taps. She looked surprised to see him. He put a finger to his lips and then jerked a thumb toward the kitchen, whispering, 'Someone's outside, I don't know who.'

She went to find her husband. Wyndham picked up the landline phone; it was dead. Getting out his Blackcurrant, he dialled the vicarage. Mrs Jenkins answered the phone and he said quickly, 'Mrs Jenkins, it's Haydn. Are you all safely home? There's someone outside the pub and the landline has been cut off.'

Mrs Jenkins answered him calmly, 'Yes, Haydn, we're home safely. I'll just get my son to speak to you now. Don't panic, you'll have plenty of help in this village.'

The vicar came to the phone and said, 'I'll take five minutes to change and get down to the church tower; the camera obscura should show me who's there, Haydn. What are your plans?'

'Mr Jenkins, I'd like to get up to Llwynywormwood as I have a weapon up there. I've got a good knife on me but that's not enough.'

'Right, Haydn. Here's what we'll do. You can't get out of the pub without bumping into whoever it is, so I'm going to ring Toff now and he'll come down in his Jeep, making a lot of racket, and he'll stop outside the pub's front door. Be ready to jump into the Jeep. In the meantime, I'll get *Mam* to ring the Director and tell him what's happening. Don't worry, you've got help.'

Wyndham thanked him and spoke to Betti and Siôn, telling them of the plan. They went to stand by the door and very quietly unlocked it, leaving the bolt across. Within a few minutes, they heard a lot of singing and noise being made as Toff's Jeep came along the road. As soon as he stopped at the door, still making an almighty noise, the Williams pair opened the door quickly and Wyndham dashed out, hearing the door close behind him. Betti locked the door and the two of them sat down shakily in the bar. Siôn had his mobile phone with him and they just sat and waited.

Outside, Wyndham had got into the Jeep successfully and stayed low in the seat as Toff drove very fast up Myrtle Hill to Llwynywormwood. Near the entrance to the old estate, he slowed down and Wyndham jumped out. Toff told him that he'd go up the road for a short distance and then come back in a few minutes to pick up Wyndham again.

Wyndham jumped over the gates and ran like the wind for the old tower. Within eight minutes, he'd got his gun and ammunition and dashed back down the steps, locked the gate to the tower and sprinted back across the open ground to the gates. Toff drove the Jeep down the hill again and Wyndham leapt in the car, again keeping low. Toff was singing at the top of his voice and lights came on in upstairs windows and words of protest were heard from some houses. Driving back toward the church, he slowed down again, enough for Wyndham to jump out and run into the churchyard.

The vicar was in the darkened porch and pulled Wyndham inside the church, locking the doors behind him. Then they went up the steep steps to the church tower and the camera obscura. The village had some street-lighting and there were still a few lights from houses and from the pub so there was some possibility of seeing an intruder.

In the meantime, two darkly-dressed figures made their way via a back path, behind village gardens, toward the pub. Very carefully, they moved toward the pub garden where they could see the shape of a medium-sized person who appeared to be trying to reach an upper window at the pub. The two figures signalled to each other and the taller one climbed over the wall, while the smaller one went into the garden via the gate, recently oiled so it was silent. The intruder had managed to climb up a few feet and the small, darkly-dressed figure ran up and slammed a hand into the intruder's right knee with tremendous force. With a cry of pain, the intruder fell to the ground and rolled over, clutching his leg. The smaller attacker knelt down and put a handkerchief into the intruder's mouth, while the larger attacker tied his hands behind his back. Then they waited silently, in case anyone else was there. There was no sound.

Up in the church tower, the vicar and Wyndham could see another figure at the side of the pub, near the steps to Wyndham's room. Whoever it was had presumably seen the padlock on the door and realised that no one could be in there. The figure seemed to hesitate, then tried the door to the pub kitchen. Slowly, the figure walked around to the front of the pub.

The vicar nodded to Wyndham and showed him a high-powered rifle. 'It's best if we take him alive, Haydn; either one of us can go down and try to capture him... the other one can stay and use the rifle if necessary. It's got a telescopic lens and infra-red light.'

Wyndham didn't hesitate, he asked the vicar to stay in the tower and cover him while he went down. Fortunately, his clothes were quite dark, if not ideal. He slipped quietly down the steps and out of the church and then ran out to the road and down the main street. He stopped and hid in a house porch while the intruder walked hesitantly around the pub. After about thirty seconds, Wyndham risked running across to the pub and, keeping close to the wall, he moved slowly round toward the steps to his room. He hoped the vicar could see him from the tower. All at once, the intruder was in front of him but facing away from Wyndham, toward the steps.

'Intelligence Officer, drop your weapon or I'll shoot,' said

Wyndham calmly. The intruder laughed and turned slowly around, although he held his gun facing down toward the ground.

'You think I'm scared of you in this small country? Not even a real country – even your ministers don't believe in you. In very little time we will have you in our power and there will be no more Welsh,' he said in what Wyndham thought was some sort of East European accent. 'You are nothing and I know that you will not shoot because you are weak, like this ridiculous country.'

He laughed again and started to raise his gun toward Wyndham. A second later, the intruder was screaming as a bullet hit his hand and something launched itself at his head, making him fall backwards. Hannibal had been in the darkness at the top of the steps and seen the man trying to hurt Wyndham; he'd jumped on the man's head and scratched his scalp and face. Having done his bit, Hannibal moved over to Wyndham and Wyndham bent down quickly to stroke him.

The vicar came running up and saw Wyndham bending down. 'Are you all right? As soon as I heard the shot, I ran down.' He went over to the intruder who was lying on the ground, moaning. 'What on earth has happened to him?' He knelt down, took some strong cord from his pocket and tied the man's hands together, then his ankles.

'I shot the gun out of his hand,' said Wyndham, 'and Hannibal attacked him at the same time! Thank heaven I didn't hit Hannibal.'

Another person came around the corner and said, 'Is everything all right?'

It was Rhian Jenkins. She and Llew had been the darkly-dressed figures who had captured the other intruder in the garden.

'Llew is in the back garden with the other one but that one's not going anywhere either, with a broken leg!'

The vicar looked at Wyndham and said, '*Mam* hasn't lost her touch in all these years!'

She chuckled as she knocked on the pub door and called out to Betti that all was well. Betti came to the kitchen door and was shocked to see the man lying on the ground.

'There's another one in the garden, Betti, but Llew is with him.'

As they were speaking, some WARF soldiers arrived. In charge was Wyndham's pal, Ryan. He went up to the group at the kitchen door and said, 'Looks like you've done our work for us!'

They told Ryan that there was another one in the garden, with a broken leg, so he sent a stretcher party to fetch him and Llew came round to join them at the kitchen door.

'This one's walking wounded,' said Ryan, 'so he can just go in the back of van and think himself lucky. What are all those scratches?'

The vicar said, 'Secret weapon, Ryan!' and looked up at Hannibal who was now at the top of the steps again.

Ryan laughed and said, 'We'll have to sort out a medal for that one.' He went on to tell them that they had found the intruders' car further up the road and it was being taken back to the WARF camp.

Someone was now running down the road and they turned to see Merle, looking very worried. 'Dad, *Mamgu*, is everything all right?'

When she saw them all standing together, and Hannibal

watching her from the top of the steps, she was so relieved that she ran and hugged her father. He stroked her hair and Betti drew her into the kitchen. The WARF soldiers wished everyone a goodnight and took the two intruders off, promising to keep Wyndham informed.

They all went into the pub where Llew told the story of Mrs Jenkins's bravery and deadly right hand. Drinks were brought in and glasses raised to the Resistance heroine.

Wyndham found a quiet corner and rang the Director to tell him about what happened. He asked if the pub's landline could be sorted out the following day and the Director promised to organise it. He told Wyndham that the East European plane was scheduled to take off again in the morning, this time from Cardiff International, and a close eye was being kept on the people at the St David's Hotel. Photographs had been taken of all the mysterious visitors for future reference; if they were all going home of their own volition, there was no point in forcing them. Before he rang off, the Director said, 'This was good work, Wyndham. Your boss will be very pleased.'

Wyndham returned to the others and told them what the Director had said.

'Who would have thought the East Europeans would have been involved?' said Mrs Jenkins. 'It's a new world now, and no mistake.'

The vicar said, 'You're coping with the new world very well, *Mam*. I'm so proud of you.'

She waved his praise away and held up her glass for another sherry. Hannibal was lapping up some cream, having been cleaned up by Merle, and Wyndham went over to stroke him and thank him for his help.

'Right, everyone, time for some sleep. I've got a service to conduct at 9.30am so I must get to my bed. Come on now.'

The vicar was firm and Merle and Mrs Jenkins followed him out of the door. Hannibal looked at his bowl and up at Wyndham, then he went out and up the steps to Wyndham's bedroom door.

In the shadows beneath the steps, Merle kissed Wyndham on the cheek and blew a kiss to Hannibal before following her father and grandmother home. Llew was offered a bed in the pub and accepted gratefully.

Half an hour later, all was still at the pub. Hannibal slept the sleep of the just, next to the second-favourite person in his little world.

Chapter 54

THE FOLLOWING MORNING, as Wyndham and Hannibal woke to the delicious scent of frying bacon and eggs in the kitchen beneath them, a DVD was being delivered to the St David's Hotel in Cardiff. A CI agent, working as a member of the hotel staff, took it upstairs and placed it on the breakfast tray for the main suite on the floor taken by the East Europeans. The tray was taken from him by a stern-faced man in a dark suit and the CI agent immediately left the floor and the building.

A few minutes later, there was a crash in the room as the tray was thrown on to the floor, and harsh words were heard by the agents patrolling the floor in the guise of cleaners, maids and valets. A long-distance call was placed and then the manager was summoned for the bill to be paid.

By 10am the entire floor was deserted and the visitors were on their way to the private plane at Cardiff. By 11.30am the plane had left Welsh airspace and was flying eastward. Whatever fate awaited them at their destination was no business of CI or WBI.

At 9.30am in Myddfai, Wyndham joined Mrs Jenkins and Merle in the front pew of the church. Hannibal was also there, sitting next to Merle on a cushion. The vicar's sermon went well that day; he spoke of friendship, trust and the generosity of the people of Myddfai, as well as the extraordinary loyalty of animals. Although most of the villagers did not know the full story of what had happened over the past few days, a few had worked out that it had had something to do with the fiasco in Westminster.

Leaving the church, Wyndham found himself being approached by people from the village and shaken by the hand. He followed the vicar and Merle to the vicarage, walking with Mrs Jenkins and Hannibal. Llew was already at the front door, waiting for them. As they walked in, Wyndham's Blackcurrant rang and he answered the phone, excusing himself from the company for a moment. It was the Director.

Wyndham learned that the two intruders they had captured in the night were Russian and that WARF had made a DVD film of both men, showing their injuries, and sent the DVD to the St David's Hotel. The people there had clearly abandoned their fellow countrymen to WARF and had left the hotel to fly home. The Director was fairly confident that it would be a long time before they tried anything similar again.

It turned out that those two men Wyndham had captured were also going to be in charge of making Aneurin assassinate The Boss so that side of things was also cleared up. He was also pleased to tell Wyndham that Aneurin was continuing to recover and should be able to rejoin CI before too long. He advised Wyndham to take a couple of days' break in Myddfai before returning to work. No sooner than he had finished his call with the Director, he received another call from The Boss. She told him that everything should start getting back to normal at CI during the following week although, of course, Iori would never return there. She and Emia were going to take time off until Wednesday and she advised Wyndham to do the same.

She did not say what was happening to Sweety, the Secretary of State for Transport and the two junior ministers although he was certain it would be a long time before they appeared in public again. He hoped RSJ Williams would be charged and tried, although it would be painful for The Boss.

He turned and went into the vicarage; already it felt like a second home to him. Hannibal was waiting in the hall and meowed at him to hurry up. The family and Llew were in the cosy sitting room, drinking coffee and looking at the Sunday papers, the front pages of which concerned themselves with the extraordinary events at the House of Commons, the stock market troubles in the light of the government's collapse and all the ramifications the country could expect from the strange disappearance of Sweety and company.

'Come and sit, Wyndham,' said Mrs Jenkins. 'I think we can use your real name now, can't we?'

He smiled and nodded. Sitting down next to that excellent lady, he took a cup of coffee from her and said, 'Yes, Mrs Jenkins, I think it's time.' He looked across at Merle. 'I think the hair dye will wear off soon, too!'

They all laughed and Hannibal walked from one person to the other to be petted.

Chapter 55

FOUR MONTHS LATER, Geraint in IT had finally organised another coracle party. Wyndham had warned Merle to take something warm to wear in case they had to stay out in the night and he ensured that he had his hip flask full of Penderyn whisky. Emia was also coming with her new man, Special Agent Lewis. Emia and Merle had become firm friends, for which Wyndham was thankful. Aneurin had been invited but turned down the invitation, with thanks; he was determined to keep away from the temptations of drink now and was quite happy with his home in Little Water Street. Besides, Nurse Nest Jones had been to see him; it turned out that she was the one who had informed WBI and CI that Aneurin was going to be released from Llanfihangel and had acted as double agent on their behalf, as well as secretly removing the implant in Aneurin's temple.

Dai Sewin shook his head at the young things playing with coracles but he was going to set off in one himself, just to keep an eye on them. This time there was plenty of beer, wine and whisky, and Merle had made sure there was food too.

It was a glorious evening and they were all allowed to take the Underground to the King Morgan Bridge steps. Will Front Row was, as always, in charge of the train and, if he objected to these flighty young people misusing CI property, he wasn't saying anything, but then he hardly ever did say anything. As they moved slowly under Quay Street and Coracle Way to the other side of the Towy, normal Carmarthen life went on above them. Few people in the town knew of how close they had come to being dominated completely by their perfidious neighbour, and, more sinisterly, by Eastern European factions. There was a new party in government in Westminster, one which had received due warning that any encroachment on Welsh territory would not be taken lightly.

The Boss didn't take part in the coracle party. She was still smarting from the betrayal by RSJ Williams and she headed home for a glass of wine in her garden, feeling a little melancholy. Outside her door, there was a familiar car and standing by the car was the Director, holding a bottle of Welsh sparkling wine. She went up to him and shook his hand; he held hers a little longer than was necessary and then they went indoors. That evening, they spent time sitting in the garden, sipping wine and talking quietly.

In Wyndham's flat in Quay Street, Hannibal was making the most of his humans' absence. He had a most enjoyable life, travelling between his homes in Myddfai and Carmarthen, and he was making himself known to the cats and rodents of Quay Street; he had even been on the Swansea Express to WBI HQ, where he'd received a special medal from the Speaker of the Senate. Wyndham's new sofa was now Hannibal's special seat and he found Wyndham's bed most comfortable. He approved of all the arrangements made on his behalf.

The same evening, in a secluded area of Snowdonia, some people could be seen in the tea plantation controlled by Welsh Intelligence, near Beddgelert. It was the end of another hot day and, among the group leaving the tea terraces was a very large man carrying a big basket of newly picked tea leaves on his back. Walking shyly toward him was a younger and much smaller man, carrying an Irish harp. They greeted each other affectionately and held hands as they walked back to the plantation house. At last, Iori and Harri had found happiness.